mc

W9-AWG-387

Praise for #1 *New York Times* bestselling author

# NORA ROBERTS

"America's favorite writer."

—*The New Yorker*

"When Roberts puts her fingers on the pulse of romance, legions of fans feel the heartbeat."

—*Publishers Weekly*

"Her stories have fueled the dreams of twenty-five million readers."

—*Chicago Tribune*

"Nora Roberts is among the best."

—*The Washington Post*

"Roberts is a storyteller of immeasurable diversity and talent."

—*Publishers Weekly*

"Roberts is indeed a word artist."

— *Los Angeles Daily News*

"Roberts' bestselling novels are some of the best in the romance genre."

—*USA TODAY*

Dear Reader,

We are excited to bring you *Once More for Love*, a special volume containing two of Nora Roberts's beloved stories about women finding themselves—and, of course, true love!

Set in glittering New York City, *Blithe Images* is the story of Hillary Baxter, a woman with the face of a model and the heart of a girl born and raised on a Kansas farm. But that small-town heart gets its first challenge when Hillary is assigned to work with sexy magazine magnate Bret Bardoff…

In *Search for Love*, Serenity Smith embarks on a journey to find her family roots, but she never expected to encounter the arrogant Count de Kergallen. Nor did she expect to be so attracted to the man who suspected her motivations from their first heated glance…

Happy reading!

The Editors
Silhouette Books

# NORA ROBERTS

# ONCE MORE for LOVE

*Silhouette Books*

Published by Silhouette Books

**America's Publisher of Contemporary Romance**

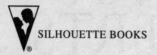 **SILHOUETTE BOOKS**

Recycling programs
for this product may
not exist in your area.

Once More for Love

ISBN-13: 978-0-373-28229-6

Copyright © 2016 by Harlequin Books S.A.

The publisher acknowledges the copyright holder
of the individual works as follows:

Blithe Images
Copyright © 1981 by Nora Roberts

Search for Love
Copyright © 1982 by Nora Roberts

Visit Silhouette Books at www.Harlequin.com

**Printed in U.S.A.**

# CONTENTS

# BLITHE IMAGES

To Ron's Patience...

# Chapter 1

The girl twisted and turned under the lights, her shining black hair swirling around her as various expressions flitted across her striking face.

"That's it, Hillary, a little pout now. We're selling the lips here." Larry Newman followed her movements, the shutter of his camera clicking rapidly. "Fantastic," he exclaimed as he straightened from his crouched position. "That's enough for today."

Hillary Baxter stretched her arms to the ceiling and relaxed. "Good, I'm beat. It's home and a hot tub for me."

"Just think of the millions of dollars in lipstick your face is going to sell, sweetheart." Switching off lights, Larry's attention was already wavering.

"Mind-boggling."

"Mmm, so it is," he returned absently. "We've got

that shampoo thing tomorrow, so make sure your hair is in its usual gorgeous state. I almost forgot." He turned and faced her directly. "I have a business appointment in the morning. I'll get someone to stand in for me."

Hillary smiled with fond indulgence. She had been modeling for three years now, and Larry was her favorite photographer. They worked well together, and as a photographer he was exceptional, having a superior eye for angles and detail, for capturing the right mood. He was hopelessly disorganized, however, and pathetically absentminded about anything other than his precious equipment.

"What appointment?" Hillary inquired with serene patience, knowing well how easily Larry confused such mundane matters as times and places when they did not directly concern his camera.

"Oh, that's right, I didn't tell you, did I?" Shaking her head, Hillary waited for him to continue. "I've got to see Bret Bardoff at ten o'clock."

"*The* Bret Bardoff?" Hillary demanded, more than a little astonished. "I didn't know the owner of *Mode* magazine made appointments with mere mortals—only royalty and goddesses."

"Well, this peasant's been granted an audience," Larry returned dryly. "As a matter of fact, Mr. Bardoff's secretary contacted me and set the whole thing up. She said he wanted to discuss plans for a layout or something."

"Good luck. From what I hear of Bret Bardoff, he's a man to be reckoned with—tough as nails and used to getting his own way."

"He wouldn't be where he is today if he were a pushover," Larry defended the absent Mr. Bardoff with a shrug. "His father may have made a fortune by starting *Mode,* but Bret Bardoff made his own twice over by expanding and developing other magazines. A very successful businessman, and a good photographer—one that's not afraid to get his hands dirty."

"You'd love anyone who could tell a Nikon from a Brownie," Hillary accused with a grin, and pulled at a lock of Larry's disordered hair. "But his type doesn't appeal to me." A delicate and counterfeit shudder moved her shoulders. "I'm sure he'd scare me to death."

"Nothing scares you, Hil," Larry said fondly as he watched the tall, willowy woman gather her things and move for the door. "I'll have someone here to take the shots at nine-thirty tomorrow."

Outside, Hillary hailed a cab. She had become quite adept at this after three years in New York. And she had nearly ceased to ponder about Hillary Baxter of a small Kansas farm being at home in the thriving metropolis of New York City.

She had been twenty-one when she had made the break and come to New York to pursue a modeling career. The transition from small-town farm girl to big-city model had been difficult and often frightening, but Hillary had refused to be daunted by the fast-moving, overwhelming city and resolutely made the rounds with her portfolio.

Jobs had been few and far between during the first year, but she had hung on, refusing to surrender and escape to the familiar surroundings of home. Slowly, she had constructed a reputation for portraying the right image for the right product, and she had become more and more in demand. When she had begun to work with Larry, everything had fallen into place, and her face was now splashed throughout magazines and, as often as not, on the cover. Her life was proceeding according to plan, and the fact that she now commanded a top model's salary had enabled her to move from the third-floor walk-up in which she had started her New York life to a comfortable high-rise near Central Park.

Modeling was not a passion with Hillary, but a job. She had not come to New York with starry-eyed dreams of fame and glamour, but with a resolution to succeed, to stand on her own. The choice of career had seemed inevitable, since she possessed a natural grace and poise and striking good looks. Her coal black hair and high cheekbones lent her a rather exotic fragility, and large, heavily fringed eyes in deep midnight blue contrasted appealingly with her golden complexion. Her mouth was full and shapely, and smiled beautifully at the slightest provocation. Along with her stunning looks, the fact that she was inherently photogenic added to her current success in her field. The uncanny ability to convey an array of images for the camera came naturally, with little conscious effort on her part. After being told the type of woman she was to portray, Hillary became just that—sophisticated, practical, sensuous—whatever was required.

Letting herself into her apartment, Hillary kicked off her shoes and sank her feet into soft ivory carpet. There was no date to prepare for that evening, and she was looking forward to a light supper and a few quiet hours at home.

Thirty minutes later, wrapped in a warm, flowing azure robe, she stood in the kitchen of her apartment preparing a model's feast of soup and unsalted crackers. A ring of the doorbell interrupted her far-from-gourmet activities.

"Lisa, hi." She greeted her neighbor from across the hall with an automatic smile. "Want some dinner?"

Lisa MacDonald wrinkled her nose in disdain. "I'd rather put up with a few extra pounds than starve myself like you."

"If I indulge myself too often," Hillary stated, patting a flat stomach, "I'd be after you to find me a job in that law firm you work for. By the way, how's the rising young attorney?"

"Mark still doesn't know I'm alive," Lisa complained as she flopped onto the couch. "I'm getting desperate, Hillary. I may lose my head and mug him in the parking lot."

"Tacky, too tacky," Hillary said, giving the matter deep consideration. "Why not attempt something less dramatic, like tripping him when he walks past your desk?"

"That could be next."

With a grin, Hillary sat and lifted bare feet to the surface of the coffee table. "Ever hear of Bret Bardoff?"

Lisa's eyes grew round. "Who hasn't? Millionaire, incredibly handsome, mysterious, brilliant businessman and still fair game." These attributes were counted off carefully on Lisa's fingers. "What about him?"

Slim shoulders moved expressively. "I'm not sure. Larry has an appointment with him in the morning."

"Face to face?"

"That's right." Amusement dawned first, then dark blue eyes regarded Lisa with curiosity. "Of course, we've both done work for his magazines before, but I can't imagine why the elusive owner of *Mode* would want to see a mere photographer, even if he is the best. In the trade, he's spoken of in reverent whispers, and if gossip columns are to be believed, he's the answer to every maiden's prayer. I wonder what he's really like." She frowned, finding herself nearly obsessed with the thought. "It's strange, I don't believe I know anyone who's had a personal dealing with him. I picture him as a giant phantom figure handing out monumental corporate decisions from *Mode*'s Mount Olympus."

"Maybe Larry will fill you in tomorrow," Lisa suggested, and Hillary shook her head, the frown becoming a grin.

"Larry won't notice anything unless Mr. Bardoff's on a roll of film."

Shortly before nine-thirty the following morning, Hillary used her spare key to enter Larry's studio. Prepared for the shampoo ad, her hair fell in soft, thick waves, shining and full. In the small cubicle in the rear she applied her makeup with an expert hand, and at nine forty-five she was impatiently switching on the lights required for indoor shots. As minutes slipped by, she began to entertain the annoying suspicion that Larry had neglected to arrange for a substitute. It was nearly ten when the door to the studio opened, and Hillary immediately pounced on the man who entered.

"It's about time," she began, tempering irritation with a small smile. "You're late."

"Am I?" he countered, meeting her annoyed expression with raised brows.

Pausing a moment, she realized how incredibly handsome the man facing her was. His hair, the color of corn silk, was full and grew just over the collar of his casual polo-necked gray sweater, a gray that exactly matched large, direct eyes. His mouth was quirked in a half smile, and there was something vaguely familiar about his deeply tanned face.

"I haven't worked with you before, have I?" Hillary asked, forced to look up to meet his eyes since he was an inch or more over six feet.

"Why do you ask?" His evasion was smooth, and she felt suddenly uncomfortable under his unblinking gray glance.

"No reason," she murmured, turning away, feeling compelled to adjust the cuff of her sleeve. "Well, let's get to it. Where's your camera?" Belatedly, she observed he carried no equipment. "Are you using Larry's?"

"I suppose I am." He continued to stand staring down at her, making no move to proceed with the task at hand, his nonchalance becoming thoroughly irritating.

"Well, come on then, let's not be all day. I've been ready for half an hour."

"Sorry." He smiled, and she was struck with the change it brought to his already compelling face. It was a carelessly slow smile, full of charm, and the thought passed through her mind that he could use it as a deadly weapon. Pivoting away from him, she struggled to ignore its power. She had a job to do. "What are the pictures for?" he asked her as he examined Larry's cameras.

"Oh, Lord, didn't he tell you?" Turning back to him, she shook her head and smiled fully for the first time. "Larry's a tremendous photographer, but he is the most exasperatingly absentminded man. I don't know how he remembers to get up in the morning." She tugged a lock of raven hair before giving her head a dramatic toss.

"Clean, shiny, sexy hair," she explained in the tone of a commercial. "Shampoo's what we're selling today."

"Okay," he returned simply, and began setting equipment to rights in a thoroughly professional manner that did much to put Hillary's mind at ease. At least he knows his job, she assured herself, for his attitude had made her vaguely uneasy. "Where is Larry, by the way?" The question startled Hillary out of her silent thoughts.

"Didn't he tell you anything? That's just like him." Standing under the lights, she began turning, shaking her head, creating a rich black cloud as he clicked the camera, crouching and moving around her to catch different angles. "He had an appointment with Bret Bardoff," she continued, tossing her hair and smiling. "Lord help him if he forgot that. He'll be eaten alive."

"Does Bret Bardoff consume photographers as a habit?" the voice behind the camera questioned with dry amusement.

"Wouldn't be surprised." Hillary lifted her hair above her head, pausing for a moment before she allowed it to fall back to her shoulders like a rich cloak. "I would think a ruthless businessman like Mr. Bardoff would have little patience with an absentminded photographer or any other imperfection."

"You know him?"

"Lord, no." She laughed with unrestrained pleasure. "And I'm not likely to, far above my station. Have you met him?"

"Not precisely."

"Ah, but we all work for him at one time or another, don't we? I wonder how many times my face has been in one of his magazines. Scillions," she calculated, receiving a raised-brow look from behind the camera. "Scillions," she repeated with a nod. "And I've never met the emperor."

"Emperor?"

"How else does one describe such a lofty individual?" Hillary demanded with a gesture of her hands. "From what I've heard, he runs his mags like an empire."

"You sound as though you disapprove."

"No," Hillary disagreed with a smile and a shrug. "Emperors just make me nervous. I'm plain peasant stock myself."

"Your image seems hardly plain or peasant," he remarked, and this time it was her brow that lifted. "That should sell gallons of shampoo." Lowering his camera, he met her eyes directly. "I think we've got it, Hillary."

She relaxed, pushed back her hair, and regarded him curiously. "You know me? I'm sorry, I can't quite seem to place you. Have we worked together before?"

"Hillary Baxter's face is everywhere. It's my business to recognize beautiful faces." He spoke with careless simplicity, gray eyes smoky with amusement.

"Well, it appears you have the advantage, Mr.—?"

"Bardoff, Bret Bardoff," he answered, and the camera clicked to capture the astonished expression on her face. "You can close your mouth now, Hillary. I think we've got enough." His smile widened as she obeyed without thinking. "Cat got your tongue?" he mocked, pleasure at her embarrassment obvious.

She recognized him now, from pictures she had seen of him in newspapers and his own magazines, and she was busily engaged in cursing herself for the stupidity she had just displayed. Anger with herself spread to encompass the man in front of her, and she located her voice.

"You let me babble on like that," she sputtered, eyes and cheeks bright with color. "You stood there taking pictures you had no business taking and just let me carry on like an idiot."

"I was merely following orders." His grave tone and sober expression added to her mounting embarrassment and fury.

"Well, you had no right following them. You should have told me who you were." Her voice quavered with indignation, but he merely moved his shoulders and smiled again.

"You never asked."

Before she could retort, the door of the studio opened and Larry entered, looking harassed and confused. "Mr. Bardoff," he began, advancing on the pair standing under the lights. "I'm sorry. I thought I was to meet you at your office." Larry ran a hand through his hair in agitation. "When I got there, I was told you were coming here. I don't know how I got it so confused. Sorry you had to wait."

"Don't worry about it," Bret assured him with an easy smile. "The last hour's been highly entertaining."

"Hillary." Her existence suddenly seeped into Larry's consciousness. "Good Lord, I knew I forgot something. We'll have to get those pictures later."

"No need." Bret handed Larry the camera. "Hillary and I have seen to them."

"You took the shots?" Larry looked at Bret and the camera in turn.

"Hillary saw no reason to waste time." He smiled and added, "I'm sure you'll find the pictures suitable."

"No question of that, Mr. Bardoff." His voice was tinged with reverence. "I know what you can do with a camera."

Hillary had an overwhelming desire for the floor to open up and swallow her. She had to get out of there quickly. Never before in her life had she felt such a fool. Of course, she reasoned silently, it was his fault. The nerve of the man, letting her believe he was a photographer! She recalled the fashion in which she had ordered him to begin, and the things she had said. She closed her eyes with an inward moan. All she wanted to do now was disappear, and with luck she would never have to come face to face with Bret Bardoff again.

She began gathering her things quickly. "I'll leave you to get on with your business. I have another session across town." Slinging her purse over her shoulder, she took a deep breath. "Bye, Larry. Nice to have met you, Mr. Bardoff." She attempted to brush by them, but Bret put out his hand and captured hers, preventing her exit.

"Goodbye, Hillary." She forced her eyes to meet his, feeling a sudden drain of power by the contact of her hand in his. "It's been a most interesting morning. We'll have to do it again soon."

When hell freezes over, her eyes told him silently, and muttering something incoherent, she dashed for the door, the sound of his laughter echoing in her ears.

Dressing for a date that evening, Hillary endeavored, without success, to block the events of the morning from her mind. She was confident that her path would never cross Bret Bardoff's again. After all, she comforted herself, it had only been through a stupid accident that they had met in the first place. Hillary prayed that the adage about lightning never striking twice would hold true. She had indeed been hit by a lightning bolt when he had casually disclosed his name to her, and her cheeks burned again, matching the color of her soft jersey dress as her careless words played back in her mind.

The ringing of the phone interrupted her reflections, and she answered, finding Larry on the other end. "Hillary, boy, I'm glad I caught you at home." His excitement was tangible over the wire, and she answered him quickly.

"You just did catch me. I'm practically out the door. What's up?"

"I can't go into details now. Bret's going to do that in the morning."

She noted the fact that *Mr. Bardoff* had been discarded since that morning and spoke wearily. "Larry, what are you talking about?"

"Bret will explain everything in the morning. You have an appointment at nine o'clock."

"What?" Her voice rose and she found it imperative to swallow twice. "Larry, what are you talking about?"

"It's a tremendous opportunity for both of us, Hil. Bret will tell you tomorrow. You know where his office is." This was a statement rather than a question, since everyone in the business knew *Mode*'s headquarters.

"I don't want to see him," Hillary argued, feeling a surge of panic at the thought of those steel gray eyes. "I don't know what he told you about this morning, but I made a total fool of myself. I thought he was a photographer. Really," she continued, with fresh annoyance, "you're partially to blame, if—"

"Don't worry about all that now," Larry interrupted confidently. "It doesn't matter. Just be there at nine tomorrow. See you later."

"But, Larry." She stopped, there was no purpose in arguing with a dead phone. Larry had hung up.

This was too much, she thought in despair, and sat down heavily on the bed. How could Larry expect her to go through with this? How could she possibly face that man after the things she had said? Humiliation, she decided, was simply something for which she was not suited. Rising from the bed, she squared her shoulders. Bret Bardoff probably wanted another opportunity to laugh at her for her stupidity. Well, he wasn't going to get the best of Hillary Baxter, she told herself with firm pride. She'd face him without cringing. This peasant would stand up to the emperor and show him what she was made of!

Hillary dressed for her appointment the next morning with studious care. The white, light wool cowl-necked dress was beautiful in its simplicity, relying on the form it covered to make it eye-catching. She arranged her hair in a loose bun on top of her head in order to add a businesslike air to her appearance. Bret Bardoff would not find her stammering and blushing this morning, she determined, but cool and confident. Slipping on soft leather shoes, she was satisfied with the total effect, the heels adding to her height. She would not be forced to look up quite so high in order to meet those gray eyes, and she would meet them straight on.

Confidence remained with her through the taxi ride and all the way to the top of the building where Bret Bardoff had his offices. Glancing at her watch on the elevator, she was pleased to see she was punctual. An attractive brunette was seated at an enormous reception desk, and Hillary stated her name and business. After a brief conversation on a phone that held a prominent position on the large desk, the woman ushered Hillary down a long corridor and through a heavy oak door.

She entered a large, well-decorated room where she was greeted by yet another attractive woman, who introduced herself as June Miles, Mr. Bardoff's secretary. "Please go right in, Miss Baxter. Mr. Bardoff is expecting you," she informed Hillary with a smile.

Walking to a set of double doors, Hillary's eyes barely had time to take in the room with its rather fabulous decor before her gaze was arrested by the man seated at a huge oak desk, a panoramic view of the city at his back.

"Good morning, Hillary." He rose and approached her. "Are you going to come in or stand there all day with your back to the door?"

Hillary's spine straightened and she answered coolly, "Good morning, Mr. Bardoff, it's nice to see you again."

"Don't be a hypocrite," he stated mildly as he led her to a seat near the desk. "You'd be a great deal happier if you never laid eyes on me again." Hillary could find no comment to this all-too-true observation, and contented herself with smiling vaguely into space.

"However," he continued, as if she had agreed with him in words, "it suits my purposes to have you here today in spite of your reluctance."

"And what are your purposes, Mr. Bardoff?" she demanded, her annoyance with his arrogance sharpening her tone.

He leaned back in his chair and allowed his cool gray eyes to travel deliberately over Hillary from head to toe. The survey was slow and obviously intended to disconcert, but she remained outwardly unruffled.

Because of her profession, her face and form had been studied before. She was determined not to let this man know his stare was causing her pulses to dance a nervous rhythm.

"My purposes, Hillary—" his eyes met hers and held "—are for the moment strictly business, though that is subject to change at any time."

This remark cracked Hillary's cool veneer enough to bring a slight blush to her cheeks. She cursed the color as she struggled to keep her eyes level with his.

"Good Lord." His brows lifted with humor. "You're blushing. I didn't think women did that anymore." His grin widened as if he were enjoying the fact that more color leaped to her cheeks at his words. "You're probably the last of a dying breed."

"Could we discuss the business for which I'm here, Mr. Bardoff?" she inquired. "I'm sure you're a very busy man, and believe it or not, I'm busy myself."

"Of course," Bret agreed. He grinned reflectively. "I remember—*'Let's not waste time.'* I'm planning a layout for *Mode,* a rather special layout." He lit a cigarette and offered Hillary one, which she declined with a shake of her head. "I've had the idea milling around in my mind for some time, but I needed the right photographer and the right woman." His eyes narrowed as he peered at her speculatively, giving Hillary the sensation of being viewed under a microscope. "I've found them both now."

She squirmed under his unblinking stare. "Suppose you give me some details, Mr. Bardoff. I'm sure it's not usual procedure for you to interview models personally. This must be something special."

"Yes, I think so," he agreed suavely. "The idea is a

layout—a picture story, if you like—on the Many Faces of Woman." He stood then and perched on the corner of the desk, and Hillary was affected by his sheer masculinity, the power and strength that exuded from his lean form clad in a fawn-colored business suit. "I want to portray all the facets of womanhood: career woman, mother, athlete, sophisticate, innocent, temptress, et cetera—a complete portrait of Eve, the Eternal Woman."

"Sounds fascinating," Hillary admitted, caught up in the backlash of his enthusiasm. "You think I might be suitable for some of the pictures?"

"I know you're suitable," he stated flatly, "for *all* of the pictures."

Finely etched brows raised in curiosity. "You're going to use one model for the entire layout?"

"I'm going to use *you* for the entire layout."

Struggling with annoyance and the feeling of being submerged by very deep water, Hillary spoke honestly. "I'd be an idiot not to be interested in a project like this. I don't think I'm an idiot. But why me?"

"Come now, Hillary." His voice mirrored impatience, and he bent over to capture her surprised chin in his hand. "You do own a mirror. Surely you're intelligent enough to know that you're quite beautiful and extremely photogenic."

He was speaking of her as if she were an inanimate object rather than a human being, and the fingers, strong and lean on her chin, were very distressing. Nevertheless, Hillary persisted.

"There are scores of beautiful and photogenic models in New York alone, Mr. Bardoff. You know that better than anyone. I'd like to know why you're considering me for your pet project."

"Not considering." He rose and thrust his hands in his pockets, and she observed he was becoming irritated. She found the knowledge rewarding. "There's no one else I would consider. You have a rather uncanny knack for getting to the heart of a picture and coming across with exactly the right image. I need versatility as well as beauty. I need honesty in a dozen different images."

"In your opinion, I can do that."

"You wouldn't be here if I weren't sure. I never make rash decisions."

No, Hillary mused, looking into his cool gray eyes, you calculate every minute detail. Aloud, she asked, "Larry would be the photographer?"

He nodded. "There's an affinity between the two of you that is obvious in the pictures you produce. You're both superior alone, but together you've done some rather stunning work."

His praise caused her smile to warm slightly. "Thank you."

"That wasn't a compliment, Hillary—just a fact. I've given Larry all the details. The contracts are waiting for your signature."

"Contracts?" she repeated, becoming wary.

"That's right," he returned, overlooking her hesitation. "This project is going to take some time. I've no intention of rushing through it. I want exclusive rights to that beautiful face of yours until the project's completed and on the stands."

"I see." She digested this carefully, unconsciously chewing on her bottom lip.

"You needn't react as if I've made an indecent proposal, Hillary." His voice was dry as he regarded her frowning concentration. "This is a business arrangement."

Her chin tilted in defiance. "I understand that completely, Mr. Bardoff. It's simply that I've never signed a long-term contract before."

"I have no intention of allowing you to get away. Contracts are obligatory, for you and for Larry. For the next few months I don't want you distracted by any other jobs. Financially, you'll be well compensated. If you have any complaints along those lines, we'll negotiate. However, my rights to that face of yours for the next six months are exclusive."

He lapsed into silence, watching the varied range of expressions on her face. She was working out the entire platform carefully, doing her best not to be intimidated by his overwhelming power. The project appealed to her, although the man did not. It would be fascinating work, but she found it difficult to tie herself to one establishment for any period of time. She could not help feeling that signing her name was signing away liberation. A long-term contract equaled a long-term commitment.

Finally, throwing caution to the winds, she gave Bret one of the smiles that made her face known throughout America.

"You've got yourself a face."

## Chapter 2

Bret Bardoff moved quickly. Within two weeks contracts had been signed, and the shooting schedule had been set to begin on a morning in early October. The first image to be portrayed was one of youthful innocence and unspoiled simplicity.

Hillary met Larry in a small park selected by Bret. Though the morning was bright and brisk, the sun filtering warm through the trees, the park was all but deserted. She wondered a moment if the autocratic Mr. Bardoff had arranged the isolation. Blue jeans rolled to mid-calf and a long-sleeved turtleneck in scarlet were Hillary's designated costume. She had bound her shining hair in braids, tied them with red ribbons, and had kept her makeup light, relying on natural, healthy skin. She was the essence of honest, vibrant youth, dark blue eyes bright with the anticipation.

"Perfect," Larry commented as she ran across the grass to meet him. "Young and innocent. How do you manage it?"

She wrinkled her nose. "I am young and innocent, old man."

"Okay. See that?" He pointed to a swing set complete with bars and a slide. "Go play, little girl, and let this old man take some pictures."

She ran for the swing, giving herself over to the freedom of movement. Stretching out full length, she leaned her head to the ground and smiled at the brilliant sky. Climbing on the slide, she lifted her arms wide, let out a whoop of uninhibited joy, and slid down, landing on her bottom in the soft dirt. Larry clicked his camera from varying angles, allowing her to direct the mood.

"You look twelve years old." His laugh was muffled, his face still concealed behind the camera.

"I am twelve years old," Hillary proclaimed, scurrying onto the crossbars. "Betcha can't do this." She hung up by her knees on the bar, her pigtails brushing the ground.

"Amazing." The answer did not come from Larry, and she turned her head and looked directly into a pair of well-tailored gray slacks. Her eyes roamed slowly upward to the matching jacket and farther to a full, smiling mouth and mocking gray eyes. "Hello, child, does your mother know where you are?"

"What are you doing here?" Hillary demanded, feeling at a decided disadvantage in her upside-down position.

"Supervising my pet project." He continued to regard her, his grin growing wider. "How long do you intend to hang there? The blood must be rushing to your head."

Grabbing the bar with her hands, she swung her legs over in a neat somersault and stood facing him. He patted her head, told her she was a good girl, and turned his attention to Larry.

"How'd it go? Looked to me as if you got some good shots."

The two men discussed the technicalities of the morning's shooting while Hillary sat back down on the swing, moving gently back and forth. She had met with Bret a handful of times during the past two weeks, and each time she had been unaccountably uneasy in his presence. He was a vital and disturbing individual, full of raw, masculine power, and she was not at all sure she wanted to be closely associated with him. Her life was well ordered now, running smoothly along the lines she designated, and she wanted no complications. There was something about this man, however, that spelled complications in capital letters.

"All right." Bret's voice broke into her musings. "Setup at the club at one o'clock. Everything's been arranged." Hillary rose from the swing and moved to join Larry. "No need for you to go now, little girl— you've an hour or so to spare."

"I don't want to play on the swings anymore, Daddy," she retorted, bristling at his tone. Picking up her shoulder bag, she managed to take two steps before he reached out and took command of her wrist. She rounded on him, blue eyes blazing.

"Spoiled little brat, aren't you?" he murmured in a mild tone, but his eyes narrowed and met the dark blue blaze with cold gray steel. "Perhaps I should turn you over my knee."

"That would be more difficult than you think, Mr.

Bardoff," she returned with unsurpassable dignity. "I'm twenty-four, not twelve, and really quite strong."

"Are you now?" He inspected her slim form dubiously. "I suppose it's possible." He spoke soberly, but she recognized the mockery in his eyes. "Come on, I want some coffee." His hand slipped from her wrist, and his fingers interlocked with hers. She jerked away, surprised and disconcerted by the warmth. "Hillary," he began in a tone of strained patience. "I would like to buy you coffee." It was more a command than a request.

He moved across the grass with long, easy strides, dragging an unwilling Hillary after him. Larry watched their progress and automatically took their picture. They made an interesting study, he decided, the tall blond man in the expensive business suit pulling the slim, dark woman-child behind him.

As she sat across from Bret in a small coffee shop, Hillary's face was flushed with a mixture of indignation and the exertion of keeping up with the brisk pace he had set. He took in her pink cheeks and bright eyes, and his mouth lifted at one corner.

"Maybe I should buy a dish of ice cream to cool you off." The waitress appeared then, saving Hillary from formulating a retort, and Bret ordered two coffees.

"Tea," Hillary stated flatly, pleased to contradict him on some level.

"I beg your pardon?" he returned coolly.

"I'll have tea, if you don't mind. I don't drink coffee; it makes me nervous."

"One coffee and one tea," he amended before he turned back to her. "How do you wake up in the morning without the inevitable cup of coffee?"

"Clean living." She flicked a pigtail over her shoulder and folded her hands.

"You certainly look like an ad for clean living now." Sitting back, he took out his cigarette case, offering her one and lighting one before going on. "I'm afraid you'd never pass for twenty-four in pigtails. It's not often one sees hair that true black—certainly not with eyes that color." He stared into them for a long moment. "They're fabulous, so dark at times they're nearly purple, quite dramatic, and the bone structure, it's rather elegant and exotic. Tell me," he asked suddenly, "where did you get that marvelous face of yours?"

Hillary had thought herself long immune to comments and compliments on her looks, but somehow his words nonplussed her, and she was grateful that the waitress returned with their drinks, giving her time to gather scattered wits.

"I'm told I'm a throwback to my great-grandmother." She spoke with detached interest as she sipped tea. "She was an Arapaho. It appears I resemble her quite strongly."

"I should have guessed." He nodded his head, continuing his intense study. "The cheekbones, the classic bone structure. Yes, I can see your Indian heritage, but the eyes are deceiving. You didn't acquire eyes like cobalt from your great-grandmother."

"No." She struggled to meet his penetrating gaze coolly. "They belong to me."

"To you," he acknowledged with a nod, "and for the next six months to me. I believe I'll enjoy the joint ownership." The focus of his study shifted to the mouth that moved in a frown at his words. "Where are you from, Hillary Baxter? You're no native."

"That obvious? I thought I had acquired a marvelous New York varnish." She gave a wry shrug, grateful that the intensity of his examination appeared to be over. "Kansas—a farm some miles north of Abilene."

He inclined his head, and his brows lifted as he raised his cup. "You appear to have made the transition from wheat to concrete very smoothly. No battle scars?"

"A few, but they're healed over." She added quickly, "I hardly have to point out New York's advantages to you, especially in the area of my career."

His agreement was a slow nod. "It's very easy to picture you as a Kansas farm girl or a sophisticated New York model. You have a remarkable ability to suit your surroundings."

Hillary's full mouth moved in a doubtful pout. "That makes me sound like I'm no person on my own, sort of…inconspicuous."

"Inconspicuous?" Bret's laughter caused several heads to turn, and Hillary stared at him in dumb amazement. "Inconspicuous," he said again, shaking his head as if she had just uttered something sublimely ridiculous. "What a beautiful statement. No, I think you're a very complex woman with a remarkable affinity with her surroundings. I don't believe it's an acquired talent, but an intrinsic ability."

His words pleased Hillary out of all proportion, and she made an issue of stirring her tea, giving it her undivided attention. *Why should a simple, impersonal compliment wrap around my tongue like a twenty-pound chain?* she wondered, careful to keep a frown from forming. *I don't think I care for the way he always manages to shift my balance.*

"You do play tennis, don't you?"

Again, his rapid altering of the conversation threw her into confusion, and she stared at him without comprehension until she recalled the afternoon session was on the tennis court of an exclusive country club.

"I manage to hit the ball over the net once in a while." Annoyed by his somewhat condescending tone, she answered with uncharacteristic meekness.

"Good. The shots will be more impressive if you have the stance and moves down properly." He glanced at the gold watch on his wrist and drew out his wallet. "I've got some things to clear up at the office." Standing, he drew her from the booth, again holding her hand in his oddly familiar manner, ignoring her efforts to withdraw from his grip. "I'll put you in a cab. It'll take you some time to change from little girl to female athlete." He looked down at her, making her feel unaccustomedly small at five foot seven in her sneakers. "Your tennis outfit's already at the club, and I assume you have all the tricks of your trade in that undersized suitcase?" He indicated the large shoulder bag she heaved over her arm.

"Don't worry, Mr. Bardoff."

"Bret," he interrupted, suddenly engrossed with running his hand down her left pigtail. "I don't intend to stop using your first name."

"Don't worry," she began again, evading his invitation. "Changing images is my profession."

"It should prove interesting," he murmured, tugging the braid he held. Then, shifting to a more professional tone he said, "The court is reserved for one. I'll see you then."

"You're going to be there?" Her question was accompanied by a frown as she found herself undeniably distressed at the prospect of dealing with him yet again.

"My pet project, remember?" He nudged her into a cab, either unaware of or unconcerned by her scowl. "I intend to supervise it very carefully."

As the cab merged with traffic, Hillary's emotions were in turmoil. Bret Bardoff was an incredibly attractive and distracting man, and there was something about him that disturbed her. The idea of being in almost daily contact with him made her decidedly uneasy.

*I don't like him,* she decided with a firm nod. *He's too self-assured, too arrogant, too...* Her mind searched for a word. *Physical.* Yes, she admitted, albeit unwillingly, he was a very sexual man, and he unnerved her. She had no desire to be disturbed. There was something about the way he looked at her, something about the way her body reacted whenever she came into contact with him. Shrugging, she stared out the window at passing cars. She wouldn't think of him. Rather, she corrected, she would think of him only as her employer, and a temporary one at that—not as an individual. Her hand still felt warm from his, and glancing down at it, she sighed. It was imperative to her peace of mind that she do her job and avoid any more personal dealings with him. Strictly business, she reminded herself. Yes, their relationship would be strictly business.

The tomboy had been transformed into the fashionable tennis buff. A short white tennis dress accented Hillary's long, slender legs and left arms bare. She covered them, as she waited on the court, with a light jacket, since the October afternoon was pleasant but cool. Her hair was tied away from her face with a dark blue scarf, leaving her delicate features unframed. Color had been added to her eyes, accenting them with sooty fringes, and her lips were tinted deep rose. Spotless white tennis shoes completed her outfit, and she held a lightweight racket in her hands. The pure white of the ensemble contrasted well with her golden skin and raven hair, and she appeared wholly feminine as well as capable.

Behind the net, she experimented with stances, swinging the racket and serving the balls to a nonexistent partner while Larry roamed around her, checking angles and meters.

"I think you might have better luck if someone hit back."

She spun around to see Bret watching her with an amused gleam in his eyes. He too was in white, the jacket of his warm-up suit pushed to the elbows. Hillary, used to seeing him in a business suit, was surprised at the athletic appearance of his body, whipcord lean, his shoulders broad, his arms hard and muscular, his masculinity entirely too prevalent.

"Do I pass?" he asked with a half smile, and she flushed, suddenly aware that she had been staring.

"I'm just surprised to see you dressed that way," she muttered, shrugging her shoulders and turning away.

"More suitable for tennis, don't you think?"

"We're going to play?" She spun back to face him, scowling at the racket in his hand.

"I rather like the idea of action…shots," he finished with a grin. "I won't be too hard on you. I'll hit some nice and easy."

With a good deal of willpower, she managed not to stick out her tongue. She played tennis often and well.

Hillary decided, with inner complacency, that Mr. Bret Bardoff was in for a surprise.

"I'll try to hit a few back," she promised, her face as ingenuous as a child's. "To give the shots realism."

"Good." He strode over to the other side of the court, and Hillary picked up a ball. "Can you serve?"

"I'll do my best," she answered, coating honey on her tongue. After glancing at Larry to see if he was ready, she tossed the ball idly in the air. The camera had already replaced Larry's face, and Hillary moved behind the fault line, tossed the ball once more, connected with the racket, and smashed a serve. Bret returned her serve gently, and she hit back, aiming deep in the opposite corner.

"I think I remember how to score," she called out with a thoughtful frown. "Fifteen-love, Mr. Bardoff."

"Nice return, Hillary. Do you play often?"

"Oh, now and again," she evaded, brushing invisible lint from her skirt. "Ready?"

He nodded, and the ball bounced back and forth in an easy, powerless volley. She realized with some smugness that he was holding back, making it a simple matter for her to make the return for the benefit of Larry's rapidly snapping camera. But she too was holding back, hitting the ball lightly and without any style. She allowed a few more laconic lobs, then slammed the ball away from him, deep in the back court.

"Oh." She lifted a finger to her lips, feigning innocence. "That's thirty-love, isn't it?"

Bret's eyes narrowed as he approached the net. "Why do I have this strange feeling that I'm being conned?"

"Conned?" she repeated, wide-eyed, allowing her lashes to flutter briefly. He searched her face until her lips trembled with laughter. "Sorry, Mr. Bardoff, I couldn't resist." She tossed her head and grinned. "You were so patronizing."

"Okay." He returned her grin somewhat to Hillary's relief. "No more patronizing. Now I'm out for blood."

"We'll start from scratch," she offered, returning to the serving line. "I wouldn't want you to claim I had an unfair advantage."

He returned her serve with force, and they kept each other moving rapidly over the court in the ensuing volley. They battled for points, reaching deuce and exchanging advantage several times. The camera was forgotten in the focus of concentration, the soft click of the shutter masked by the swish of rackets and thump of balls.

Cursing under her breath at the failure to return a ball cleanly, Hillary stooped to pick up another and prepared to serve.

"That was great." Larry's voice broke her concentration, and she turned to gape at him. "I got some fantastic shots. You look like a real pro, Hil. We can wrap it up now."

"Wrap it up?" She stared at him with incredulous exasperation. "Have you lost your mind? We're at deuce." She continued to regard him a moment as if his brain had gone on holiday, and shaking her head and muttering, she resumed play.

For the next few minutes, they fought for the lead until Bret once more held the advantage and once more placed the ball down the line to her backhand.

Hillary put her hands on her hips and let out a deep breath after the ball had sailed swiftly past her. "Ah, well, the agony of defeat." She smiled, attempted to catch her wind, and approached the net. "Congratulations." She offered both hand and smile. "You play a very demanding game."

He accepted her hand, holding it rather than shaking it. "You certainly made me earn it, Hillary. I believe I'd like to try my luck at doubles, with you on my side of the net."

"I suppose you could do worse."

He held her gaze a moment before his eyes dropped to the hand still captive in his. "Such a small hand." He lifted it higher and examined it thoroughly. "I'm astonished it can swing a racket like that." He turned it palm up and carried it to his lips.

Odd and unfamiliar tingles ran up her spine at his kiss, and she stared mesmerized at her hand, unable to speak or draw away. "Come on." He smiled into bemused eyes, annoyingly aware of her reaction. "I'll buy you lunch." His gaze slid past her. "You too, Larry."

"Thanks, Bret." He was already gathering his equipment. "But I want to get back and develop this film. I'll just grab a sandwich."

"Well, Hillary." He turned and commanded her attention. "It's just you and me."

"Really, Mr. Bardoff," she began, feeling near to panic at the prospect of having lunch with him and wishing with all her heart that he would respond to the effort she was currently making to regain sole possession of her hand. "It's not necessary for you to buy me lunch."

"Hillary, Hillary." He sighed, shaking his head. "Do you always find it difficult to accept an invitation, or is it only with me?"

"Don't be ridiculous." She attempted to maintain a

casual tone while she became more and more troubled by the warmth of his hand over hers. She stared down at the joined hands, feeling increasingly helpless as the contact continued. "Mr. Bardoff, may I please have my hand back?" Her voice was breathless, and she bit her lip in vexation.

"Try Bret, Hillary," he commanded, ignoring her request. "It's easy enough, only one syllable. Go ahead."

The eyes that held hers were calm, demanding, and arrogant enough to remain steady for the next hour. The longer her hand remained in his, the more peculiar she felt, and knowing that the sooner she agreed, the sooner she would be free, she surrendered.

"Bret, may I please have my hand back?"

"There, now, we've cleared the first hurdle. That didn't hurt much, did it?" The corner of his mouth lifted as he released her, and immediately the vague weakness began to dissipate, leaving her more secure.

"Nearly painless."

"Now about lunch." He held up his hand to halt her protest. "You do eat, don't you?"

"Of course, but—"

"No buts. I rarely listen to buts or nos."

In short order Hillary found herself seated across from Bret at a small table inside the club. Things were not going as she had planned. It was very difficult to maintain a businesslike and impersonal relationship when she was so often in his company. It was useless to deny that she found him interesting, his vitality stimulating, and he was a tremendously attractive man. But, she admonished herself, he certainly wasn't her type. Besides, she didn't have time for entanglements at this point of her life. Still, the warning signals in her brain told her to tread carefully, that this man was capable of upsetting her neatly ordered plans.

"Has anyone ever told you what a fascinating conversationalist you are?" Hillary's eyes shot up to find Bret's mocking gaze on her.

"Sorry." Color crept into her face. "My mind was wandering."

"So I noticed. What will you have to drink?"

"Tea."

"Straight?" he inquired, his smile hovering.

"Straight," she agreed, and ordered herself to relax. "I don't drink much. I'm afraid I don't handle it well. More than two and I turn into Mr. Hyde. Metabolism."

Bret threw back his head and laughed with the appearance of boundless pleasure. "That's a transformation I would give much to witness. We'll have to arrange it."

Lunch, to Hillary's surprise, was an enjoyable meal, though Bret met her choice of salad with open disgust and pure masculine disdain. She assured him it was adequate, and made a passing comment on the brevity of overweight models' careers.

Fully relaxed, Hillary enjoyed herself, the resolution to keep a professional distance between herself and Bret forgotten. As they ate, he spoke of the next day's shooting plans. Central Park had been designated for more outdoor scenes in keeping with the outdoor, athletic image.

"I've meetings all day tomorrow and won't be able to supervise. How do you exist on that stuff?" He changed the trend of conversation abruptly, waving a superior finger at Hillary's salad. "Don't you want some food? You're going to fade away."

She shook her head, smiling as she sipped her tea, and he muttered under his breath about half-starved models before resuming his previous conversation. "If all goes according to schedule, we'll start the next segment Monday. Larry wants to get an early start tomorrow."

"Always," she agreed with a sigh. "If the weather holds."

"Oh, the sun will shine." She heard the absolute confidence in his voice. "I've arranged it."

Sitting back, she surveyed the man across from her with uninhibited curiosity. "Yes." She nodded at length, noting the firm jaw and direct eyes. "I believe you could. It wouldn't dare rain."

They smiled at each other, and as the look held, she experienced a strange, unfamiliar sensation running through her—something swift, vital, and anonymous.

"Some dessert?"

"You're determined to fatten me up, aren't you?" Grateful that his casual words had eliminated the strange emotion, she summoned up an easy smile. "You're a bad influence, but I have a will of iron."

"Cheesecake, apple pie, chocolate mousse?" His smile was wicked, but she tossed her head and lifted her chin.

"Do your worst. I don't break."

"You're bound to have a weakness. A little time, and I'll find it."

"Bret, darling, what a surprise to see you here." Hillary turned and looked up at the woman greeting Bret with such enthusiasm.

"Hello, Charlene." He granted the shapely, elegantly dressed redhead a charming smile. "Charlene Mason, Hillary Baxter."

"Miss Baxter." Charlene nodded in curt greeting, and green eyes narrowed. "Have we met before?"

"I don't believe so," Hillary returned, wondering why she felt a surge of gratitude at the fact.

"Hillary's face is splashed over magazine covers everywhere," Bret explained. "She's one of New York's finest models."

"Of course." Hillary watched the green eyes narrow further, survey her, and dismiss her as inferior merchandise. "Bret, you should have told me you'd be here today. We could have had some time."

"Sorry," he answered with a casual move of his shoulders. "I won't be here long, and it was business."

Ridiculously deflated by his statement, Hillary immediately forced her spine to straighten. *Didn't I tell you not to get involved?* she reminded herself. He's quite right, this was a business lunch. She gathered her things and stood.

"Please, Miss Mason, have my seat. I was just going." She turned to Bret, pleased to observe his annoyance at her hasty departure. "Thanks for lunch, Mr. Bardoff," she added politely, flashing a smile at the frown that appeared at her use of his surname. "Nice to have met you, Miss Mason." Giving the woman occupying the seat she had just vacated a professional smile, Hillary walked away.

"I didn't realize taking employees to lunch was part of your routine, Bret." Charlene's voice carried to Hillary as she made her exit. Her first instinct was to whirl around and inform the woman to mind her own business, but grasping for control, she continued to move away without hearing Bret's reply.

\* \* \*

The following day's session was more arduous. Using the brilliant fall color in Central Park for a backdrop, Larry's ideas for pictures were varied and energetic. It was a bright, cloudless day, as Bret had predicted, one of the final, golden days of Indian summer. Gold, russet, and scarlet dripped from the branches and covered the ground. Against the varied fall hues, Hillary posed, jogged, threw Frisbees, smiled, climbed trees, fed pigeons, and made three costume changes as the day wore on. Several times during the long session she caught herself looking for Bret, although she knew he was not expected. Her disappointment at his absence both surprised and displeased her, and she reminded herself that life would run much more smoothly if she had never laid eyes on a certain tall, lean man.

"Lighten up, Hil. Quit scowling." Larry's command broke into her musings. Resolutely, she shoved Bret Bardoff from her mind and concentrated on her job.

That evening she sank her tired body into a warm tub, sighing as the scented water worked its gentle magic on aching muscles. *Oh, Larry,* she thought wearily, *with a camera in your hands you become Simon Legree. What you put me through today. I know I've been snapped from every conceivable angle, with every conceivable expression, in every conceivable pose. Thank heavens I'm through until Monday.*

This layout was a big assignment, she realized, and there would be many more days like this one. The project could be a big boost to her career. A large layout in a magazine of *Mode*'s reputation and quality would bring her face to international recognition, and with Bret's backing she would more than likely be on her way to becoming one of the country's top models.

A frown appeared from nowhere. *Why doesn't that please me? The prospect of being successful in my profession has always been something I wanted.* Bret's face entered her mind, and she shook her head in fierce rejection.

"Oh, no you don't," she told his image. "You're not going to get inside my head and confuse my plans. You're the emperor, and I'm your lowly subject. Let's keep it that way."

Hillary was seated with Chuck Carlyle in one of New York's most popular discos. Music filled every corner, infusing the air with its vibrancy, while lighting effects played everchanging colors over the dancers. As the music washed over them, Hillary reflected on her reasoning for keeping her relationship with Chuck platonic.

It wasn't as though she didn't enjoy male companionship, she told herself. It wasn't as though she didn't enjoy a man's embrace or his kisses. A pair of mocking gray eyes crept into her mind unbidden, and she scowled fiercely into her drink.

If she shied away from more intimate relationships, it was only because no one had touched her deeply enough or stirred her emotions to a point where she felt any desire to engage in a long-term or even a short-term affair. Love, she mused, had so far eluded her, and she silently asserted that she was grateful. With love came commitments, and commitments did not fit into her plans for the immediate future. No, an involvement with a man would bring complications, interfere with her well-ordered life.

"It's always a pleasure to take you out, Hillary."
Thoughts broken, she glanced over to see Chuck grin
and look pointedly down at the drink she had been
nursing ever since their arrival. "You're so easy on my
paycheck."

She returned his grin and pushed soul-searching
aside. "You could look far and wide and never find another woman so concerned about your financial wel-
fare."

"Too true." He sighed and adopted a look of great
sadness. "They're either after my body or my money,
and you, sweet Hillary, are after neither." He grabbed
both of her hands and covered them with kisses. "If only
you'd marry me, love of my life, and let me take you
away from all this decadence." His hand swept over the
dance floor. "We'll find a vine-covered cottage, two-
point-seven kids, and settle down."

"Do you know," Hillary said slowly, "if I said yes,
you'd faint dead away?"

"When you're right, you're right." He sighed again.
"So instead of sweeping you off your feet to a vine-
covered cottage, I'll drag you back to the decadence."

Admiring eyes focused on the tall, slim woman with
the dress as blue as her eyes. Hillary's skirt was slit high
to reveal long, shapely legs as she turned and spun with
the dark man in his cream-colored suit. Both dancers
possessed a natural grace and affinity with the music,
and they looked spectacular on the dance floor. They
ended the dance with Chuck lowering Hillary into a
deep, dramatic dip, and when she stood again, she was
laughing and flushed with the excitement of the dance.
They wove their way back to their table, Chuck's arm
around her shoulders, and Hillary's laughter died as she

found herself confronted with the gray eyes that had disturbed her a short time before.

"Hello, Hillary." Bret's greeting was casual, and she was grateful for the lighting system, which disguised her change of color.

"Hello, Mr. Bardoff," she returned, wondering why her stomach had begun to flutter at the sight of him.

"You met Charlene, I believe."

Her eyes shifted to the redhead at his side. "Of course, nice to see you again." Hillary turned to her partner and made quick introductions. Chuck pumped Bret's hand with great enthusiasm.

"Bret Bardoff? *The* Bret Bardoff?" Hillary cringed at the undisguised awe and admiration.

"The only one I know," he answered with an easy smile.

"Please—" Chuck indicated their table "—join us for a drink."

Bret's smile widened as he inclined his head to Hillary, laughter lighting his eyes as she struggled to cover her discomfort.

"Yes, please do." She met his eyes directly, and her voice was scrupulously polite. She was determined to win the silent battle with the strange, uncommon emotions his mere presence caused. Flicking a quick glance at his companion, her discomfort changed to amusement as she observed Charlene Mason was no more pleased to share their company than she was. Or perhaps, Hillary thought idly as they slid behind the table, she was not pleased with sharing Bret with anyone, however briefly.

"A very impressive show the two of you put on out there," Bret commented to Chuck, indicating the dance floor with a nod of his head. His gaze roamed over to include Hillary. "You two must dance often to move so well together."

"There's no better partner than Hillary," Chuck declared magnanimously, and patted her hand with friendly affection. "She can dance with anyone."

"Is that so?" Bret's brows lifted. "Perhaps you'll let me borrow her for a moment and see for myself."

An unreasonable panic filled Hillary at the thought of dancing with him and it was reflected in her expressive eyes.

She rose with a feeling of helpless indignation as Bret came behind her and pulled out her chair without waiting for her assent.

"Stop looking like such a martyr," he whispered in her ear as they approached the other dancers.

"Don't be absurd," she stated with admirable dignity, furious that he could read her so effortlessly.

The music had slowed, and he turned her to face him, gathering her into his arms. At the contact, an overpowering childish urge to pull away assailed her, and she struggled to prevent the tension from becoming noticeable. His chest was hard, his basic masculinity overwhelming, and she refused to allow herself the relief of swallowing in nervous agitation. The arm around her waist held her achingly close, so close their bodies seemed to melt together as he moved her around the floor. She had unconsciously shifted to her toes, and her cheek rested against his, the scent of him assaulting her senses, making her wonder if she had perhaps sipped her drink too quickly. Her heart was pounding erratically against his, and she fought to control the leaping of her pulses as she matched her steps to his.

"I should have known you were a dancer," he mur-

mured against her ear, causing a fresh flutter of her
heartbeat.

"Really," she countered, battling to keep her tone
careless and light, attempting to ignore the surge of excitement of his mouth on the lobe of her ear. "Why?"

"The way you walk, the way you move. With a sensuous grace, and effortless rhythm."

She intended to laugh off the compliment and tilted
her head to meet his eyes. She found herself instead
staring wordlessly into their gray depths. His hold on
her did not lessen as they faced, their lips a breath apart,
and she found the flip remark she had been about to
make slip into oblivion.

"I always thought gray eyes were like steel," she
murmured, hardly aware she was voicing her thoughts.
"Yours are more like clouds."

"Dark and threatening?" he suggested, holding her
gaze.

"Sometimes," she whispered, caught in the power he
exuded. "And others, warm and soft like an early mist.
I never know whether I'm in for a storm or a shower.
Never know what to expect."

"Don't you?" His voice was quiet as his gaze dropped
to her lips, tantalizingly close to his. "You should by
now."

She struggled with the weakness invading her at his
softly spoken retort and clutched for sophistication. "Really, Mr. Bardoff, are you attempting to seduce me in
the middle of a crowded dance floor?"

"One must make use of what's available," he answered, then lifted his brow. "Have you somewhere
else in mind?"

"Sorry," she apologized, and turned her head so their

faces no longer met. "We're both otherwise engaged, and," she added, attempting to slip away, "the dance is over."

He did not release her, pulling her closer and speaking ominously in her ear. "You'll not get away until you drop that infuriatingly formal Mr. Bardoff and use my name." When she did not reply, he went on, an edge sharpening his voice. "I'm perfectly content to stay like this. You're a woman who was meant for a man's arms. I find you suit mine."

"All right," Hillary said between her teeth. "Bret, would you please let me go before I'm crushed beyond recognition?"

"Certainly." His grip slacked, but his arm remained around her. "Don't tell me I'm really hurting you." His smile was wide and triumphant as he gazed into her resentful face.

"I'll let you know after I've had my X-rays."

"I doubt if you're as fragile as all that." He led her back to the table, his arm still encircling her waist.

They joined their respective partners, and the group spoke generally for the next few minutes. Hillary felt unmistakable hostility directed toward her from the other woman, which Bret was either blissfully unaware of or ignored. Between frosty green eyes and her own disquieting awareness of the tall, fair man whose arms had held her so intimately, Hillary was acutely uncomfortable. It was a relief when the couple rose to leave, and Bret refused Chuck's request that they stay for another round. Charlene looked on with undisguised boredom.

"Charlene's not fond of discos, I'm afraid," Bret explained, grinning as he slipped an arm casually around the redhead's shoulders, causing her to look up at him with a smile of pure invitation. The gesture caused a sudden blaze of emotions to flare in Hillary that she refused to identify as jealousy. "She merely came tonight to please me. I'm thinking of using a disco background for the layout." Bret gazed down at Hillary with an enigmatic smile. "Wasn't it a stroke of luck that I was able to see you here tonight. It gives me a much clearer picture of how to set things up."

Hillary's gaze narrowed at his tone, and she caught the gleam of laughter in his eyes. Luck nothing, she thought suddenly, realizing with certainty that Bret rarely depended on luck. Somehow he had known she would be here tonight, and he had staged the accidental meeting. This layout must be very important to him, she mused, feeling unaccountably miserable. What other reason would he have for seeking her out and dancing with her while he had the obviously willing Charlene Mason hanging all over him?

"See you Monday, Hillary," Bret said easily as he and his lady made to leave.

"Monday?" Chuck repeated when they were once more alone. "Aren't you the fox." His teeth flashed in a grin. "Keeping the famous Mr. Bardoff tucked in your pocket."

"Hardly," she snapped, irritated by his conclusion. "Our relationship is strictly business. I'm working for his magazine. He's my employer, nothing more."

"Okay, okay." Chuck's grin only widened at her angry denial. "Don't take my head off. It's a natural mistake, and I'm not the only one who made it."

Hillary looked up sharply. "What are you talking about?"

"Sweet Hillary," he explained in a patient tone, "didn't you feel the knives stabbing you in the back when you were dancing with your famous employer?" At her blank stare, he sighed deeply. "You know, even after three years in New York, you're still incredibly naive." The corners of his mouth lifted, and he laid a brotherly hand on her shoulder. "A certain redhead was shooting daggers into you from her green eyes the entire time you were dancing. Why, I expected you to keel over in a pool of blood at any second."

"That's absurd." Hillary swirled the contents of her glass and frowned at them. "I'm sure Miss Mason knew very well Bret's purpose in seeing me was merely for research, just background for his precious layout."

Chuck regarded her thoroughly and shook his head. "As I said before, Hillary, you are incredibly naive."

# Chapter 3

Monday morning dawned cool, crisp, and gray. In the office of *Mode,* however, threatening skies were not a factor. Obviously, Hillary decided, Bret had permitted nature to have a tantrum now that shooting had moved indoors.

At his direction, she was placed in the hands of a hairdresser who would assist in the transformation to smooth, competent businesswoman. Jet shoulder-length hair was arranged in a sleek chignon that accented classic bone structure, and the severely tailored lines of the three-piece gray suit, instead of appearing masculine, only heightened Hillary's femininity.

Larry was immersed in camera equipment, lighting, and angles when she entered Bret's office. Giving the room a quick survey, she was forced to admit it was both an elegant and suitable background for the morning's session. She watched with fond amusement as Larry, oblivious to her presence, adjusted lenses and tested meters, muttering to himself.

"The genius at work," a voice whispered close to her ear, and Hillary whirled, finding herself staring into the eyes that had begun to haunt her.

"That's precisely what he is," she retorted, furious with the way her heart began to drum at his nearness.

"Testy this morning, aren't we?" Bret observed with a lifted brow. "Still hungover from the weekend?"

"Certainly not." Dignity wrapped her like a cloak. "I never drink enough to have a hangover."

"Oh, yes, I forgot, the Mr. Hyde syndrome."

"Hillary, there you are." Larry interrupted Hillary's search for a suitable retort. "What took you so long?"

"Sorry, Larry, the hairdresser took quite some time."

The amused gleam in Bret's eyes demanded and received her answer. As their gazes met over Larry's head with the peculiar intimacy of a shared joke, a sweet weakness washed over her, like a soft, gentle wave washing over a waiting shore. Terrified, she dropped her eyes, attempting to dispel the reaction he drew from her without effort.

"Do you always frighten so easily?" Bret's voice was calm, with a hint of mockery, the tone causing her chin to lift in defiance. She glared, helplessly angry with his ability to read her thoughts as if they were written on her forehead. "That's better," he approved, fending off the fire with cool composure. "Anger suits you. It darkens your eyes and puts rose in your cheeks. Spirit is an essential trait for women and—" his mouth lifted at the corner as he paused "—for horses."

She choked and sputtered over the comparison, willing her temper into place with the knowledge that if she lost it she would be powerless against him in a verbal battle. "I suppose that's true," she answered carelessly after swallowing the words that had sprung into her head. "In my observation, men appear to fall short of the physical capacity of one and the mental capacity of the other."

"Well, that hairstyle certainly makes you look competent." Larry turned to study Hillary critically, oblivious to anything that had occurred since he had last spoken. With a sigh of defeat, Hillary gazed at the ceiling for assistance.

"Yes," Bret agreed, keeping his features serious. "The woman executive, very competent, very smart."

"Assertive, aggressive, and ruthless," Hillary interrupted, casting him a freezing look. "I shall emulate you, Mr. Bardoff."

His brows rose fractionally. "That should be fascinating. I'll leave you then to get on with your work, while I get on with mine."

The door closed behind him, and the room was suddenly larger and strangely empty. Hillary shook herself and got to work, attempting to block out all thoughts of Bret Bardoff from her mind.

For the next hour Larry moved around the room, clicking his camera, adjusting the lighting, and calling out directions as Hillary assumed the poses of a busy woman executive.

"That's a wrap in here." He signaled for her to relax, which she did by sinking into a soft leather chair in a casual, if undignified, pose.

"Fiend!" she cried as he snapped the camera once

more, capturing her as she sprawled, slouched in the chair, legs stretched out in front of her.

"It'll be a good shot," he claimed with an absent smile. "Weary woman wiped out by woesome work."

"You have a strange sense of humor, Larry," Hillary retorted, not bothering to alter her position. "It comes from having a camera stuck to your face all the time."

"Now, now, Hil, let's not get personal. Heave yourself out of that chair. We're going into the boardroom, and you, my love, can be chairman of the board."

"Chairperson," she corrected, but his mind was already involved with his equipment. Groaning, she stood and left him to his devices.

The remainder of the day's shooting was long and tedious. Dissatisfied with the lighting, Larry spent more than half an hour rearranging and resetting until it met with his approval. After a further hour under hot lights, Hillary felt as fresh as week-old lettuce and was more than ready when Larry called an end to the day's work.

She found herself searching for Bret's lean form as she made her way from the building, undeniably disappointed when there was no sign of him and angry with her own reaction. Walking for several blocks, she breathed in the brisk autumn air, determined to forget the emotions stirred by the tall man with sharp gray eyes. Just a physical attraction, she reasoned, tucking her hands in her pockets and allowing her feet to take her farther down the busy sidewalk. Physical attraction happens all the time; it would pass like a twenty-four-hour virus.

A diversion was what she required, she decided—something to chase him from her mind and set her thoughts back on the track she had laid out for herself.

Success in the field she had chosen, independence, security—these were her priorities. There was no room for romantic entanglements. When the time came for settling down, it certainly would not be with a man like Bret Bardoff, but with someone safe, someone who did not set her nerves on end and confuse her at every encounter. Besides, she reminded herself, ignoring the sudden gloom, he wasn't interested in her romantically in any case. He seemed to prefer well-proportioned redheads.

Shooting resumed the next morning, once again in *Mode*'s offices. Today, dressed in a dark blue shirt and boot-length skirt of a lighter shade, Hillary was to take on the role of working girl. The session was to take place in Bret's secretary's office, much to that woman's delight.

"I can't tell you how excited I am, Miss Baxter. I feel like a kid going to her first circus."

Hillary smiled at the young woman whose eyes were alight with anticipation. "I'll admit to feeling like a trained elephant from time to time—and make it Hillary."

"I'm June. This is all routine to you, I suppose." Her head shook, causing chestnut curls to bounce and sway. "But it seems very glamorous and exciting to me." Her eyes drifted to where Larry was setting up for the shooting with customary absorption. "Mr. Newman's a real expert, isn't he? He's been fiddling with all those dials and lenses and lights. He's very attractive. Is he married?"

Hillary laughed, glancing carelessly at Larry. "Only to his Nikon."

"Oh." June smiled, then frowned. "Are you two, ah, I mean, are you involved?"

"Just master and slave," Hillary answered, seeing Larry as an attractive, eligible man for the first time. Looking back at June's appealing face, she smiled in consideration. "You know the old adage, 'The way to a man's heart is through his stomach.' Take my advice. The way to that man's heart is through his lenses. Ask him about f-stops."

Bret emerged from his office. He broke into a slow, lazy smile when he saw Hillary. "Ah, man's best friend, the efficient secretary."

Ignoring the pounding of her heart, Hillary forced her voice into a light tone. "No corporate decisions today. I've been demoted."

"That's the way of the business world." He nodded understandingly. "Executive dining room one day, typing pool the next. It's a jungle out there."

"All set," Larry announced from across the room. "Where's Hillary?" He turned to see the trio watching him and grinned. "Hello, Bret, hi, Hil. All set?"

"Your wish is my command, O master of the thirty-five millimeter," Hillary said, moving to join him.

"Can you type, Hillary?" Bret inquired cheerily. "I'll give you some letters, and we can kill two birds with one stone."

"Sorry, Mr. Bardoff," she replied, allowing herself to enjoy his smile. "Typewriters and I have a longstanding agreement. I don't pound on them, and they don't pound on me."

"Is it all right if I watch for a while, Mr. Newman?" June requested. "I won't get in the way. Photography just fascinates me."

Larry gave an absent assent, and, after casting his secretary a puzzled look, Bret turned to reenter his office. "I'll need you in a half hour, June—the Brookline contract."

The session went quickly with Larry and Hillary progressing with professional ease. The model followed the photographer's instructions, often anticipating a mood before he spoke. After a time, June disappeared unobtrusively through the heavy doors leading to Bret's office. Neither Hillary nor Larry noticed her silent departure.

Sometime later, Larry lowered his camera and stared fixedly into space. Hillary maintained her silence, knowing from experience this did not signal the end, but a pause while a fresh idea formed in his mind.

"I want to finish up with something here," he muttered, staring through Hillary as if she were intangible. His face cleared with inspiration. He focused his eyes. "I know. Change the ribbon in the typewriter."

"Surely you jest." She began an intense study of her nails.

"No, it'll be good. Go ahead."

"Larry," she protested in patient tones. "I haven't the foggiest notion how to change a ribbon."

"Fake it," Larry suggested.

With a sigh, Hillary seated herself behind the desk and stared at the typewriter.

"Ever harvested wheat, Larry?" she hazarded, attempting to postpone his order. "It's a fascinating process."

"Hillary," he interrupted, drawing his brows together.

With another sigh, she surrendered to artistic temperament. "I don't know how to open it," she muttered, pushing buttons at random. "It has to open, doesn't it?"

"There should be a button or lever under it," Larry returned patiently. "Don't they have typewriters in Kansas?"

"I suppose they do. My sister... Oh!" she cried, and grinned, delighted out of all proportion, like a small child completing a puzzle, when the release was located. Lifting the lid, she frowned intently at the inner workings. "Scalpel," she requested, running a finger over naked keys.

"Keep going, Hil," Larry commanded. "Just pretend you know what you're doing."

She found herself falling into the spirit of things and attacked the thin black ribbon threaded through various guides with enthusiasm. Her smooth brow was puckered in concentration as she forgot the man and his camera and gave herself over to the job of dislodging ribbon from machine. The more she unraveled, the longer the ribbon became, growing with a life of its own. Absently, she brushed a hand across her cheek, smearing it with black ink.

An enormous, ever-growing heap tangled around her fingers. Realization dawned that she was fighting a losing battle. With a grin for Larry, she flourished the mess of ribbon as he clicked a final picture.

"Terrific," he answered her grin as he lowered his camera. "A classic study in ineptitude."

"Thanks, friend, and if you use any of those shots, I'll sue." Dumping the mass of loose ribbon on the open typewriter, she expelled a long breath. "I'll leave it to you to explain to June how this catastrophe came about. I'm finished."

"Absolutely." Bret's voice came from behind, and Hillary whirled in the chair to see both him and June staring at the chaos on the desk. "If you ever give up modeling, steer clear of office work. You're a disaster."

Hillary attempted to resent his attitude, but one glance at the havoc she had wrought brought on helpless giggles. "Well, Larry, get us out of this one. We've been caught red-handed at the scene of the crime."

Bret closed the distance between them with lithe grace and gingerly lifted one of Hillary's hands. "Blackhanded, I'd say." Putting his other hand under her chin, he smiled in the lazy way that caused Hillary's reluctant heart to perform a series of somersaults. "There's quite a bit of evidence on that remarkable face as well."

She shook off the sweet weakness invading her and peered down at her hands. "Good Lord, how did I manage that? Will it come off?" She addressed her question to June, who assured her soap and water would do the trick. "Well, I'm going to wash away the evidence, and I'm leaving you—" she nodded to Larry "—to make amends for the damage." She encompassed June's desk with a sweeping gesture. "Better do some fast talking, old man," she added in a stage whisper, and gave June the present of her famous smile.

Reaching the door before her, Bret opened it and took a few steps down the long hall beside her. "Setting up a romance for my secretary, Hillary?"

"Could be," she returned enigmatically. "Larry could do with more than cameras and darkrooms in his life."

"And what could you use in yours, Hillary?" His question was soft, putting a hand on her arm and turning her to face him.

"I've… I've got everything I need," she stammered, feeling like a pinned butterfly under his direct gaze.

"Everything?" he repeated, keeping her eyes locked on his. "Pity I've an appointment, or we could go into this in more detail." Pulling her close, his lips brushed hers, then formed a crooked smile that was devastatingly appealing. "Go wash your face—you're a fine mess." Turning, he strode down the hall, leaving Hillary to deal with a mixture of frustration and unaccustomed longing.

She spent her free afternoon shopping, a diversionary tactic for soothing jangled nerves, but her mind constantly floated back to a brief touch of lips, a smile lighting gray eyes. The warmth seemed to linger on her mouth, stirring her emotions, arousing her senses. A cold blast of wind swirling in her face brought her back to reality. Cursing her treacherous imagination, she hailed a cab. She would have to hurry in order to make her dinner date with Lisa.

It was after five when Hillary entered her apartment and dumped her purchases on a chair in the bedroom. She released the latch on the front door for Lisa's benefit and made her way to the bath, filling the tub with hot, fragrant water. She intended to soak for a full twenty minutes. Just as she stepped from the tub and grabbed a towel, the bell sounded at the front door.

"Come on in, Lisa. Either you're early, or I'm late." Draping the towel saronglike around her slim body, she walked from the room, the scent of strawberries clinging to her shining skin. "I'll be ready in a minute. I got carried away in the tub. My feet were…" She stopped dead in her tracks, because instead of the small, blond Lisa, she was confronted by the tall, lean figure of Bret Bardoff.

"Where did you come from?" Hillary demanded when she located her voice.

"Originally or just now?" he countered, smiling at her confusion.

"I thought you were Lisa."

"I got that impression."

"What are you doing here?"

"Returning this." He held up a slim gold pen. "I assumed it was yours. The initials H.B. are engraved on it."

"Yes, it's mine," she concurred, frowning at it. "I must have dropped it from my bag. You needn't have bothered. I could have gotten it tomorrow."

"I thought you might have been looking for it." His eyes roamed over the figure scantily clad in the bath towel and lingered on her smooth legs, then rested a moment on the swell of her breast. "Besides, it was well worth the trip."

Hillary's eyes dropped down to regard her state of disarray and widened in shock. Color stained her cheeks as his eyes laughed at her, and she turned and ran from the room. "I'll be back in a minute."

Hastily, she pulled on chocolate brown cords and a beige mohair sweater, tugged a quick brush through her hair, and applied a touch of makeup with a deft hand. Taking a deep breath, she returned to the living room, attempting to assume a calm front that she was far from feeling. Bret was seated comfortably on the sofa, smoking a cigarette with the air of someone completely at home.

"Sorry to keep you waiting," she said politely, fighting back the embarrassment that engulfed her. "It was kind of you to take the trouble to return the pen to me." He handed it to her and she placed it on the low mahogany table. "May I...would you..." She bit her lip in frustration, finding her poise had vanished. "Can I get you a drink? Or maybe you're in a hurry—"

"I'm in no hurry," he answered, ignoring her frown. "Scotch, neat, if you have it."

Her frown deepened. "I may have. I'll have to check." She retreated to the kitchen, searching through cupboards for her supply of rarely used liquor. He had followed her, and she turned, noting with a quickening of pulse how his presence seemed to dwarf the small room. She felt an intimacy that was both exciting and disturbing. She resumed her search, all too conscious of his casual stance as he leaned against the refrigerator, hands in pockets.

"Here." Triumphantly, she brandished the bottle. "Scotch."

"So it is."

"I'll get you a glass. Neat, you said?" She pushed at her hair. "That's with no ice, right?"

"You'd make a marvelous bartender," he returned, taking both bottle and glass and pouring the liquid himself.

"I'm not much of a drinker," she muttered.

"Yes, I remember—a two-drink limit. Shall we go sit down?" He took her hand with the usual familiarity, and her words of protest died. "A very nice place, Hillary," he commented as they seated themselves on the sofa. "Open, friendly, colorful. Do the living quarters reflect the tenant?"

"So they say."

"Friendliness is an admirable trait, but you should know better than to leave your door unlatched. This is New York, not a farm in Kansas."

"I was expecting someone."

"But you got someone unexpected." He looked into her eyes, then casually swept the length of her. "What do you think would have happened if someone else had come across that beautiful body of yours draped in a very insufficient towel?" The blush was immediate and impossible to control, and she dropped her eyes. "You should keep your door locked, Hillary. Not every man would let you escape as I did."

"Yes, O mighty emperor," Hillary retorted before she could bite her tongue, and his eyes narrowed dangerously. He captured her with a swift movement, but whatever punishment he had in mind was postponed by the ringing of the phone. Jumping up in relief, Hillary hurried to answer.

"Lisa, hi. Where are you?"

"Sorry, Hillary." The answering voice was breathless. "The most wonderful thing happened. I hope you don't mind, but I have to beg off tonight."

"Of course not—what happened?"

"Mark asked me to have dinner with him."

"So you took my advice and tripped him, right?"

"More or less."

"Oh, Lisa," Hillary cried in amused disbelief, "you didn't really!"

"Well, no," she admitted. "We were both carrying all these law books and ran smack into each other. What a beautiful mess."

"I get the picture." Her laughter floated through the room. "It really has more class than a mugging."

"You don't mind about tonight?"

"Do you think I'd let a pizza stand in the way of true love?" Hillary answered. "Float along and have fun. I'll see you later."

She replaced the receiver and turned to find Bret regarding her with open curiosity. "I must admit that was the most fascinating one-ended conversation I've ever heard." She flashed him a smile with full candle-power and told him briefly of her friend's long unrequited love affair.

"So your solution was to land the poor guy on his face at her feet," he concluded.

"It got his attention."

"Now you're stood up. A pizza, was it?"

"My secret's out," she said, carefully seating herself in a chair across from him. "I hope I can trust you never to breathe a word of this, but I am a pizza junkie. If I don't have one at well-ordered intervals, I go into a frenzy. It's not a pretty sight."

"Well, we can't have you foaming at the mouth, can we?" He set down his empty glass and stood with a fluid motion. "Fetch a coat, I'll indulge you."

"Oh, really, there's no need," she began with quick panic.

"For heaven's sake, let's not go through this again. Get a coat and come on," he commanded, pulling her from her chair. "I could do with some food myself."

She found herself doing his bidding, slipping on a short suede jacket as he picked up his own brown leather. "Got your keys?" he questioned, reengaging the latch and propelling her through the door.

Soon they were seated in the small Italian restaurant that Hillary had indicated. The small table was covered with the inevitable red and white checkered cloth, a candle flickering in its wine bottle holder.

"Well, Hillary, what will you have?"

"Pizza."

"Yes, I know that," he countered with a smile. "Anything on it?"

"Extra cholesterol."

White teeth flashed as he grinned at her. "Is that all?"

"I don't want to overdo—these things can get out of hand."

"Some wine?"

"I don't know if my system can handle it." She considered, then shrugged. "Well, why not, you only live once."

"Too true." He signaled the waiter and gave their order. "You, however," he continued when they were once more alone, "look as though you had lived before. You are a reincarnation of an Indian princess. I bet they called you Pocahontas when you were a kid."

"Not if they were smart," Hillary returned. "I scalped a boy once for just that."

"Do tell?" Bret's attention was caught, and he leaned forward, his head on his hands as his elbows rested on the table. "Please elaborate."

"All right, if you can handle such a bloodthirsty subject over dinner." Pushing back her hair with both hands, she mirrored his casual position. "There was this boy, Martin Collins. I was madly in love with him, but he preferred Jessie Winfield, a cute little blond number with soulful brown eyes. I was mad with jealousy. I was also too tall, skinny, all eyes and elbows, and eleven years old. I passed them one day, devastated because he was carrying her books, and he called out 'Head for the hills, it's Pocahontas.' That did it, I was a woman scorned. I planned my revenge. I went home and got the small scissors my mother used for mending, painted my face with her best lipstick, and returned to stalk my prey.

"I crept up behind him stealthily, patiently waiting for the right moment. Springing like a panther, I knocked my quarry to the ground, holding him down with my body and cutting off as much hair as I could grab. He screamed, but I showed no mercy. Then my brothers came and dragged me off and he escaped, running like the coward he was, home to his mother."

Bret's laughter rang out as he threw back his head. "What a monster you must have been!"

"I paid for it." She lifted the glass of wine that Bret had poured during her story. "I got the tanning of my life, but it was worth it. Martin wore a hat for weeks."

Their pizza arrived, and through the meal their conversation was more companionable and relaxed than Hillary would have believed possible. When the last piece was consumed, Bret leaned back and regarded her seriously.

"I'd never have believed you could eat like that."

She grinned, relaxed by the combination of wine, good food, and easy company. "I don't often, but when I do, I'm exceptional."

"You're a constant amazement. I never know what to expect. A study of contradictions."

"Isn't that why you hired me, Bret?" She used his name for the first time voluntarily without conscious thought. "For my versatility?"

He smiled, lifted his glass to his lips, and left her question unanswered.

Hillary felt her earlier nervousness return as they walked down the carpeted hall toward her apartment. Determined to remain calm, she bent her head to fish out her keys, using the time to assume a calm veneer.

"Would you like to come in for coffee?"

He took the keys from her hand, unlocked the door, and gave her a slow smile. "I thought you didn't drink coffee."

"I don't, but everyone else in the world does, so I keep some instant."

"With the Scotch, no doubt," he said, leading her into the apartment.

Removing her jacket, Hillary assumed the role of hostess. "Sit down. I'll have coffee out in a minute."

He had shed his own coat, carelessly dropping it down over the arm of a chair. Once more she was aware of the strong build beneath the dark blue rib-knit sweater and close-fitting slacks. She turned and made for the kitchen.

Her movements were deft and automatic as she set the kettle on the burner and removed cups and saucers from cupboards. She set a small sugar bowl and creamer on the glass and wicker tray, and prepared tea for herself and coffee for the man in her living room. She moved with natural grace to the low table, to set the ladened tray down. She smiled with professional ease at the tall man who stood across the room leafing casually through her collection of record albums.

"Quite an assortment." He addressed her from where he stood, looking so at ease and blatantly masculine that Hillary felt her veneer cracking rapidly and fought back a flutter of panic. "Typical of you though," he went on, sparing her from the necessity of immediate comment. "Chopin when you're romantic, Denver when you're homesick, B. B. King when you're down, McCartney when you're up."

"You sound like you know me very well." She felt a strange mixture of amusement and resentment that he had pinpointed her mood music with such uncanny accuracy.

"Not yet," he corrected, putting down an album and coming over to join her. "But I'm working on it."

Suddenly, he was very close, and there was an urgent need in Hillary to be on a more casual footing. "Your coffee's getting cold." She spoke quickly and bent to remove the clutter from the tray, dropping a spoon in her agitation. They bent to retrieve it simultaneously, his strong, lean fingers closing over her fine-boned hand. At the contact, a current of electricity shot down her arm and spread through her body, and her eyes darkened to midnight. She raised her face to his.

There were no words as their eyes met, and she realized the inevitability of the movement. She knew they had been drifting steadily toward this since the first day in Larry's studio. There was a basic attraction between them, an undefinable need she did not pause to question as he lifted her to her feet, and she stepped into his arms.

His lips were warm and gentle on hers as he kissed her slowly, then with increasing pressure, his tongue parted her lips, and his arms tightened around her, crushing her breasts against the hardness of his chest. Her arms twined around his neck. She responded as she had never responded to any man before. The thought ran through her clouded brain that no one had ever kissed her like this, no one had ever held her like this. Then all thought was drowned in a tidal wave of passion.

She made no resistance as she felt herself lowered onto the cushions of the couch, her mouth still the captive of his. The weight of his body pushed hers deep into the sofa as his legs slid between hers, making no secret of his desire. His mouth began to roam, exploring the smooth skin of her neck. The fire of a new and ageless need raged through her veins. She felt the thudding of a heart—hers or his, she could not tell—as his lips caressed her throat and face before meeting hers with possessing hunger. His hand moved under her sweater to cup the breast that swelled under his touch. She sighed and moved under him.

She was lost in a blaze of longing such as she had never known, responding with a passion she had kept buried until that moment, as his lips and hands moved with expertise over her warm and willing body.

His hands moved to the flatness of her stomach, and when she felt his fingers on the snap of her pants, she began to struggle against him. Her protests were ignored, his mouth devouring hers, then laying a trail of heat along her throat.

"Bret, please don't. You have to stop."

He lifted his head from the curve of her neck to look into the deep pools of her eyes, huge now with fear and desire. His own breathing was ragged. She knew a sharp fear that the decision to stop or go on would be taken out of her hands.

"Hillary," he murmured, and bent to claim her lips again, but she turned her head and pushed against him.

"No, Bret, no more."

A long breath escaped from his lips as he removed his body from hers, standing before removing a cigarette from the gold case he had left on the table. Hillary sat up, clutching her hands together in her lap, keeping her head lowered to avoid his eyes.

"I knew you were many things, Hillary," he said after expelling a swift and violent stream of smoke. "I never thought you were a tease."

"I'm not!" she protested, her head snapping up at the harshness of his tone. "That's unfair. Just because I stopped, just because I didn't let you…" Her voice broke. She was filled with confusion and embarrassment, and a perverse longing to be held again in his arms.

"You are not a child," he began with an anger that caused her lips to tremble. "What is the usual outcome when two people kiss like that, when a woman allows a man to touch her like that?" His eyes were dark with barely suppressed fury, and she sat mutely, having been unprepared for the degree his temper could reach. "You wanted me as much as I wanted you. Stop playing games. We've both been well aware that this would happen eventually. You're a grown woman. Stop behaving like an innocent young girl."

The remark scored, and the telltale flush crept to her cheeks before she could lower her lashes to conceal painful discomfort. Bret gaped at her, anger struggling with stunned disbelief. "Good heavens, you've never been with a man before, have you?"

Hillary shut her eyes in humiliation, and she remained stubbornly silent.

"How is that possible?" he asked in a voice tinged with reluctant amusement. "How does a woman reach the ripe old age of twenty-four with looks like yours and remain as pure as the driven snow?"

"It hasn't been all that difficult," she muttered, and looked anywhere in the room but at him. "I don't normally let things get so out of hand." She made a small, helpless shrug.

"You might let a man know of your innocence before things get out of hand," he advised caustically, crushing out his cigarette with undue force.

"Maybe I should paint a red V for virgin on my forehead—then there'd be no confusion," Hillary flared, lifting her chin in bold defiance.

"You know, you're gorgeous when you're angry." He spoke coolly, but the steel vibrated in his tone, casual elegance wrapped around a volatile force. "Watch yourself, or I'll have another go at changing your status."

"I don't think you would ever stoop to forcing a woman," she retorted as he moved to pick up his jacket.

Pausing, he turned back to her, gray eyes narrowing into slits as he hauled her to her feet, possessing her again until her struggles had transformed into limp clinging.

"Don't count on it." His voice was deadly soft as he gave her a firm nudge back onto the couch. "I make a point of getting what I want." His eyes moved lazily over her slim body, pausing on the lips still soft from his. "Make no mistake," he went on as she began to tremble under his prolonged gaze. "I could have you here and now without forcing, but—" he moved to the door "—I can afford to wait."

# Chapter 4

For the next few weeks shooting moved along with few complications. Larry was enthusiastic about the progress that was being made and brought Hillary a file of work prints so that she could view the fruits of their labor.

Studying the pictures with a professional objectivity, she admitted they were excellent, perhaps the best work Larry and she had done together or separately. There was a touch of genius in his choice of angles and lighting, using shadows and filters with a master hand. Added to this was Hillary's ability to assume varied roles. The pictures were already beginning to form a growing study of womanhood. They were nearly halfway through the planned shooting. If everything continued to go as well, they would be finished ahead of schedule. Bret was now planning a crash publication, which would put the issue on the stands in early spring.

Sessions would resume following the Thanksgiving weekend, while the art director and staff, with Bret's approval, began the selection of what would be printed in the final copy. Hillary was grateful for the time off, not only for the rest, but for the separation from the man who filled her thoughts and invaded her dreams.

She had expected some constraint between them when she returned to work after their evening together, but Bret had greeted her in his usual way, so casually, in fact, that she thought for a moment that she had imagined the feel of his lips on hers. There was no mention of their meal together or the scene that followed, while he slipped with apparent ease into the partly professional, partly mocking attitude he invariably directed toward her.

It was not as simple a task for Hillary to mirror his nonchalance after the emotions he had awakened in her—emotions that had lain sleeping within her until his touch had brought them to life—but outwardly she displayed a casualness at odds with her inner turmoil.

All in all, the remainder of the shooting time passed easily, and if Larry was forced to admonish her from time to time to relax and not to scowl, he was characteristically preoccupied and saw nothing amiss.

Hillary stood staring from the window of her apartment, her state of mind as bleak as the scene that greeted her. The late November sky was like lead, casting a depressing spell over the city, the buildings and skyscrapers taking on a dismal hue. Leaves had long since deserted the trees, leaving them naked and cheerless, and the grass, where sidewalks made room for it, had lost its healthy green tone, looking instead a sad, dreary yellow. The somberness of the day suited her mood precisely.

A sudden wave of homesickness washed over her, a strong desire for golden wheat fields. Moving to the stereo, she placed a Denver album on the turntable, halting in her movements when the image of Bret standing in the very spot she now occupied swept through her mind. The memory of the hardness of his body against hers and the intimacy briefly shared filled her with a painful longing, replacing homesickness. With a flash of insight, she realized that her attraction for him was more than physical. She switched on the player, filling the room with soft music.

Falling in love had not been in her plans, she reminded herself, and falling for Bret was out of the question, now or ever. That road would lead nowhere but to disaster and humiliation. But she could not quiet the voice that hammered in her brain telling her it was already too late. She sank down in a chair, confusion and depression settling over her like a fog.

It had grown late when Hillary let herself into her apartment after having joined Lisa and Mark for Thanksgiving dinner. The meal had been superb, but she had hidden her lack of appetite under the guise of keeping a careful watch on her figure. She had hidden her depression and concentrated on appearing normal and content. As she closed the door behind her, she breathed a sigh of relief, at last removing the frozen smile and relaxing. Before she could move to the closet to hang up her coat, the phone rang.

"Hello." Her voice reflected her weariness and annoyance.

"Hello, Hillary. Been out on the town?"

There was no need for the caller to identify himself. Hillary recognized Bret immediately, glad that the thumping of her heart was not audible over the wire.

"Hello, Mr. Bardoff." She schooled her voice to coolness. "Do you always call your employees so late?"

"Grouchy, aren't we?" He seemed unperturbed. The thrill of hearing his voice warred with irritation at his composure. "Did you have a nice day?"

"Lovely," she lied. "I'm just home from having dinner with a friend. And you?"

"Spectacular. I'm very fond of turkey."

"Did you call to compare menus or was there something on your mind?" Her voice grew sharp at the picture of Bret and Charlene enjoying a beautifully catered dinner in elegant surroundings.

"Oh, yes, I've something on my mind. To begin with, I had thought to share a holiday drink with you, if you still have that bottle of Scotch."

"Oh." Her voice cracked, panic-filled. Clearing her throat, she stumbled on. "No, I mean, yes, I have the Scotch, but it's late and…"

"Afraid?" he interrupted quietly.

"Certainly not," she snapped. "I'm just tired. I'm on my way to bed."

"Oh, really?" She could hear the amusement in his voice.

"Honestly." To her disgust, she felt herself blushing. "Must you continually make fun of me?"

"Sorry." His apology lacked conviction. "But you will insist on taking yourself seriously. Very well, I won't dip into your liquor supply." Pausing, he added, "Tonight. I'll see you Monday, Hillary, sleep well."

"Good night," she murmured, filled with regret as

she replaced the receiver. Glancing around the room, she felt a swift desire to have him there, filling the emptiness with the excitement of his presence. She sighed and pushed at her hair, realizing she could hardly call him back and issue the invitation had she known where to reach him.

*It's better this way,* she rationalized, *better to avoid him whenever possible. If I'm going to get over this infatuation, distance is my best medicine. He'll tire soon enough without encouragement. I'm sure he gets an ample supply of it from other quarters. Charlene is more his style,* she went on, digging at the wound. *I could never compete with her sophistication, I haven't the knack. She probably speaks French and knows about wines and can drink more than one glass of champagne before she starts to babble.*

On Saturday Hillary met Lisa for lunch, hoping the short outing would boost her flagging spirits. The elegant restaurant was crowded. Spotting Lisa at a small table, Hillary waved and made her way through the room.

"Sorry, I know I'm late," Hillary apologized, picking up the menu set before her. "Traffic was dreadful, and I had a terrible time getting a cab. Winter's definitely on its way. It's freezing out there."

"Is it?" Lisa grinned. "It feels like spring to me."

"Love has apparently thrown you off balance. But," she added, "even if it's affected your brain, it's done wonders for the rest of you. I believe you could glow in the dark."

The blissful smile that lighted Lisa's face was a heart-catching sight, and Hillary's depression evaporated.

"I know my feet haven't touched the ground in weeks. I guess you're sick of watching me float around."

"Don't be silly. It's given me a tremendous lift watching you light up like a neon sign."

The two women ordered their meal, slipping into the easy camaraderie they enjoyed.

"I really should find a friend with warts and a hooked nose," Lisa commented.

Hillary's fork paused on its journey to her mouth. "Come again?"

"The most fascinating man just came in. I might as well be invisible for all the attention he paid me. He was too busy staring at you."

"He's probably just looking for someone he knows."

"He's got someone he knows hanging on to his arm like an appendage," Lisa declared, staring boldly at the couple across the room. "His attention, however, is riveted on you. No, don't turn around," she hissed as Hillary started to turn her head. "Oh, good grief, he's coming over. Quick," she whispered desperately, "look natural."

"You're the one standing on her head, Lisa," Hillary returned calmly, amused by her friend's rapid capitulation.

"Well, Hillary, we just can't keep away from each other, can we?"

Hillary heard the deep voice and her wide eyes met Lisa's startled ones before she looked up to meet Bret's crooked smile. "Hello." Her voice was oddly breathless. Her glance took in the shapely redhead on his arm. "Hello, Miss Mason, nice to see you again," she said quietly.

Charlene merely nodded. From the expression in her

frosty green eyes, it was apparent she couldn't have disagreed more. There was a short pause. Bret raised his brow in inquiry.

"Lisa MacDonald, Charlene Mason and Bret Bardoff," Hillary introduced quickly.

"Oh, you're *Mode* magazine," Lisa blurted out, her eyes shining with excitement. Hillary looked in vain for a hole to open up and swallow her.

"More or less."

Hillary watched, helpless, as Bret turned his most charming smile on Lisa.

"I'm a great fan of your magazine, Mr. Bardoff," Lisa bubbled. She appeared to be unaware of the darts shooting at her from Charlene's narrowed eyes. "I can barely wait for this big layout of Hillary's. It must be very exciting."

"It's been quite an experience so far." He turned to Hillary with an annoying grin. "Don't you agree, Hillary?"

"Quite an experience," she agreed carelessly, forcing her eyes to remain level.

"Bret," Charlene interrupted. "We really must get to our table and let these girls get on with their lunch." Her eyes swept both Hillary and Lisa, dismissing them as beneath notice.

"Nice to have met you, Lisa. See you later, Hillary." His lazy smile had Hillary's heart pounding in its now familiar way. But she managed to murmur goodbye. Nervously, she reached for her tea, hoping Lisa would not discuss the encounter.

Lisa stared at Bret's retreating back for several seconds. "Wow," she breathed, turning huge brown eyes on Hillary. "You didn't tell me he was so terrific! I was literally liquified when he smiled at me."

Dear heaven, Hillary thought wearily, does he affect all women that way? Aloud, she spoke with mock censure. "Shame on you—your heart's supposed to be taken."

"It is," Lisa affirmed. "But I'm still a woman." Looking at Hillary, she went on shrewdly, "Don't tell me he leaves you unmoved. We know each other too well."

A deep sigh escaped. "I'm not immune to Mr. Bardoff's devastating charm, but I'll have to develop some kind of antidote during the next couple of months."

"Don't you think the interest might be mutual? You're not without substantial charm yourself."

"You did notice the redhead clinging to him like ivy on a brick wall?"

"Couldn't miss her." Lisa grimaced. "I had the feeling she expected me to rise and curtsy. Who is she, anyway? The Queen of Hearts?"

"Perfect match for the emperor," Hillary murmured.

"What?"

"Nothing. Are you done? Let's get out of here." Rising without waiting for an answer, Hillary gathered her purse and the two women left the restaurant.

The following Monday Hillary walked to work. She lifted her face to the first snow of the season. Cold flakes drifted to kiss her upturned face, and she felt a thrill of anticipation watching soft white swirl from the lead-colored sky. Snow brought memories of home, sleigh rides, and snow battles. Sluggish traffic was powerless against her mood of excitement, and Hillary arrived at Larry's studio as bright and exuberant as a child.

"Hi, old man. How was your holiday?" Wrapped in a calf-length coat, a matching fur hat pulled low over her head, and cheeks and eyes glowing with the combination of cold and excitement, she was outrageously beautiful.

Larry paused in his lighting adjustment to greet her with a smile. "Look what the first snow blew in. You're an ad for winter vacations."

"You're incorrigible." She slipped out of her outdoor clothing and wrinkled her nose. "You see everything cropped and printed."

"Occupational hazard. June says my eye for a picture is fascinating," he added smugly.

"*June* says?" Delicate brows rose inquiringly.

"Well, yeah, I've, uh, been teaching her a little about photography."

"I see." The tone was ironic.

"She's, well, she's interested in cameras."

"Ah, her interest is limited to shutter speeds and wide-angle lenses," Hillary agreed with a wise nod.

"Come on, Hil," Larry muttered, and began to fiddle with dials.

Gliding over, she hugged him soundly. "Kiss me, you fox. I knew you had it in you somewhere."

"Come on, Hil," he repeated, disentangling himself. "What are you doing here so early? You've got half an hour."

"Amazing, you noticed the time." She batted her eyes, received a scowl, and subsided. "I thought I might look over the work prints."

"Over there." He indicated his overloaded desk in the back corner of the room. "Go on now and let me finish."

"Yes, master." She retreated to search out the file

filled with the prints of the layout. After a few moment's study, she drew out one of herself on the tennis court. "I want a copy of this," she called to him. "I look fiercely competitive." Receiving no response, she glanced over, seeing him once more totally involved and oblivious to her presence. "Certainly, Hillary, my dear," she answered for him. "Anything you want. Look at that stance," she continued with deep enthusiasm, glancing back at the picture in her hands. "The perfect form and intense concentration of a champion. Look out, Wimbledon, here I come. You'll tear them apart, Hil." She again assumed Larry's role. "Thanks, Larry. All that talent and beauty too. Please, Larry, you're embarrassing me."

"They lock people up for talking to themselves," a deep voice whispered in her ear. Hillary jumped. The picture dropped from her hands to the pile on the desk. "Nervous, too—that's a bad sign."

She whirled and found herself face to face with Bret—so close, in fact, she took an instinctive step in retreat. The action did not go unnoticed, and the corner of his mouth twitched into a disarmingly crooked smile.

"Don't creep up on me like that."

"Sorry, but you were so engrossed in your dialogue." His shoulders moved eloquently, and he allowed his voice to trail away.

A reluctant smile hovered on Hillary's lips. "Sometimes Larry lets the conversation drag a mite, and I'm obliged to carry him." She gestured with a slender hand. "Just look at that. He doesn't even know you're here."

"Mmm, perhaps I should take advantage of his preoccupation." He tucked a silky strand of hair behind her ear. The warmth of his fingers shot through her as he made the disturbingly gentle gesture, and her pulse began to jump at an alarming rate.

"Oh, hi, Bret. When did you get in?"

At Larry's words, Hillary let out a sigh, unsure whether it was born of relief or frustration.

December was slipping slowly by. Progress on the layout was more advanced than expected, and it appeared that actual shooting would be completed before Christmas. Hillary's contract with Bret ran through March, and she speculated on what she would do when the shooting stage was over and she was no longer needed. It was possible that Bret would release her, though she admitted this was highly unlikely. He would hardly wish her to work for a competitor before his pet project was on the stands.

Maybe he'll find some other work for me through the next couple of months, she theorized during a short break in a session. Or maybe she could be idle for a time. Oddly, the latter prospect appealed to her, and this surprised her. She enjoyed her work, didn't she? Hard work, yes, but rarely boring. Of course she enjoyed her work. It was enough for her, and she intended to keep it first in her life for the next few years. After that, she could retire if she liked or take a long vacation, travel—whatever. Then, when everything was in order, there would be time for a serious romance. She'd find someone nice, someone safe, someone she could marry and settle down with. That was her plan, and it made perfect sense. Only now, when thought through, it sounded horribly cold and dull.

\* \* \*

Larry's studio was more crowded than usual during the second week of December. This particular morning, voices and bodies mingled in the room in delightful chaos. In this shooting, Hillary was sharing the spotlight with an eight-month-old boy as she portrayed the young mother.

A small section of the room was set to resemble part of a living area. When Hillary emerged from the hairdresser's hands, Larry was busy double-checking his equipment. Bret worked with him, discussing ideas for the session, and she chided herself for staring at his strong, lean back.

Leaving the men to their duties, she went over to meet the young mother and the child who would be hers for a few minutes in front of the camera. She was both surprised and amused by the baby's resemblance to her. Andy, as his mother introduced him, had a tuft of hair as dark and shining as Hillary's, and his eyes, though not as deep as hers, were startlingly blue. She would be taken without question for his mother by any stranger.

"Do you know how hard it was to find a child with your looks?" Bret asked, approaching from across the room to where Hillary sat with Andy on her lap. Bret stopped in front of her as she laughed and bounced the baby on her knee, and both woman and child raised deep blue eyes. "A person could be struck blind by all that brilliance. Perhaps you two should turn down the wattage."

"Isn't he beautiful?" Her voice was warm as she rubbed her cheeks against the soft down of his hair.

"Spectacular," he agreed. "He could be yours."

A shadow clouded over dark blue, and Hillary lowered her lashes on the sudden longing his words aroused. "Yes, the resemblance is amazing. Are we ready?"

"Yes."

"Well, partner." She stood and rested Andy on her hip. "Let's get to work."

"Just play with him," Larry instructed. "Do what comes naturally. What we're looking for is spontaneity." He looked down at the round face, and Andy's eyes met his levelly. "I think he understands me."

"Of course," Hillary agreed with a toss of her head. "He's a very bright child."

"We'll keep the shots candid and hope he responds to you. We can only work with children a few minutes at a time."

And so they began, with the two dark heads bent near each other as they sat on the carpeted area with Hillary building alphabet blocks and Andy gleefully destroying her efforts. Soon both were absorbed in the game and each other, paying scant attention to Larry's movements or the soft click of the camera. Hillary lay on her stomach, feet in the air, constructing yet another tower for ultimate demolition. The child reached out, diverted by a strand of silky hair. His stubby fingers curled around the softness, tugging on it and bringing it to his mouth wrapped in a small fist.

Rolling on her back, she lifted the child over her head, and he gurgled in delight at the new game. Setting him on her stomach, he soon became enchanted by the pearl buttons on her pale green blouse. She watched his concentration, tracing his features with her fingertip. Again, she felt the pull of sudden longing. She lifted the baby over her body, making the sounds of a plane as she swayed him over her. Andy squealed in delight and she stood him on her stomach, letting him bounce to his own music.

She stood with him, swinging him in a circle before hugging him against her. *This is what I want,* she realized suddenly, holding the child closer. *A child of my own, tiny arms around my neck, a child with the man I love.* She closed her eyes as she rubbed her cheek against Andy's round one. When she opened them again, she found herself staring up into Bret's intense gaze.

She held her eyes level a moment as it drifted over her quietly that this was the man she loved, the man whose child she wanted to feel in her arms. She had known the truth for some time, but had refused to acknowledge it. Now, there was no denying it.

Andy's none-too-gentle tug on her hair broke the spell, and Hillary turned away, shaken by what she had just been forced to admit to herself. This was not what she had planned. How could this happen? She needed time to think, time to sort things out. Right now she felt too confused.

She was profoundly relieved when Larry signaled the finish. With a supreme effort, Hillary kept her professional smile in place while inside she trembled at her new awareness.

"Outstanding," Larry declared. "You two work together like old friends."

Not work, Hillary corrected silently, a fantasy. She had been acting out a fantasy. Perhaps her entire career was a fantasy, perhaps her entire life. A hysterical giggle bubbled inside her, and she choked it back. She could not afford to make a fool of herself now. She could not allow herself to think about the feelings running through her or the questions buzzing inside her brain.

"It's going to take some time to break down and set up for the next segment, Hil." Larry consulted his watch. "Go grab a bite before you change. Give it an hour."

Hillary assented with a wave of relief at the prospect of some time alone.

"I'll go with you."

"Oh, no," she protested, picking up her coat and hurrying out. His brow lifted at her frantic tone. "I mean, don't bother. You must have work to do. You must have to get back to your office or something."

"Yes, my work never ceases," he acknowledged with a heavy dose of mockery. "But once in a while I have to eat."

He took her coat to help her with it. His hands rested on her shoulders, their warmth seeping through the material and burning her skin, causing her to stiffen defensively. His fingers tightened and he turned her to face him.

"It was not my intention to have *you* for lunch, Hillary." The words were soft, at odds with the temper darkening his eyes. "Will you never cease to be suspicious of me?"

The streets were clear, but there was a light covering of white along the sidewalks and on the cars parked along the curb. Hillary felt trapped in the closed car sitting so close to the man who drove, long fingers closed over the steering wheel of the Mercedes. He skirted Central Park, and she endeavored to ease her tension and slow the incessant drumming of her heart.

"Look, it's beautiful, isn't it?" She indicated the

trees, their bare branches now robed in white, glittering as if studded with diamonds. "I love the snow," she chattered on, unable to bear the silence. "Everything seems clean and fresh and friendly. It makes it seem more like..."

"Home?" he supplied.

"Yes," she said weakly, retreating from his penetrating gaze.

Home, she thought. Home could be anywhere with this man. But she must not reveal her weakness. He must never know the love that rushed through her, tossing her heart like the winds of a tornado that swept through Kansas in late spring.

Sitting in a small booth, Hillary babbled about whatever innocuous subject came to mind. Chattering to avoid a lull where he might glimpse the secret she held within her, securely locked like a treasure in a fortress.

"Are you okay, Hillary?" Bret asked suddenly when she paused to take a breath. "You've been very jumpy lately." His eyes were sharp and probing, and for a terrifying moment Hillary feared they would penetrate her mind and read the secret written there.

"Sure, I am." Her voice was admirably calm. "I'm just excited about the layout." She grasped at the straw of an excuse. "We'll be finished soon, and the issue will be on the stands. I'm anxious about the reception."

"If it's only business that bothers you," he said abruptly, "I believe I'm qualified to predict the reaction will be tremendous." His eyes reached out and held hers. "You'll be a sensation, Hillary. Offers will come pouring in—magazines, television, products for your endorsement. You'll be in a position to pick and choose."

"Oh" was all that she could manage.

His brows knitted dangerously. "Doesn't it excite you? Isn't that what you've always wanted?" he asked brusquely.

"Of course it is," she stated with a great deal more enthusiasm than she was feeling. "I'd have to be demented not to be thrilled, and I'm grateful for the opportunity you gave me."

"Save your gratitude." He cut her off curtly. "This project has been a result of teamwork. Whatever you gain from it, you've earned." He drew out his wallet. "If you're finished, I'll drop you back before I return to the office."

She nodded mutely, unable to comprehend what she had said to arouse his anger.

The final phase of shooting was underway. Hillary changed in the small room off Larry's main studio. Catching sight of her reflection in the full-length mirror, she held her breath. She had thought the negligee lovely but uninspired when she had lifted it from its box, but now, as it swirled around her, she was awed by its beauty. White and filmy, it floated around her slim curves, falling in gentle folds to her ankles. It was low cut, but not extreme, the soft swell of her breasts merely hinted at above the neckline. Yes, Hillary decided as she moved, the drifting material following in a lovingly lazy manner, it's stunning.

Earlier that day, she had modeled an exquisite sable coat. She remembered the feel of the fur against her chin and sighed. Larry had captured the first expression of delight and desire as she had buried her face against the collar. But Hillary knew now that she would rather have this negligee than ten sables. There was something special about it, as though it had been created with her in mind.

She walked from the dressing room and stood watching as Larry completed his setup. He has outdone himself this time, she mused with admiration. The lighting was soft and gentle, like a room lit with candles, and he had set up backlighting, giving the illusion of moonlight streaming. The effect was both romantic and subtle.

"Ah, good, you're ready." Larry turned from his task, then, focusing on her directly, let out a low whistle. "You're gorgeous. Every man who sees your picture will be dying for love of you, and every woman will be putting herself in your place. Sometimes you still amaze me."

She laughed and moved to join him as the studio door opened. Turning, the gown drifting about her, she saw Bret enter the room with Charlene on his arm. Blue eyes locked with gray before his traveled slowly over her with the intensity of a physical caress.

He took his time in bringing his eyes back to her face. "You look extraordinary, Hillary."

"Thanks." She swallowed the huskiness of her voice and her gaze moved from his to encounter Charlene's icy stare. The shock was like a cold shower and Hillary wished with all her heart that Bret had not chosen to bring his shapely companion with him.

"We're just getting started." Larry's matter-of-fact tone shattered the spell, and three heads turned to him.

"Don't let us hold things up," Bret said easily. "Charlene wanted to see the project that's been keeping me so busy."

His implication that Charlene had a stake in his life caused Hillary's spirits to plummet. Shaking off encroaching depression, she reminded herself that what she felt for Bret was strictly one-sided.

"Stand here, Hil," Larry directed, and she drifted to the indicated spot.

Muted lighting lent a glow to her skin, as soft on her cheek as a lover's caress. Soft backlighting shone through the filmy material, enticingly silhouetting her curves.

"Good," Larry stated, and, switching on the wind machine, he added, "perfect."

The easy breeze from the machine lifted her hair and rippled her gown. Picking up his camera, Larry began to shoot. "That's good, now lift your hair. Good, good, you'll drive them crazy." His instructions came swiftly, and her expressions and stances changed in rapid succession. "Now, look right into the camera—it's the man you love. He's coming to take you into his arms." Her eyes flew to the back of the studio where Bret stood linked with Charlene. Her eyes met his and a tremor shook her body. "Come on, Hillary, I want passion, not panic. Come on now, baby, look at the camera."

She swallowed and obeyed. Slowly, she allowed her dreams to take command, allowed the camera to become Bret. A Bret looking at her not only with desire, but with love. He came to her with love and need. He was holding her close as she remembered him holding her. His hands moved gently over her as his lips claimed hers after he whispered the words she longed to hear.

"That does it, Hillary."

Lost in her own world, she blinked and stared at Larry without comprehension.

"That was great. I fell in love with you myself."

Letting out a deep breath, she shut her eyes a moment

and sighed at her own imagination. "I suppose we could get married and breed little lenses," she murmured as she headed for the dressing room.

"Bret, that negligee is simply marvelous." Charlene's words halted Hillary's progress. "I really must have it, darling. You can get it for me, can't you?" Charlene's voice was low and seductive as she ran a well-manicured hand along Bret's arm.

"Hmm? Sure," he assented, his eyes on Hillary. "If you want it, Charlene."

Hillary's mouth fell open with astonishment. His casual gift to the woman at his side wounded her beyond belief. She stared at him for a few moments before fleeing to her dressing room.

In the privacy of the dressing room, she leaned against the wall battling the pain. How could he? she cried inwardly. The gown was special, it was hers, she belonged in it. She closed her eyes and stifled a sob. She had even imagined him holding her in it, loving her, and now...it would be Charlene's. He would look at Charlene, his eyes dark with desire. His hands would caress Charlene's body through the misty softness. Now a fierce anger began to replace the pain. If that was what he wanted, well, they were welcome to it—both of them. She stripped herself from frothy white folds and dressed.

When she left the dressing room, Bret was alone in the studio, sitting negligently behind Larry's desk. Summoning all her pride, Hillary marched to him and dropped the large box on its cluttered surface.

"For your friend. You'll want to have it laundered first."

She turned to make her exit with as much dignity

as possible, but was outmaneuvered as his hand closed over her wrist.

"What's eating you, Hillary?" He stood, keeping his grip firm and towering over her.

"Eating me?" she repeated, glaring up at him. "Whatever do you mean?"

"Drop it, Hillary," he ordered, the familiar steel entering both voice and eyes. "You're upset, and I mean to know why."

"Upset?" She tugged fiercely at her arm. As her efforts for liberation proved fruitless, her anger increased. "If I'm upset, it's my own affair. It's not in my contract that I'm obliged to explain my emotions to you." Her free hand went to his in an attempt to pry herself free, but he merely transferred his hold to her shoulders and shook her briskly.

"Stop it! What's gotten into you?"

"I'll tell you what's gotten into me," she snapped as her hair tumbled around her face. "You walk in here with your redheaded girlfriend and just hand over that gown. She just bats her eyes and says the word, and you hand it over."

"Is that what all this is about?" he demanded, exasperated. "Good heavens, woman, if you want the damn thing, I'll get you one."

"Don't you patronize me," she raged at him. "You can't buy my good humor with your trinkets. Keep your generosity for someone who appreciates it and let me go."

"You're not going anywhere until you calm down and we get to the root of the problem."

Her eyes were suddenly filled with uncontrollable tears. "You don't understand." She sniffed as tears coursed down her cheeks. "You just don't understand anything."

"Stop it!" He began to brush her tears away with his hand. "Tears are my downfall. I can't handle them. Stop it, Hillary, don't cry like that."

"It's the only way I know how to cry," she said, weeping miserably.

He swore under his breath. "I don't know what this is all about. A nightgown can't be worth all this! Here, take it—it's obviously important to you." He picked up the box, holding it out to her. "Charlene has plenty." The last words, uttered in an attempt to lighten her mood, had precisely the reverse effect.

"I don't want it. I don't ever want to see it again," she shouted, her voice made harsh by tears. "I hope you and your lover thoroughly enjoy it." With this, she whirled, grabbed her coat, and ran from the studio with surprising speed.

Outside, she stood on the sidewalk, stomping her feet against the cold. Stupid! she accused herself. Stupid to get so attached to a piece of cloth. But no more stupid than getting attached to an arrogant, unfeeling man whose interests lay elsewhere. Spotting a cab, she stepped forward to flag it down when she was spun around to face the buttons on Bret's leather coat.

"I've had enough of your tantrums, Hillary, and I don't tolerate being walked out on." His voice was low and dangerous, but Hillary tilted back her head to meet his gaze boldly.

"We have nothing more to say."

"We have plenty more to say."

"I don't expect you to understand." She spoke with

the exaggerated patience an adult uses when addressing a slow-witted child. "You're just a man."

She heard the sharp intake of his breath as he moved toward her.

"You're right about one thing, I am a man," she heard him whisper before he pulled her close, crushing her mouth in an angry kiss, forcing her lips to open to his demands. The world emptied but for his touch, and the two stood locked together, oblivious to the people who walked the sidewalk behind them.

When at last he freed her, she drew back from him, her breath coming quickly. "Now that you've proven your masculinity, I really must go."

"Come back upstairs. We'll finish our discussion."

"Our discussion is finished."

"Not quite." He began to drag her back toward the studio.

*I can't be alone with him now,* she thought wildly. *Not now, when I'm already so vulnerable.* He could see too much too easily.

"Really, Bret." She was proud of the calmness of her voice. "I do hate to create a scene, but if you continue to play the caveman I shall be forced to scream. And I can scream very loud."

"No, you wouldn't."

"Yes," Hillary corrected, digging in her heels. "I would."

"Hillary." He turned, maintaining possession of her arm. "We have things to clear up."

"Bret, it's gotten blown out of proportion." She spoke sweetly, ignoring the weakness in her legs. "We've both had our outburst of temper—let's just leave it at that. The entire thing was silly anyway."

"It didn't seem silly to you upstairs."

The slender hold on her control was slipping rapidly, and she looked up at him in a last ditch attempt. "Please, Bret, drop it. We're all temperamental sometimes."

"Very well," he agreed after a pause. "We'll drop it for the time being."

Hillary sighed tremulously. She felt that if she stayed any longer she ran the risk of agreeing to whatever he asked. Out of the corner of her eye she glimpsed a passing cab, and she put her fingers to her mouth to whistle it down.

Bret's mouth lifted in irrepressible amusement. "You never cease to surprise me."

Her answer was lost as she slammed the cab door behind her.

## Chapter 5

Christmas was approaching, and the city was decorated in its best holiday garb. Hillary watched from her window as cars and people bustled through the brightly lit streets. The snow fell upon city sidewalks, the drifting white adding to her holiday mood. She watched the huge flakes float to earth like down from a giant pillow.

Shooting of the layout was complete, and she had seen little of Bret in the past few days. She would be seeing less of him, she realized, a shaft of gloom darkening her cheerful mood. Now that her part in the project was over, there would be no day-to-day contact, no chance meetings. She sighed and shook her head. I'm going home tomorrow, she reminded herself, home for Christmas.

That was what she needed, she told herself, closing her eyes on the image of Bret's handsome features. A complete change of scene. Ten days to help heal her heart, time to reevaluate all the plans she had laid out, which now seemed hopelessly dull and unsatisfying.

The knock on the door caused her to remove her face, which had been pressed against the glass. "Who is it?" she called as she placed her hand on the knob.

"Santa Claus."

"B-Bret?" she stammered, thrown off balance. "Is that you?"

"Just can't fool you, can I?" After a slight pause, he asked, "Are you going to let me in, or do we have to talk through the door?"

"Oh, sorry." She fumbled with the latch and opened the door, staring at his lean form, which leaned negligently against the frame.

"You're locking up these days." His eyes swept her pearl-colored velour housecoat before he brought them back to hers. "Are you going to let me in?"

"Oh, sure." Hillary stood back to let him enter, desperately searching for lost composure. "I, ah, I thought Santa came down the chimney."

"Not this one," he returned dryly, and removed his coat. "I could use some of your famous Scotch. It's freezing out there."

"Now I'm totally disillusioned. I thought Santa thrived on cookies and milk."

"If he's half the man I think he is, he's got a flask in that red suit."

"Cynic," she accused, and retreated to the kitchen. Finding the Scotch easily this time, she poured a measure into a glass.

"Very professional." Bret observed from the doorway. "Aren't you going to join me in some holiday cheer?"

"Oh, no." Hillary wrinkled her nose in disgust. "This stuff tastes like the soap I had my mouth washed out with once."

"You've got class, Hillary," he stated wryly, and took the glass from her hand. "I won't ask you what your mouth was washed out for."

"I wouldn't tell you anyway." She smiled, feeling at ease with the casual banter.

"Well, have something, I hate to drink alone."

She reached into the refrigerator and removed a pitcher of orange juice.

"You do live dangerously, don't you?" he commented as she poured. She raised the glass in toast and they returned to the living room.

"I heard you're off to Kansas in the morning," he said as he seated himself on the sofa. Hillary strategically made use of the chair facing him.

"That's right, I'll be home until the day after New Year's."

"Then I'll wish you both a Merry Christmas and a Happy New Year early." He lifted his glass to her. "I'll think of you when the clock strikes twelve."

"I'm sure you'll be too busy to think of me at the stroke of midnight," she retorted, and cursed herself for losing the calm, easy tone.

He smiled and sipped his Scotch. "I'm sure I'll find a minute to spare." Hillary frowned into her glass and refrained from a comment. "I've something for you, Hillary." He rose and, picking up his jacket, removed a small package from its pocket. Hillary stared at it dumbly, then raised her expressive eyes to his.

"Oh, but… I didn't think…that is… I don't have anything for you."

"Don't you?" he asked lazily, and color rushed to her cheeks.

"Really, Bret, I can't take it. I wouldn't feel right."

"Think of it as a gift from the emperor to one of his subjects." He took the glass from her hand and placed the package in its stead.

"You have a long memory." She smiled in spite of herself.

"Like an elephant," he said, then, with a touch of impatience: "Open it. You know you're dying to."

She stared at the package, conceding with a sigh. "I never could resist anything wrapped in Christmas paper." She tore the elegant foil away, then caught her breath as she opened the box and revealed its contents. Earrings of deep sapphire stones blinked up from their backing of velvet.

"They reminded me of your eyes, brilliantly blue and exquisite. It seemed a crime for them to belong to anyone else."

"They're beautiful, really very beautiful," she murmured when she found her voice. Turning her sapphire eyes to his, she added, "You really shouldn't have bought them for me, I—"

"I shouldn't have," he interrupted, "but you're glad I did."

She had to smile. "Yes, I am. It was a lovely thing to do. I don't know how to thank you."

"I do." He drew her from the chair, his arms slipping around her. "This will do nicely." His lips met hers and, after a moment's hesitation, she responded, telling herself she was only showing her gratitude for his thoughtfulness. As the kiss lingered, her gratitude was forgotten. He lifted his mouth, and dazedly she made to move from the warm circle of his arms. "There are two earrings, love." His mouth claimed possession again, now more demanding, and her lips parted beneath his insistence. Her body seemed to melt against his, her arms twining around his neck, fingers tangling in his hair. She was lost in the feel of him, all thought ceasing, her only reality his mouth on hers, and his hard body blending with her yielding softness.

When at last their lips separated, he looked down at her, his eyes darkened with emotion. "It's a pity you've only got two ears." His voice was husky, and his head lowered toward hers.

She dropped her forehead to his chest and attempted to catch her breath. "Please, Bret," she whispered, her hands slipping from his neck to his shoulders. "I can't think when you kiss me."

"Can't you now?" His mouth tarried a moment in her hair. "That's very interesting." He brought his hand under her chin and lifted her face, his eyes moving over her features slowly. "You know, Hillary, that's a very dangerous admission. I'm tempted to press my advantage." He paused, continuing to study the fragile, vulnerable face. "Not this time." He released her, and she checked the impulse to sway toward him. Walking to the table, he downed the remainder of his Scotch and lifted his coat. At the door, he turned, giving her his charming smile. "Merry Christmas, Hillary."

"Merry Christmas, Bret," she whispered at the door he closed behind him.

The air was brisk and cold, carrying the clean, pure scent that meant home, the sky brilliantly blue and naked of clouds. Hillary let herself into the rambling farmhouse and for a moment gave in to memories.

"Tom, what are you doing coming in all the way around the front?" Sarah Baxter bustled from the kitchen, wiping her hands on a full white apron. "Hillary." She stopped as she caught sight of the slim, dark woman in the center of the room. "Well, time's just gotten away from me."

Hillary ran and enveloped her mother in a fierce hug. "Oh, Mom, it's good to be home."

If her mother noticed the desperate tone of Hillary's words, she made no comment, but returned the embrace with equal affection. Standing back, she examined Hillary with a mother's practiced eye. "You could use a few pounds."

"Well, look what the wind blew in all the way from New York City." Tom Baxter entered through the swinging kitchen door and caught Hillary in a close embrace. She breathed deeply, reveling in the smell of fresh hay and horses that clung to him. "Let me look at you." He drew her away and repeated his wife's survey. "What a beautiful sight." He glanced over Hillary's head and smiled at his wife. "We grew a real prize here, didn't we, Sarah?"

Later, Hillary joined her mother in the large kitchen that served the farm. Pots were simmering on a well-used range, filling the air with an irresistible aroma. Hillary allowed her mother to ramble about her brothers and their families, fighting back the deep longing that welled inside her.

Her hand went unconsciously to the blue stones at her ears, and Bret's image flooded her mind, bringing him almost close enough to touch. She averted her face, hoping that the bright tears that sprung to her eyes would not be observed by her mother's sharp glance.

\* \* \*

On Christmas morning, Hillary woke with the sun and snuggled lazily in her childhood bed. She had fallen into the bed late the night before, but, having slipped between the covers, had been unable to sleep. Tossing and turning, she had stared at a dark ceiling until the early hours. Bret had remained in her mind no matter how strenuously she had tried to block him out. His image broke through her defenses like a rock through plate glass. To her despair, she found herself aching to be close to him, the need an ache deep inside her.

In the morning, in the clear light of day, she once more stared at the ceiling. *There's nothing I can do,* she realized hopelessly. *I love him. I love him and I hate him for not loving me back. Oh, he wants me all right—he's made no secret of that—but wanting's not loving. How did it happen? Where did all my defenses go? He's arrogant,* she began, mentally ticking off faults in an effort to find an escape hatch in her solitary prison. *He's short-tempered, demanding, and entirely too self-assured. Why doesn't any of that matter? What's happened to my brain? Why can't I stop thinking about him for more than five minutes at a time?*

*It's Christmas,* she reminded herself, shutting her eyes against his intrusion. *I am not going to let Bret Bardoff spoil my day!*

Rising, she threw back the quilt, slipped on a fleece robe, and hurried from the room.

The house was already stirring, the quiet morning hush vanishing into activity. For the next hour, the scene around the Christmas tree was filled with gaiety, exclamations for the gifts that were revealed, and the exchange of hugs and kisses.

Later Hillary slipped outside, the thin blanket of frost crunching under her boots as she pulled her father's worn work jacket tighter around her slimness. The air tasted of winter, and the quiet seemed to hang like a soft curtain. Joining her father in the barn, she automatically began to measure out grain, her movements natural, the routine coming back as if she had performed the tasks the day before.

"Just an old farm hand after all, aren't you?" Though the words had been spoken in jest, Hillary halted and looked at her father seriously.

"Yes, I think I am."

"Hillary." His tone softened as he noticed the clouding of her eyes. "What's wrong?"

"I don't know." She let out a deep sigh. "Sometimes New York seems so crowded. I feel closed in."

"We thought you were happy there."

"I was… I am," she amended, and smiled. "It's a very exciting place, busy and filled with so many different kinds of people." She forced back the image of clear gray eyes and strong features. "Sometimes I just miss the quiet, the openness, the peace. I'm being silly." She shook her head and scooped out more grain. "I've been a bit homesick lately, that's all. This layout I just finished was fascinating, but it took a lot out of me." Not the layout, she corrected silently, but the man.

"Hillary, if you're unhappy, if there's anything on your mind, I want to help you."

For a moment, she longed to lean on her father's shoulder and pour out her doubts and frustrations. But what good would it do to burden him? What could he do about the fact that she loved a man who saw her only as a temporary diversion, a marketable commodity for selling magazines? How could she explain that she was unhappy because she had met a man who had broken and captured her heart unknowingly and effortlessly? All these thoughts ran through her brain before she shook her head, giving her father another smile.

"It's nothing. I expect it's just a letdown from finishing the layout. Postphotography depression. I'll go feed the chickens."

The house was soon overflowing with people, echoing with mixed voices, laughter, and the sound of children. Familiar tasks and honest affection helped to erase the ache of emptiness that still haunted her....

When only the echoes of the holiday lingered, Hillary remained downstairs alone, unwilling to seek the comfort of her bed.

Curled in a chair, she stared at the festive lights of the tree, unable to prevent herself from speculating on how Bret had celebrated his holiday. A quiet day with Charlene, perhaps, or a party at the country club? Right now they were probably sitting in front of a roaring fire, and Charlene was snuggled in his arms draped in that beautiful negligee.

A pain shot through her, sharp as the point of an arrow, and she was enveloped by a torturous combination of raging jealousy and hopeless despair. But the image would not fade.

The days at home went quickly. They were good days, following a soothing routine that Hillary dropped into gratefully. Kansas wind blew away a portion of her depression. She took long, quiet walks, gazing out at the rolling hills and acres of winter wheat.

People from the city would never understand, she

mused. How could they comprehend this? Her arms were lifted wide as she spun in a circle. In their elegant apartments looking out at steel and concrete they could never feel the exuberation of being a part of the land. The land; she surveyed its infinity with wondering eyes. The land is indomitable; the land is forever. There had been Indians here, and plainsmen and pioneers and farmers. They came and went, lived and died, but the land lived on. And when she was gone, and another generation born, wheat would still wave in the bright summer sun. The land gave them what they needed, rich and fertile, generously giving birth to acres of wheat year after year, asking only for honest labor in return.

*And I love it,* she reflected, hugging herself tightly. *I love the feel of it in my hands and under my bare feet in the summer. I love the rich, clean smell of it. I suppose, for all my acquired sophistication, I'm still just a farm girl. She retraced her steps toward the house. What am I going to do about it? I have a career; I have a place in New York as well. I'm twenty-four. I can't just throw in the towel and come back to live on the farm. No.* She shook her head vigorously, sending her hair swirling in a black mist. *I've got to go back and do what I'm qualified to do.* Firmly, she ignored the small voice that asserted her decision was influenced by another resident of New York.

The phone jangled on the wall as she entered the house, and, slipping off her jacket, she lifted it.

"Hello."

"Hello, Hillary."

"Bret?" She had not known pain could come so swiftly at the sound of a voice.

"Very good." She heard the familiar mockery and pressed her forehead to the wall. "How are you?"

"Fine, I'm just fine." She groped for some small island of composure. "I... I didn't expect to hear from you. Is there a problem?"

"Problem?" he returned in a voice that mirrored his smile. "No permanent one in any case. I thought you might be needing a reminder of New York about now. We wouldn't want you to forget to come back."

"No, I haven't forgotten." Taking a deep breath, she made her voice lightly professional. "Have you something in mind for me?"

"In mind? You might say I had one or two things in mind." There was a slight pause before he continued. "Anxious to get back to work?"

"Uh, yes, yes, I am. I wouldn't want to get stale."

"I see."

You couldn't see through a chain-link fence, she thought with growing frustration.

"We'll see what we can do when you get back. It would be foolish not to put your talents to use." He spoke absently, as though his mind was already formulating a suitable project.

"I'm sure you'll think of something advantageous for both of us," she stated, trying to emulate his businesslike tone.

"Mmm, you'll be back at the end of the week?"

"Yes, on the second."

"I'll be in touch. Keep your calendar clear." The order was casual, confident, and brisk. "We'll get you in front of the camera again, if that's what you want."

"All right. I...well...thanks for calling."

"My pleasure. I'll see you when you get back."

"Yes. Bret…" She searched for something to say, wanting to cling to the small contact, perhaps just to hear him say her name one more time.

"Yes?"

"Nothing, nothing." Shutting her eyes, she cursed her lack of imagination. "I'll wait to hear from you."

"Fine." He paused a moment, and his voice softened. "Have a good time at home, Hillary."

## Chapter 6

The first thing Hillary did upon returning to her New York apartment was to put a call through to Larry. When greeted by a feminine voice, she hesitated, then apologized.

"Sorry, I must have the wrong number…"

"Hillary?" the voice interrupted. "It's June."

"June?" she repeated, confused, then added quickly, "How are you? How were your holidays?"

"Terrific to both questions. Larry told me you went home. Did you have a good time?"

"Yes, I did. It's always good to get home again."

"Hang on a minute. I'll get Larry."

"Oh, well, no, I'll…"

Larry's voice broke into her protestations. She immediately launched into an apology, telling him she would call back.

"Don't be dumb, Hil, June's just helping me sort out my old photography magazines."

It occurred to Hillary that their relationship must be moving along at light speed for Larry to allow June to get her hands on his precious magazines. "I just wanted you to know I was back," she said aloud. "Just in case anything comes up."

"Mmm, well, I guess you really should get in touch with Bret." Larry considered. "You're still under contract. Why don't you give him a call?"

"I won't worry about it," she returned, striving to keep her tone casual. "I told him I'd be back after the first." Her voice dropped. "He knows where to find me."

Several days passed before Bret contacted Hillary. Much of the interim she spent at home because of the snow, which seemed to fall unceasingly over the city, alternating with a penetrating, bitter sleet. The confinement, coming on the heels of the open freedom she had experienced in Kansas, played havoc with her nerves, and she found herself staring down from her window at ice-covered sidewalks with increasing despair.

One evening, as the sky dropped the unwelcome gift of freezing rain, Lisa arranged to have dinner and spend a few hours in Hillary's company. Standing in the kitchen, Hillary was separating a small head of lettuce when the phone rang. Looking down at her wet, leaf-filled hands, she rubbed her nose on her shoulder and asked Lisa to answer the ring.

Lifting the receiver, Lisa spoke into it in her most formal voice. "Miss Hillary Baxter's residence, Lisa MacDonald speaking. Miss Baxter will be with you as soon as she gets her hands out of the lettuce."

"Lisa." Hillary laughed as she hurried into the room. "I just can't trust you to do anything."

"It's all right," she announced loudly, holding out the receiver. "It's only an incredibly sexy male voice."

"Thanks," Hillary returned with deep sincerity, and rescued the phone. "Go, you're banished back into the kitchen." Pulling a face, Lisa retreated, and Hillary gave her attention to her caller. "Hello, don't mind my friend, she's just crazy."

"On the contrary, that's the most interesting conversation I've had all day."

"Bret?" Until that moment, Hillary had not realized how much she needed to hear his voice.

"Right the first time." She could almost see the slow smile spread across his features. "Welcome back to the concrete jungle, Hillary. How was Kansas?"

"Fine," she stammered. "It was just fine."

"Mmm, how illuminating. Did you enjoy your Christmas?"

"Yes, very much." Struggling to regain the composure that had fled at the sound of his voice, she spoke quickly. "And you? Did you have a nice holiday?"

"Delightful, though I'm sure it was a great deal quieter than yours."

"Different anyway," Hillary rejoined, annoyed.

"Ah, well, that's behind us now. Actually, I'm calling about this weekend."

"Weekend?" Hillary repeated dumbly.

"Yes, a trip to the mountains."

"Mountains?"

"You sound like a parrot," he said shortly. "Do you have anything important scheduled from Friday through Sunday?"

"Well, I…ah…"

"Lord, what an astute conversationalist you are." His voice reflected growing annoyance.

Swallowing, she attempted to be more precise. "No. That is, nothing essential. I—"

"Good," he interrupted. "Ever been skiing?"

"In Kansas?" she retorted, regaining her balance. "I believe mountains are rather essential for skiing."

"So they are," he agreed absently. "Well, no matter. I had an idea for some pictures of a lovely lady frolicking in the snow. I've a lodge in the Adirondacks near Lake George. It'll make a nice setting. We can combine business with pleasure."

"We?" Hillary murmured weakly.

"No need for panic," he assured her, his words heavy with mockery. "I'm not abducting you to the wilderness to ravish you, although the idea does have some interesting angles." He paused, then laughed outright. "I can feel you blushing right through the phone."

"Very funny," she retorted, infuriated that he could read her so easily. "I'm beginning to recall an urgent engagement for the weekend, so—"

"Hold on, Hillary," he interrupted again, his words suddenly brooking no argument. "You're under contract. My rights hold for a couple more months. You wanted to get back to work; I'm putting you back to work."

"Yes, but—"

"Read the fine print if you like, but keep this weekend clear. And relax," he continued as she remained silent. "You'll be well protected from my dishonorable advances. Larry and June will be coming with us. Bud Lewis, my assistant art director, will be joining us later."

"Oh," she replied inadequately, unsure whether she was relieved or disappointed.

"I—the magazine, that is—will provide you with suitable snow gear. I'll pick you up at seven-thirty Friday morning. Be packed and ready."

"Yes, but—" Hillary stared at the dead receiver with a mixture of annoyance and trepidation. He had not given her the opportunity to ask questions or formulate a reasonable excuse to decline. Hanging up, she turned around, her face a study in bewilderment.

"What was all that? You look positively stunned." Lisa regarded her friend from the kitchen doorway.

"I'm going to the mountains for the weekend," she answered slowly, as if to herself.

"The mountains?" Lisa repeated. "With the owner of that fascinating voice?"

Hillary snapped back and attempted to sound casual. "It's just an assignment. That was Bret Bardoff. There'll be plenty of others along," she added.

Friday morning dawned clear and cloudless and cold. Hillary was packed and ready as instructed, sipping a second cup of tea, when the doorbell sounded.

"Good morning, Hillary," Bret said as she opened the door. "Ready to brave the uncharted wilderness?"

He looked quite capable of doing just that in a hip-length sheepskin jacket, heavy corded jeans, and sturdy boots. Now he appeared rugged, not the cool, calculating businessman to whom she had grown accustomed. Gripping the doorknob tightly, she maintained a cool exterior and invited him in.

Assuring him she was quite ready, she walked away

to place the empty cup in the sink and fetch her coat. Slipping her coat over her sweater and jeans, she pulled a dark brown ski hat over her hair. Bret looked on silently.

"I'm ready." Suddenly aware of his intense regard, she moistened her lips nervously with her tongue. "Shall we go?"

Inclining his head, he bent to pick up the case she had waiting beside the sofa, his movements coinciding with hers. Straightening with a jerk, she flushed awkwardly. His brow lifted with his smile as he captured her hand and led her to the door.

They soon left the city as Bret directed the Mercedes north. He drove quickly and skillfully along the Hudson, keeping up a light conversation. Hillary found herself relaxing in the warm interior, forgetting her usual inhibition at being in close contact with the man who stirred her senses. As they began to pass through small towns and villages, she could hardly believe they were still in New York, her experience with the state having been limited exclusively to Manhattan and the surrounding area. Ingenuously, she voiced her thoughts, pulling off her hat and shaking out her rich fall of hair.

"There's more in New York than skyscrapers," he informed her with a crooked smile. "Mountains, valleys, forests—it has a bit of everything. I suppose it's time we changed your impression."

"I've never thought of it except as a place to work," she admitted, shifting in her seat to face him more directly. "Noisy, busy, and undeniably exciting, but draining at times because it's always moving and never seems to sleep. It always makes the sound of the silence at home that much more precious."

"And Kansas is still home, isn't it?" He seemed to

be thinking of something else as he asked, his expression brooding on the road ahead. Hillary frowned at his change of mood, then gave her attention to the scenery without answering.

They continued northward, and she lost track of time, intoxicated by the newness and beauty of her surroundings. At her first glimpse of the Catskills, she let out a small cry of pleasure, spontaneously tugging on Bret's arm and pointing. "Oh, look—mountains!"

Turning her eyes from the view, she gave him her special smile. He returned the smile, and her heart did a series of acrobatics. She turned back to the scene out the window. "I suppose I must seem terribly foolish, but when you've only known acres of wheat and rolling hills, this is quite a revelation."

"Not foolish, Hillary." His voice was gentle, and she turned to face him, surprised at the unfamiliar tone. "I find you utterly charming."

Picking up her hand, he turned it upward and kissed her palm, sending shooting arrows of flame up her arm and down to her stomach. Dealing with his mockery and amusement was one thing, she pondered dizzily, she was quite used to that by now. But these occasional gentle moods turned her inside out, making her spark like a lighted match. This man was dangerous, she concluded, very dangerous. Somehow she must build up an impregnable defense against him. But how? How could she fight both him and the part of herself that wanted only to surrender?

"I could do with some coffee," Bret said suddenly, bringing Hillary back from her self-interrogation. "How about you?" He turned to her and smiled. "Want some tea?"

"Sure," she answered casually.

The Mercedes rolled into the small village of Catskill and Bret parked in front of a cafe. He opened his door and stepped from the car, and she quickly followed suit before he circled the front and joined her on the curb. Her eyes were fixed on the overpowering encircling mountains.

"They look higher than they are," Bret commented. "Their bases are only a few hundred feet above sea level. I'd love to see the expression on that beautiful face of yours when you encounter the Rockies or the Alps."

Interlocking his hand with hers, he led her out of the cold and into the warmth of the cafe. When the small table was between them, Hillary shrugged out of the confines of her coat, concentrating on the view, attempting to erect a wall of defense between herself and Bret.

"Coffee for me and tea for the lady. Are you hungry, Hillary?"

"What? Oh no,...well, yes, actually a little." She grinned, remembering the lack of breakfast that morning.

"They serve an outstanding coffee cake here." He ordered two slices before Hillary could protest.

"I don't usually eat that kind of thing." She frowned, thinking of the half grapefruit she had had in mind.

"Hillary, darling," Bret broke in with exaggerated patience. "One slice of cake is hardly likely to affect your figure. In any case," he added with irritating bluntness, "a few pounds wouldn't hurt you."

"Really," she retorted, chin rising with indignation. "I haven't had any complaints so far."

"I'm sure you haven't, and you'll get none from me.

I've become quite enchanted with tall, willowy women. Though," he continued, reaching over to brush a loose strand of hair from her face, "the air of frailty is sometimes disconcerting."

Hillary decided to ignore both gesture and remark. "I don't know when I've enjoyed a drive more," she said, determined to remain casual. "How much farther do we have to go?"

"We're at the halfway point." Bret added cream to his coffee. "We should arrive around noon."

"How is everyone else coming? I mean, are they driving together?"

"Larry and June are coming up together." He smiled and ate a forkful of cake. "I should say Larry and June are accompanying Larry's equipment. I'm amazed he allowed her to travel in the same car with his precious cameras and lenses."

"Are you?" Hillary questioned, grinning into her tea.

"I suppose I shouldn't be," he admitted wryly. "I have noticed our favorite photographer's increasing preoccupation with my secretary. He seemed inordinately pleased to have her company on the drive."

"When I phoned him the other day, he was actually allowing her to sort out his photography magazines." Hillary's voice was tinged with disbelief. "That's tantamount to a bethrothal." She gestured with her fork. "It might even be binding. I'm not sure of the law. I still can't believe it." She swallowed a piece of cake and looked at Bret in amazement. "Larry's actually serious about a flesh-and-blood woman."

"It happens to the best of us, love," Bret agreed gently.

But would it ever to Bret? She could not meet his eyes.

\* \* \*

On the road once more, Hillary contented herself with the scenery as Bret kept up a general conversation. The warmth of the Mercedes' interior and its smooth, steady ride had lulled her into a state of deep relaxation, and leaning back, she closed her suddenly heavy lids as they crossed the Mohawk River. Bret's deep voice increased her peaceful mood, and she murmured absently in response until she heard no more.

Hillary stirred restlessly as the change in road surface disturbed her slumber. Her eyes blinked open, and after a moment's blankness, reality returned. Her head was nestled against his shoulder, and, sitting up quickly, she turned her sleep-flushed face and heavy dark eyes to him.

"Oh, I'm sorry. Did I fall asleep?"

"You might say that," he said, glancing over as she pushed at tumbled hair. "You've been unconscious for an hour."

"Hour?" she repeated, attempting to clear the cobwebs. "Where are we?" she mumbled, gazing around her. "What did I miss?"

"Everything from Schenectady on, and we're on the road that leads to my lodge."

"Oh, it's beautiful." She came quickly awake as she focused on her surroundings.

The narrow road they traveled was flanked with snow-covered trees and rugged outcroppings of rock. Snow draped the green needles of pine, and what would have been dark, empty branches glistened with icicles and pure, sparkling white. Dense and thick, they seemed to be everywhere, rising majestically from a brilliant virgin blanket.

"There're so many." She scooted in her seat to experiment with the view from Bret's window, her knees brushing his thigh.

"The forest is full of them."

"Don't make fun." She punched his shoulder and continued to stare. "This is all new to me."

"I'm not making fun," he said, rubbing his shoulder with exaggerated care. "I'm delighted with your enthusiasm."

The car halted, and Hillary turned from Bret to look out the front window of the car. With a cry of pleasure, she spotted the large A-frame dwelling nestled in a small clearing so much a part of the surroundings it might have grown there. Picture windows gleamed and glistened in the filtered sunlight.

"Come get a closer look," Bret invited, stepping from the car. He held his hand out to her, and she slipped hers into his grasp as they began to crunch through the untouched snow. An ice-crusted stream tumbled swiftly on the far side of the house and, like a child wishing to share a new toy, Hillary pulled Bret toward it.

"How marvelous, how absolutely marvelous," she proclaimed, watching water force its way over rocks, its harsh whisper the only disturbance of peace. "What a fabulous place." She made a slow circle. "It's so wild and powerful, so wonderfully untouched and primitive."

Bret's eyes followed her survey before staring off through a dense outcropping of trees. "Sometimes I escape here, when my office begins to close in on me. There's such blessed peace—no urgent meetings, no deadlines, no responsibilities."

Hillary regarded him in open amazement. She had never imagined his needing to escape from anything or seeking deliberate solitude in a place so far from the city and its comforts and pleasures. To her, Bret Bardoff had represented the epitome of the efficient business-man, with employees rushing to do his bidding at the snap of his imperious finger. Now, she began to see another aspect of his nature, and she found the knowledge brought her a swift rush of pleasure.

He turned and encountered her stare, locking her eyes to his with a force that captured her breath. "It's also quite isolated," he added, in such a swift change of mood it took her a moment to react.

Blue eyes deepened and widened and she looked away, staring at the trees and rocks. She was here in the middle of nowhere, she realized, unconsciously chewing on her lip. He had told her the others were coming, but there was only his word. She had not thought to check with Larry. What if he had made the whole thing up? She would be trapped with him, completely alone. What would she do if…

"Keep calm, Hillary." Bret laughed wryly. "I haven't kidnapped you, the others will be along to protect you." He had deliberately provoked her reaction, and Hillary whirled to tell him what she thought of him, but he went on before she could speak. "That is, if they can find the place," he muttered, his brow creasing before his features settled in a wide smile. "It would be a shame if my directions were inadequate, wouldn't it?" Taking her hand once more, he led a confused and uneasy Hillary toward the lodge.

The interior was spacious, with wide, full windows bringing the mountains inside. The high ceiling with exposed beams added to the openness. Rough wooden stairs led to a balcony that ran the length of the living room. A stone fireplace commanded an entire wall, with furniture arranged strategically around it. Oval braid rugs graced the dark pine floor, their bright colors the perfect accent for the rustic, wood-dominated room.

"It's charming," Hillary said with delight as she gazed about her. She walked over to the huge expanse of glass. "You can stand here and be inside and out at the same time."

"I've often felt that way myself," Bret agreed, moving to join her and slipping her coat from her shoulders. "What is that scent you wear?" he murmured, his fingers massaging the back of her neck, their strength throbbing through her. "It's always the same, very delicate and appealing."

"It's, ah, it's apple blossom." She swallowed and kept her eyes glued to the window.

"Mmm, you mustn't change it, it suits you…. I'm starving," he announced suddenly, turning her to face him. "How about opening a can or something, and I'll start the fire? The kitchen's well stocked. You should be able to find something to ward off starvation."

"All right," she agreed, smiling. "We wouldn't want you to fade away. Where's the kitchen?" He pointed, and leaving him still standing by the window, she set off in the direction he indicated.

The kitchen was full of old-fashioned charm, with a small brick fireplace of its own and copper-bottomed pots hanging along the wall. The stove itself Hillary regarded doubtfully, thinking it resembled something her grandmother might have slaved over, until she observed that it had been adapted for modern use. The large pantry was well stocked, and she located enough cans for an adequate midday meal. Not precisely a gourmet feast, she reflected as she opened a can of soup, but it will have to do. She was spooning soup into a pan when she heard Bret's footsteps behind her.

"That was quick!" she exclaimed. "You must have been a terrific Boy Scout."

"It's a habit of mine to set the fire before I leave," he explained, standing behind her as she worked. "That way all I have to do is open the flue and light a match."

"How disgustingly organized," Hillary observed with a sniff, and switched the flame under the soup.

"Ah, ambrosia," he proclaimed, slipping his arms around her waist. "Are you a good cook, Hillary?"

The hard body pressed into her back was very distracting. She struggled to remain cool. "Anyone can open a can of soup." The last word caught in her throat as his hand reached up to part the dark curtain of her hair, his lips warm as they brushed the back of her neck. "I'd better make some coffee." She attempted to slip away, but his arms maintained possession, his mouth roaming over her vulnerable skin. "I thought you were hungry." The words came out in a babbling rush as her knees melted, and she leaned back against him helplessly for support.

"Oh, I am," he whispered, his teeth nibbling at her ear. "Ravenous."

He buried his face in the curve of her neck, and the room swayed as his hands slid upward under her sweater.

"Bret, don't," she moaned as a rush of desire swept over her, and she struggled to escape before she was lost.

He muttered savagely and spun her around, roughly crushing her lips under his.

Though he had kissed her before, demanding, arousing kisses, there had always been a measure of control in his lovemaking. Now it was as if the wildness of their surroundings had entered him. Like a man whose control has been too tightly bound, he assaulted her mouth, parting hers and taking possession. His hands pressed her hips against him, molding them together into one form. She was drowning in his explosion of passion, clinging to him as his hands roamed over her, seeking, demanding, receiving. The fire of his need ignited hers, and she gave herself without reservation, straining against him, wanting only to plunge deeper into the heat.

The sound of a car pulling up outside brought a muffled curse from Bret. Lifting his mouth from hers, he rested his chin on top of her head and sighed.

"They found us, Hillary. Better open another can."

## Chapter 7

Voices drifted through the building, June's laughter and Larry's raised tones in some shared joke. Bret moved off to greet them, leaving Hillary battling to regain some small thread of composure. The urgent demand of Bret's lovemaking had awakened a wild, primitive response in her. She was acutely aware that, had they been left undisturbed, he would not have held back, and she would not have protested. The need had been too vital, too consuming. The swift beginning and sudden end of the contact left her trembling and unsteady. Pressing hands to burning cheeks, she went back to the stove, to attend to soup and coffee, hoping the simple mechanical tasks would restore her equilibrium.

"So, he's got you slaving away already." June entered the kitchen, arms ladened with a large paper bag. "Isn't that just like a man?"

"Hi." Hillary turned around, showing a fairly normal countenance. "It appears we've both been put in our places. What's in the bag?"

"Supplies for the long, snowbound weekend." Unpacking the bag, June revealed milk, cheese, and other fresh goods.

"Always efficient," Hillary stated, and, feeling the tension melt away, flashed her smile.

"It is difficult being perfect," June agreed with a sigh. "But some of us are simply born that way."

Meal preparations complete, they carried bowls and plates into the adjoining room to a large, rectangular wooden table with long benches running along each side. The group devoured the simple meal as though months had passed since they had seen a crust of bread. Mirroring Bret's now casual manner was at first difficult, but, summoning all her pride, Hillary joined in the table talk, meeting his occasional comments with an easy smile.

She retreated with June upstairs as the men launched into a technical discussion on the type of pictures required, and found the room they would share as charmingly rustic as the remainder of the house. The light, airy room with a breathtaking view of forest and mountains held two twin beds covered in patchwork quilts. Again wood predominated, the high sloping ceiling adding to the space. Brass lamps ensured soft lighting once the sun had descended behind the peaks outside.

Hillary busied herself with the case containing her wardrobe for the photo session as June threw herself heavily on a bed.

"Isn't this place fantastic?" Stretching her arms to the ceiling, June heaved a deep sigh of contentment.

"Far from the maddening crowd and typewriters and telephones. Maybe it'll snow like crazy, and we'll be here until spring."

"We'd only be able to stick it out if Larry brought enough film for a couple of months. Otherwise, he'd go into withdrawal," Hillary commented. Removing a red parka and bibbed ski pants from the case, she studied them with a professional eye. "Well, this should stand out in the snow."

"If we painted your nose yellow, you'd look like a very large cardinal," June commented, clasping her hands behind her head. "That color will look marvelous on you. With your hair and complexion, and the snow as a backdrop, you'll be smashing. The boss never makes a mistake."

The sound of a car caught their attention, and they moved to the window looking down as Bud Lewis assisted Charlene from the vehicle. "Well—" June sighed and grimaced at Hillary "—maybe one."

Stunned, Hillary stared at the top of Charlene's glossy red head. "I didn't… Bret didn't tell me Charlene was coming." Infuriated by the intrusion on her weekend, Hillary turned from the window and busied her hands with unpacking.

"Unless I'm very much mistaken, he didn't know." Scowling, June turned and leaned against the windowsill. "Maybe he'll toss her out in the snow."

"Maybe," Hillary countered, relieving some of her frustration by slamming the top of her suitcase, "he'll be glad to see her."

"Well, we won't find out anything standing around up here." June started toward the door, grabbing Hillary's arm along the way. "Come on, let's go see."

Charlene's voice drifted to Hillary as she descended the stairs. "You really don't mind that I came to keep you company, do you, Bret? I thought it would be such a lovely surprise."

Hillary entered the room in time to see Bret's shrug. He was seated on a love seat in front of the blazing fire, Charlene's arm tucked possessively through his. "I didn't think the mountains were your style, Charlene." He gave her a mild smile. "If you'd wanted to come, you should have asked instead of spinning a tale to Bud about my wanting him to drive you up."

"Oh, but, darling, it was just a little fib." Tilting her head, she fluttered darkened lashes. "A little intrigue is so amusing."

"Let's hope your 'little intrigue' doesn't lead you to 'a lot of boredom.' We're a long way from Manhattan."

"I'm never bored with you."

Soft and coaxing, the voice grated on Hillary's nerves. Perhaps she made some small sound of annoyance for Bret's eyes shifted to where she stood with June in the doorway. Charlene followed his gaze, her lips tightening for a moment before settling into a vague smile.

There followed an unenthusiastic exchange of greetings. Opting for distance, Hillary seated herself across the room with Bud as Charlene again gave Bret her full attention.

"I thought we'd never get here," Charlene complained with a petulant pout. "Why you would own a place in this godforsaken wilderness is beyond me, darling." She glanced up at Bret with cool green eyes. "All this snow, and nothing but trees and rocks, and so cold." With a delicate shiver, she huddled against him. "Whatever do you find to do up here all alone?"

"I manage to find diversions," Bret drawled, and lit a cigarette. "And I'm never alone—the mountains are teeming with life." He gestured toward the window. "There are squirrels, chipmunks, rabbits, foxes—all manner of small animal life."

"That's not precisely what I meant by company," Charlene murmured, using her most seductive voice. Bret granted her a faint smile.

"Perhaps not, but I find them entertaining and undemanding. I've often seen deer pass by as I stood by that window, and bear."

"Bears?" Charlene exclaimed, and tightened her hold on his arm. "How dreadful."

"Real bears?" Hillary demanded, eyes bright with adventure. "Oh, what kind? Those huge grizzlies?"

"Black bear, Hillary," he corrected, smiling at her reaction. "But big enough just the same. And safely in hibernation at the moment," he added with a glance at Charlene.

"Thank heaven," she breathed with genuine feeling.

"Hillary's quite taken to the mountains, haven't you?"

"They're fabulous," she agreed with enthusiasm. "So wild and untamed. All this must look nearly the same as it did a century ago, unspoiled by buildings and housing developments. Nothing but undisturbed nature for miles and miles."

"My, my, you are enthusiastic," Charlene observed. Hillary shot her a deadly glance.

"Hillary grew up on a farm in Kansas," Bret explained, observing danger signals in dark blue eyes. "She'd never seen mountains before."

"How quaint," Charlene murmured, lips curving in a smile. "They grow wheat or something there, don't they? I would imagine you're quite accustomed to primitive conditions coming from a little farm."

The superior tone had Hillary bristling with anger, her rising temper reflected in her voice. "The farm is hardly little or primitive, Miss Mason. Impossible, I suppose, for one of your background to visualize the eternity of wheat, the miles of gently rolling hills. Not as sophisticated as New York, perhaps, but hardly prehistoric. We even manage to have hot and cold running water right inside the house most of the time. There are those who appreciate the land and respect it in all forms."

"You must be quite the outdoor girl," Charlene said in a bored voice. "I happen to prefer the comforts and culture of the city."

"I think I'll take a walk before it gets dark." Hillary rose quickly, needing to put some distance between herself and the other woman before her temper was irrevocably lost.

"I'll go with you." Bud stood, moving to join her as she slipped on her outdoor clothing. "I've been cooped up with that woman all day," he whispered with a conspirator's smile. "I think the fresh air will do me a world of good."

Hillary's laughter floated through the room as she strolled through the door, arm in arm with Bud. She was oblivious of the frown that darkened the gray eyes that followed her.

Once outside, the two breathed deeply, then giggled

like children at their private joke. By mutual consent, they headed for the stream, following its tumbling progress downstream as they ambled deeper into the forest. Sunlight winked sporadically through the trees, glistening on the velvet snow. Bud's easy conversation soothed Hillary's ruffled spirits.

They stopped and rested on a mound of rock for a moment of companionable silence.

"This is nice," Bud said simply, and Hillary made a small sound signifying both pleasure and agreement. "I begin to feel human again," he added with a wink. "That woman is hard to take. I can't imagine what the boss sees in her."

Hillary grinned. "Isn't it strange that I agree with you?"

They walked home in the subtle change of light that signified encroaching dusk. Again, they followed the stream, easily retracing the footsteps they had left in the pure, white snow. They were laughing companionably as they entered the A-frame.

"Don't either of you have more sense than to wander about the mountains after dark?" Bret asked them, scowling.

"Dark? Don't be silly." Hillary hopped on one foot as she pried off a boot. "We only followed the stream a little way, and it's barely dusk." Losing her balance, she collided with Bud, who slipped an arm around her waist to right her, keeping it there while she struggled with her other boot.

"We left a trail in the snow," Bud stated with a grin. "Better than bread crumbs."

"Dusk turns to dark quickly, and there's no moon tonight," Bret said. "It's a simple matter to get lost."

"Well, we're back, and we didn't," Hillary told him. "No need for a search party or a flask of brandy. Where's June?"

"In the kitchen, starting dinner."

"I better go help then, hadn't I?" She gave him a radiant smile and brushed past them, leaving Bud to deal with his boss's temper.

"A woman's work is never done," Hillary observed with a sigh as she entered the kitchen.

"Tell that to Miss Nose-in-the-Air." June wrinkled her own as she unwrapped the steaks. "She was so fatigued from the arduous drive—" June placed a dramatic hand to her forehead "—she simply had to lie down before dinner."

"That's a blessing. Anyway," Hillary went on as she joined in the meal preparation, "who voted us in charge of kitchen duty? I'm quite sure it's not in my contract."

"I did."

"Voluntarily?"

"It's like this," June explained, searching through cupboards. "I've had a small example of Larry's talents, culinary talents, and I don't want another bout of ptomaine. The boss even makes lousy coffee. And as for Bud—well, he might be Chef Boy-Ar-Dee as far as I know, but I was unwilling to take the chance."

"I see what you mean."

In easy companionship they prepared the meal. The kitchen came to life with the clatter of dishes and sizzling of meat. Larry materialized in the doorway, breathing deeply.

"Ah, exquisite torture. I'm starving," he announced. "How much longer?"

"Here." June thrust a stack of dishes in his hands. "Go set the table—it'll keep your mind off your stomach."

"I knew I should have stayed out of here." Grumbling, he vanished into the adjoining room.

"I guess it's the mountain air," Hillary commented between bites as the group sat around the long table. "I'm absolutely ravenous."

The slow smile that drifted across Bret's face brought back the memory of the earlier scene in the kitchen, and warm color seeped into her cheeks. Picking up her glass containing a red wine Bret had produced from some mysterious place, she took a deep, impulsive swallow and firmly gave her attention to the meal.

The clearing up was confused and disorganized as the men, through design or innocence, served only to get in the way, causing June to throw up her hands and order them away.

"I'm the boss," Bret reminded her. "I'm supposed to give the orders."

"Not until Monday," June returned, giving him a firm shove. She watched with a raised brow as Charlene floated with him.

"Just as well," she observed, turning back to Hillary. "I probably couldn't have prevented myself from drowning her in the sink."

The party later spread out with lazy contentment in the living room. Refusing Bret's offer of brandy, Hillary settled herself on a low stool near the fire. She watched the dancing flames, caught up in their images, unaware of the picture she created, cheeks and hair glowing with flickering light, eyes soft and dreamy. Her mind floated, only a small portion of it registering the quiet hum of conversation, the occasional clink of glass. Elbows on knees, head on palms, she drifted with the fire's magic away from conscious thought.

"Are you hypnotized by the flames, Hillary?" Bret's lean form eased down beside her as he stretched out on the hearth rug. Tossed suddenly into reality, she started at his voice, then smiled as she brushed at her hair.

"Yes, I am. There're pictures there if you look for them," she answered, inclining her head toward the blaze. "There's a castle there with turrets all around, and there's a horse with his mane lifted in the wind."

"There's an old man sitting in a rocker," Bret said softly, and she turned to stare at him, surprised that he had seen the image too. He returned her look, with the intensity of an embrace, and she rose, flustered by the weakness his gaze could evoke.

"It's been a long day," she announced, avoiding his eyes. "I think I'll go up to bed. I don't want Larry to complain that I look washed out in the morning."

Calling her good nights, she went swiftly from the room without giving Bret the opportunity to comment.

The room was dim in early morning light when she awoke. She stretched her arms to the ceiling and sat up, knowing sleep was finished. When she had slipped under the blankets the night before, her emotions had been in turmoil, and she had been convinced the hours would be spent tossing and turning. She was amazed that she had slept not only immediately but deeply, and the mood with which she greeted the new day was cheerful.

June was still huddled under her quilt, the steady rhythm of her breathing the only sound in the absolute silence. Easing from the bed, Hillary began to dress quietly. She tugged a heavy sweater in muted greens over her head, mating it with forest green cords that fit with slim assurance. Forgoing makeup, she donned the snowsuit Bret had provided, pulling the matching ski cap over her hair.

Creeping down the stairs, she listened for the sounds of morning stirring, but the house remained heavy in slumber. Pulling on boots and gloves, Hillary stepped outside into the cold, clear sunlight.

The woods were silent, and she looked about her at the solitude. It was as if time had stopped—the mountains were a magic fairyland without human habitation. Her companions were the majestic pines, robed in glistening ermine, their tangy scent permeating the air.

"I'm alone," she said aloud, flinging out her arms. "There's not another soul in the entire world." She raced through the snow, drunk with power and liberation. "I'm free!" She tossed snow high above her head, whirling in dizzying circles before flinging herself into the cold snow.

Once more, she contemplated the white-topped mountains and dense trees, realizing her heart had expanded and made room for a new love. She was in love with the mountains as she was with the free-flowing wheat fields. The new and old love filled her with jubilation. Scrambling up, she sped once more through the snow, kicking up mists of white before she stopped and fell on her back, the soft surface yielding beneath her. She lay, spread-eagle, staring up at the sky until a face moved into her view, gray eyes laughing down at her.

"What are you doing, Hillary?"

"Making an angel," she informed him, returning his

smile. "You see, you fall down, and then you move your arms and legs like this." She demonstrated, and her smile faded. "The trick is to get up without making a mess of it. It requires tremendous ability and perfect balance." Sitting up carefully, she put her weight on her feet and started to stand, teetering on her heels. "Give me a hand," she demanded. "I'm out of practice." Grabbing his arm, she jumped clear, then turned back to regard her handiwork. "You see," she stated with arrogant pride, "an angel."

"Beautiful," he agreed. "You're very talented."

"Yes, I know. I didn't think anyone else was up," she added, brushing snow from her bottom.

"I saw you dancing in the snow from my window. What game were you playing?"

"That I was alone in all this." She whirled in circles, arms extended.

"You're never alone up here. Look." He pointed into the woods, and her eyes widened at the large buck that stared back at her, his rack adorning his head like a crown.

"He's magnificent." As if conscious of her admiration, the stag lifted his head before he melted into the cover of the woods. "Oh, I'm in love!" she exclaimed, racing across the snow. "I'm absolutely madly in love with this place. Who needs a man when you've got all this?"

"Oh, really?" A snowball thudded against the back of her head, and she turned to stare at him narrowly.

"You know, of course, this means war."

She scooped up a handful of snow, balling it swiftly and hurling it back at him. They exchanged fire, snow landing on target as often as it missed, until he closed the gap between them, and she engaged in a strategic retreat. Her flight was interrupted as he caught her, tossing her down and rolling on top of her. Her cheeks glowed with the cold, her eyes sparkled with laughter, as she tried to catch her breath.

"All right, you win, you win."

"Yes, I did," he agreed. "And to the victor go the spoils." He touched her mouth with his, his lips moving with light sensuality, stilling her laughter. "I always win sooner or later," he murmured, kissing her eyes closed. "We don't do this nearly often enough," he muttered against her mouth, deepening the kiss until her senses whirled. "You've snow all over your face." His mouth roamed to her cheek, his tongue gently removing flakes, instilling her with exquisite terror. "Oh, Hillary, what a delectable creature you are." Lifting his face, he stared into her wide, anxious eyes. He let out a deep breath and brushed the remaining snow from her cheeks with his hand. "The others should be stirring about now. Let's go have some breakfast."

"Stand over there, Hil." Hillary was once more out in the snow, but this time it was Larry and his camera joining her.

He had been taking pictures for what seemed to Hillary hours. Fervently, she wished the session would end, her mind lingering on the thought of steaming chocolate in front of the fire.

"All right, Hillary, come back to earth. You're supposed to be having fun, not floating in a daze."

"I hope your lenses freeze." She sent him a brilliant smile.

"Aw, cut it out, Hil," he mumbled, continuing to crouch around her.

"That'll do," he announced at last, and she fell over backwards in a mock faint. Larry leaned over her, taking still another picture. Shutting her eyes in amusement, she laughed up at him.

"Are the sessions getting longer, Larry, or is it just me?"

"It's you," he answered, shaking his head, allowing the camera to dangle by its strap. "You're over the hill, past your prime. It's all downhill from here."

"I'll show you who's over the hill." Hillary scrambled up, grabbing a handful of snow.

"No, Hil." Placing a protective hand over his camera, Larry backed away. "Remember my camera, don't lose control." Turning, he ran through the snow toward the lodge.

"Past my prime, am I?" The snowball hit him full on the back as Hillary gave chase. Catching him, she leaped on his back, beating him playfully on the top of the head.

"Go ahead," he told her, carrying her without effort. "Strangle me, give me a concussion—just don't touch my camera."

"Hello, Larry." Bret strolled over as they approached the house. "All finished?"

Hillary noted with some satisfaction that, with the advantage of being perched on Larry's back, she could meet Bret's eyes on level.

"I shall have to speak to you, Mr. Bardoff, about a new photographer. This one has just inferred that I am over the hill."

"I can't help it if your career's shot," Larry protested.

"I've been carrying you figuratively for months, and now that I've carried you literally, I think you're putting on weight."

"That does it," Hillary decided. "Now I have no choice—I have to kill him."

"Put it off for a while, would you?" June requested, joining them by the door. "He doesn't know it yet, but I'm dragging him off for a walk in the woods."

"Very well," Hillary agreed. "That should give me time to consider. Put me down, Larry—you've been reprieved."

"Cold?" Bret asked as Hillary began to strip off her outdoor clothing.

"Frozen. There are those among us who have developing fluid rather than blood in their veins."

"Modeling is not all glamour and smiles, is it?" he commented as she shook snow from her hair. "Are you content with it?" he asked suddenly, capturing her chin with his hand, his eyes narrowed and serious. "Is there nothing else you want?"

"It's what I do," she countered. "It's what I'm able to do."

"Is it what you *want* to do?" he persisted. "Is it *all* you want to do?"

"All?" she repeated, and, battling the urgent longing, she shrugged. "It's enough, isn't it?"

He continued to stare down at her before he mirrored her shrug and walked away. He moved, even in jeans, with a rather detached elegance. Puzzled, Hillary watched him disappear down the hall.

The afternoon passed in vague complacency. Hillary sipped the hot chocolate of her dreams and dozed in a chair by the fire. She watched Bret and Bud play a long game of chess, the three of them unconcerned by Larry's occasional, irrepressible intrusions with his camera.

Charlene remained stubbornly by Bret's side, following the contest with ill-concealed boredom. When the match was over, she insisted that he show her through the forest. It was apparent to Hillary that her mind was not on trees and squirrels.

The day drifted away into darkness. Charlene, looking disgruntled after her walk, complained about the cold, then stated regally that she would soak in a hot tub for the next hour.

Dinner consisted of beef stew, which left the redhead aghast. She compensated by consuming an overabundance of wine. Her complaints were genially ignored, and the meal passed with the casual intimacy characteristic of people who have grown used to each other's company.

Again accepting kitchen detail, Hillary and June worked in the small room, the latter stating she felt she was due for a raise. The job was near completion when Charlene strolled in, yet another glass of wine in her hand.

"Almost done with your womanly duties?" she demanded with heavy sarcasm.

"Yes. Your assistance was greatly appreciated," June answered, stacking plates in a cupboard.

"I should like to have a word with Hillary, if you don't mind."

"No, I don't mind," June returned, and continued to clatter dishes.

Charlene turned to where Hillary was now wiping the surface of the stove. "I will not tolerate your behavior any longer."

"Well, all right—if you'd rather do it yourself." Hillary offered the dishcloth with a smile.

"I saw you this morning," Charlene flung out viciously, "throwing yourself at Bret."

"Did you?" Hillary shrugged, turning back to give the stove her attention. "Actually, I was throwing snowballs. I thought you were asleep."

"Bret woke me when he got out of bed." The voice was soft, the implication all too clear.

Pain throbbed through Hillary. How could he have left one woman's arms and come so easily into hers? How could he degrade and humiliate her that way? She shut her eyes, feeling the color drain from her face. The simple fun and precious intimacy they had shared that morning now seemed cheap. Holding on to her pride desperately, she turned to face Charlene, meeting triumphant green eyes with blue ice. "Everyone's entitled to his own taste." She shrugged indifferently, tossing the cloth on the stove.

Charlene's color rose dramatically. With a furious oath, she threw the contents of her glass, splattering the red liquid over Hillary's sweater.

"That's going too far!" June exploded, full of righteous anger on Hillary's behalf. "You're not going to get away with this one."

"I'll have your job for speaking to me that way."

"Just try it, when the boss sees what you—"

"No more," Hillary broke in, halting her avenger. "I don't want any more scenes, June."

"But, Hillary."

"No, please, just forget it." She was torn between the need to crawl away and lick her wounds and the urge to pull out handfuls of red hair. "I mean it. There's no need to bring Bret into this. I've had it."

"All right, Hillary," June agreed, casting Charlene a disgusted look. "For your sake."

Hillary moved quickly from the room, wanting only to reach the sanctuary of her bedroom. Before she reached the stairs, however, she met Bret.

"Been to war, Hillary?" he asked, glancing at the red splatters on her sweater. "Looks like you lost."

"I never had anything to lose," she mumbled, and started to walk by him.

"Hey." He halted her, taking her arms and holding her in front of him. "What's wrong?"

"Nothing," she retorted, feeling her precious control slipping with each passing moment.

"Don't hand me that—look at you." His hand reached out to tilt her chin, but she jerked back. "Don't do that," he commanded. His fingers gripped her face and held her still. "What's wrong with you anyway?"

"Nothing is the matter with me," she returned, retreating behind a sheet of ice. "I'm simply a bit weary of being pawed."

She watched, his eyes darkening to a thunderous gray. His fingers tightened painfully on her flesh. "You're darned lucky there're other people in the house, or I'd give you a fine example of what it's really like to be pawed. It's a pity I had a respect for fragile innocence. I shall certainly keep my hands off you in the future."

He relaxed his grip, and with chin and arm aching from the pressure, she pushed by him and calmly mounted the stairs.

# Chapter 8

February had drifted into March. The weather had been as cold and dreary as Hillary's spirits. Since the fateful weekend in the Adirondacks, she had received no word from Bret, nor did she expect to.

The issue of *Mode* with Hillary's layout was released, but she could build up no enthusiasm as she studied the tall, slim woman covering the pages. The smiling face on the glossy cover seemed to belong to someone else, a stranger Hillary could neither recognize nor relate to. The layout was, nevertheless, a huge success, with the magazines selling as quickly as they were placed on the stands. She was besieged by offers as the weeks went by, but none of them excited her. She found the pursuit of her career of supreme indifference.

A call from June brought an end to her listlessness. The call brought a summons from the emperor. She debated refusing the order, then, deciding she would rather face Bret in his office than to have him seek her out at home, she obeyed.

She dressed carefully for the meeting, choosing a discreetly elegant pale yellow suit. She piled her hair up from her neck, covering it with a wide-brimmed hat. After a thorough study, she was well pleased with the calm, sophisticated woman reflected in her mirror.

During the elevator ride to Bret's office, Hillary schooled herself to remain aloof and detached, setting her expression into coolly polite lines. He would not see the pain, she determined. Her vulnerability would be well concealed. Her ability to portray what the camera demanded would be her defense. Her years of experience would not betray her.

June greeted her with a cheery smile. "Go right on in." She pushed the button on her phone. "He's expecting you."

Swallowing fear, Hillary fixed a relaxed smile on her face and entered the lion's den.

"Good afternoon, Hillary," Bret greeted her, leaning back in his chair but not rising. "Come sit down."

"Hello, Bret." Her voice matched the polite tone of his. Her smile remained in place though her stomach had begun to constrict at the first contact with his eyes.

"You're looking well," he commented.

"Thank you, so are you." She thought giddily, *What absurd nonsense!*

"I've just been looking over the layout again. It's certainly been every bit as successful as we had hoped."

"Yes, I'm glad it worked out so well for everyone."

"Which of these is you, Hillary?" he muttered absently, frowning over the pictures. "Free-spirited tomboy, elegant socialite, dedicated career woman, loving wife, adoring mother, exotic temptress?" He raised his eyes suddenly, boring into hers, the power almost shattering her frail barrier.

She shrugged carelessly. "I'm just a face and body doing what I'm told, projecting the image that's required. That's why you hired me in the first place, isn't it?"

"So, like a chameleon, you change from one color to the next on command."

"That's what I'm paid to do," she answered, feeling slightly ill.

"I've heard you've received quite a number of offers." Once more leaning back in his chair, Bret laced his fingers and studied her through half-closed eyes. "You must be very busy."

"Yes," she began, feigning enthusiasm. "It's been very exciting. I haven't decided which ones to accept. I've been told I should hire a manager to sort things out. There's an offer from a perfume manufacturer—" she named a well-known company "—that involves a long-term contract—three years endorsing on TV and, of course, magazines. It's by far the most interesting, I think." It was at the moment the only one she could clearly remember.

"I see. I'd heard you'd been approached by one of the networks."

"Oh, yes." She made a dismissive gesture, racking her brains for the details. "But that involves acting. I have to give that a great deal of thought." *I'd win an Oscar for this performance,* she added silently. "I doubt if it would be wise to jump into something like that."

He stood and turned his back, staring out at the steel

and glass. She studied him without speaking, wondering what was going on in his mind, noting irrelevantly how the sunlight combed his thick blond hair.

"Your contract with me is finished, Hillary, and though I'm quite prepared to make you an offer, it would hardly be as lucrative as a television contract."

An offer, Hillary thought, her mind whirling, and she was grateful his back was to her so that he could not observe her expression. At least she knew why he had wanted to see her—to offer her another contract, another piece of paper. She would have to refuse, even though she had no intention of accepting any of the other contracts. She could never endure continuous contact with this man. Even after this brief meeting, her emotions were torn.

She rose before answering, and her voice was calm, even professional. "I appreciate your offer, Bret, but I must consider my career. I'm more than grateful to you for the opportunity you gave me, but—"

"I told you before, I don't want your gratitude!" He spun to face her, the all-too-familiar temper darkening his eyes. "I'm not interested in perfunctory expressions of gratitude and appreciation. Whatever you receive as a result of this—" he picked up the magazine with Hillary's face on the cover "—you earned yourself. Take that hat off so I can look at you." He whipped the hat from her head and thrust it into her hands.

Hillary resisted the need to swallow. She met his angry, searching gaze without flinching.

"Your success, Hillary, is of your own making. I'm not responsible for it, nor do I want to be." He seemed to struggle for a measure of control and went on in calm, precise tones. "I don't expect you to accept an offer from me. However, if you change your mind, I'd be willing to negotiate. Whatever you decide, I wish you luck—I should like to think you're happy."

"Thank you." With a light smile, she turned and headed for the door.

"Hillary."

Hand on knob, she shut her eyes a moment and willed herself the strength to face him again. "Yes?"

He stared at her, giving her the sensation that he was filing each of her features separately in his brain. "Goodbye."

"Goodbye," she returned, and turning the knob, she escaped.

Shaken, she leaned her back against the smooth other side of the door. June glanced up from her work.

"Are you all right, Hillary? What's the matter?"

Hillary stared without comprehension, then shook her head. "Nothing," she whispered. "Oh, everything." With a muffled sob, she streaked from the room.

Hillary hailed a cab a few nights later with little enthusiasm. She had allowed herself to be persuaded by Larry and June to attend a party across town in Bud Lewis's penthouse apartment. She must not wallow in self-pity, cut off from friends and social activities, she had decided. It was time, she told herself, pulling her shawl closer against the early April breeze, to give some thought to the future. Sitting alone and brooding would not do the job.

As a result of her self-lecturing, she arrived at the already well-moving party determined to enjoy herself. Bud swung a friendly arm over her shoulders and, leading her to the well-stocked bar, inquired what was her pleasure. She started to request her usual well-diluted drink when a punch bowl filled with a sparkling rose pink liquid caught her eye.

"Oh, that looks nice—what is it?"

"Planter's punch," he informed her, already filling a glass.

Sounds safe enough, she decided as Bud was diverted by another of his guests. With a tentative sip, Hillary thought it remarkably good. She began to mingle with the crowd.

She greeted old and new faces, pausing occasionally to talk or laugh. She glided from group to group, faintly amazed at how light and content was her mood. Depression and unhappiness dissolved like a summer's mist. This is what she needed all along, she concluded—some people, some music, a new attitude.

She was well into her third glass, having a marvelous time, flirting with a tall, dark man who introduced himself as Paul, when a familiar voice spoke from behind her.

"Hello, Hillary, fancy running into you here."

Turning, Hillary was only somewhat surprised to see Bret. She had only agreed to attend the party when June had assured her Bret had other plans. She smiled at him vaguely, wondering momentarily why he was slightly out of focus.

"Hello, Bret, joining the peasants tonight?"

His eyes roamed over her flushed cheeks and absent smile before traveling down the length of her slim form. He lifted his gaze back to her face, one brow lifting slightly as he answered. "I slum it now and then—it's good for the image."

"Mmm." She nodded, draining the remainder of her

glass and tossing back an errant lock of hair. "We're both good with images, aren't we?" She turned to the other man at her side with a brilliant smile that left him slightly dazed. "Paul, be a darling and fetch me another of these. It's the punch over there—" she gestured largely "—in that bowl."

"How many have you had, Hillary?" Bret inquired, tilting her chin with his finger as Paul melted into the crowd. "I thought two was your limit."

"No limit tonight." She tossed her head, sending raven locks trembling about her neck and shoulders. "I am celebrating a rebirth. Besides, it's just fruit punch."

"Remarkably strong fruit I'd say from the looks of you," he returned, unable to prevent a grin. "Perhaps you should consider the benefits of coffee after all."

"Don't be stuffy," she ordered, running a finger down the buttons of his shirt. "Silk," she proclaimed and flashed another smile up at him. "I've always had a weakness for silk. Larry's here, you know, and," she added with dramatic emphasis, "he doesn't have his camera. I almost didn't recognize him."

"It won't be long before you have difficulty recognizing your own mother," he commented.

"No, my mother only takes Polaroid shots on odd occasions," she informed him as Paul returned with her drink. Taking a long sip, she captured Paul's arm. "Dance with me. I really love to dance. Here—" she handed her glass to Bret "—hang on to this for me."

She felt light and free as she moved to the music and marveled how she had ever let Bret Bardoff disturb her. The room spun in time to the music, drifting with her in a newfound sense of euphoria. Paul murmured something in her ear she could not quite understand, and she gave an indefinite sigh in response.

When the music halted briefly, a hand touched her arm, and she turned to find Bret standing beside her.

"Cutting in?" she asked, pushing back tumbled hair.

"Cutting out is more what I had in mind," he corrected, pulling her along with him. "And so are you."

"But I'm not ready to leave." She tugged at his arm. "It's early, and I'm having fun."

"I can see that." He continued to drag her after him, not bothering to turn around. "But we're going anyway."

"You don't have to take me home. I can call a cab, or maybe Paul will take me."

"Like hell he will," Bret muttered, pulling her purposefully through the crowd.

"I want to dance some more." She did a quick spin and collided full in his chest. "You want to dance with me?"

"Not tonight, Hillary." Sighing, he looked down at her. "I guess we do this the hard way."

In one swift movement, he had her slung over his shoulder and began weaving his way through the amused crowd. Instead of suffering from indignation, Hillary began to giggle.

"Oh, what fun, my father used to carry me like this."

"Terrific."

"Here, boss." June stood by the door holding Hillary's bag and wrap. "Got everything under control?"

"I will have." He shifted his burden and strode down the hall.

Hillary was carried from the building and dumped without ceremony into Bret's waiting car. "Here." He thrust her shawl into her hands. "Put this on."

"I'm not cold." She tossed it carelessly into the back seat. "I feel marvelous."

"I'm sure you do." Sliding in beside her, he gave her one despairing glance before the engine sprang to life. "You've enough alcohol in your system to heat a two-story building."

"Fruit punch," Hillary corrected, and snuggled back against the cushion. "Oh, look at the moon." She sprang up to lean on the dash, staring at the ghostly white circle. "I love a full moon. Let's go for a walk."

He pulled up at a stoplight, turned to her, and spoke distinctly. "No."

Tilting her head, she narrowed her eyes as if to gain a new perspective. "I had no idea you were such a wet tire."

"Blanket," he corrected, merging with the traffic.

"I told you, I'm not cold." Sinking back into the seat, she began to sing.

Bret parked the car in the garage that serviced Hillary's building, turning to her with reluctant amusement. "All right, Hillary, can you walk or do I carry you?"

"Of course I can walk. I've been walking for years and years." Fumbling with the door handle, she got out to prove her ability. *Funny,* she thought, *I don't remember this floor being tilted.* "See?" she said aloud, weaving dangerously. "Perfect balance."

"Sure, Hillary, you're a regular tightrope walker." Gripping her arm to prevent a spill, he swept her up, cradled against his chest. She lay back contented as he carried her to the elevator, twining her arms around his neck.

"I like this much better," she announced as the elevator began its slow climb. "Do you know what I've always wanted to do?"

"What?" His answer was absent, not bothering to turn his head. She nuzzled his ear with her lips. "Hillary," he began, but she cut him off.

"You have the most fascinating mouth." The tip of her finger traced it with careful concentration.

"Hillary, stop it."

She continued as if he had not spoken. "A nicely shaped face too." Her finger began a slow trip around it. "And I've positively been swallowed up by those eyes." Her mouth began to roam his neck, and he let out a long breath as the elevator doors opened. "Mmm, you smell good."

He struggled to locate her keys, hampered with the bundle in his arms and the soft mouth on his earlobe.

"Hillary, stop it," he ordered. "You're going to make me forget the game has rules."

At last completing the complicated process of opening the door, he leaned against it a moment, drawing in a deep breath.

"I thought men liked to be seduced," she murmured, brushing her cheek against his.

"Listen, Hillary." Turning his face, he found his mouth captured.

"I just love kissing you." She yawned and cradled her head against his neck.

"Hillary...for heaven's sake!"

He staggered for the bedroom while Hillary continued to murmur soft, incoherent words in his ear.

He tried to drop her down on the spread, but her arms remained around his neck, pulling him off balance and down on top of her. Tightening her hold, she once more pressed her lips to his.

He swore breathlessly as he struggled to untangle himself. "You don't know what you're doing." With a drowsy moan, she shut her eyes. "Have you got anything on under that dress?" he demanded as he removed her shoes.

"Mmm, a shimmy."

"What's that?"

She gave him a misty smile and murmured. Taking a deep breath, he shifted her over, released the zipper at the back of her dress, pulled the material over smooth shoulders, and continued down the length of the slimly curved body.

"You're going to pay for this," he warned. His cursing became more eloquent as he forced himself to ignore the honey skin against the brief piece of silk. He drew the spread over the inert form on the bed. Hillary sighed and snuggled into the pillow.

Moving to the door, he leaned wearily on the frame, allowing his eyes to roam over Hillary as she lay in blissful slumber. "I don't believe this. I must be out of my mind." His eyes narrowed as he listened to her deep breathing. "I'm going to hate myself in the morning." Taking a long, deep breath, he went to search out Hillary's hoard of Scotch.

# Chapter 9

Hillary awoke to bright invading sunlight. She blinked in bewilderment attempting to focus on familiar objects. She sat up and groaned. Her head ached and her mouth felt full of grit. Placing her feet on the floor, she attempted to stand, only to sink back moaning, as the room revolved around her like a carousel. She gripped her head with her hands to keep it stationary.

What did I drink last night? she wondered, squeezing her eyes tight to jar her memory. What kind of punch was that? She staggered unsteadily to her closet to secure a robe.

Her dress was tossed on the foot of the bed, and she stared at it in confusion. I don't remember undressing, she thought. Shaking her head in bemusement, she pressed a hand against her pounding temple. Aspirin, juice, and a cold shower, she decided. With slow, care-

ful steps, she walked toward the kitchen. She stopped
abruptly and leaned against the wall for support as a
pair of men's shoes and a jacket stared at her in accusation from her living room sofa.

"Good heavens," she whispered as a partial memory floated back. Bret had brought her home, and she
had… She shuddered as she remembered her conduct
on the elevator. But what happened? She could only recall bits and pieces, like a jigsaw puzzle dumped on the
floor—and the thought of putting them together was
thoroughly upsetting.

"Morning, darling."

She turned slowly, her already pale face losing all
color as Bret smiled at her, clad only in slacks, a shirt
carelessly draped over his shoulder. The dampness of
his hair attested to the fact that he had just stepped from
the shower. *My shower.* Hillary's brain pounded out as
she stared at him.

"I could use some coffee, darling." He kissed her
lightly on the cheek in a casual intimate manner that
tightened her stomach. He strode past her into the
kitchen, and she followed, terrified. After placing the
kettle to boil, he turned and wrapped his arms around
her waist. "You were terrific." His lips brushed her
brow, and she knew a moment's terror that she would
faint dead away. "Did you enjoy yourself as much as
I did?"

"Well, I—I guess, I don't… I don't remember…ex-
actly."

"Don't remember?" He stared in disbelief. "How
could you forget? You were amazing."

"I was… Oh." She covered her face with her hands.
"My head."

"Hungover?" he asked, full of solicitude. "I'll fix you up." Moving away, he rummaged in the refrigerator.

"Hungover?" she repeated, supporting herself in the doorway. "I only had some punch."

"And three kinds of rum."

"Rum?" she echoed, screwing up her eyes and trying to think. "I didn't have anything but—"

"Planter's punch." He was busily involved in his remedy, keeping his back toward her. "Which consists, for the most part, of rum—amber, white, and dark."

"I didn't know what it was." She leaned more heavily on the doorway. "I had too much to drink. I'm not used to it. You—you took advantage of me."

"I took advantage?" Glass in hand, he regarded her in astonishment. "Darling, I couldn't hold you off." He lifted his brow and grinned. "You're a real tiger when you get going."

"What a dreadful thing to say," she exploded, then moaned as her head hammered ruthlessly.

"Here, drink." He offered the concoction, and she regarded it with doubtful eyes.

"What's in it?"

"Don't ask," he advised. "Just drink."

Hillary swallowed in one gulp, then shivered as the liquid poured down her throat. "Ugh."

"Price you pay, love," he said piously, "for getting drunk."

"I wasn't drunk exactly," she protested. "I was just a little…a little muddled. And you—" she glared at him "—you took advantage of me."

"I would swear it was the other way around."

"I didn't know what I was doing."

"You certainly seemed to know what you were

doing—and very well too." His smile prompted a groan from Hillary.

"I can't remember. I just can't remember."

"Relax, Hillary," he said as she began to sniffle. "There's nothing to remember."

"What do you mean?" She sniffed again and wiped her eyes with the back of her hand.

"I mean, I didn't touch you. I left you pure and unsullied in your virginal bed and slept on that remarkably uncomfortable couch."

"You didn't…we didn't…"

"No to both." He turned in response to the shrilling kettle and poured boiling water into a mug.

The first flood of relief changed into irritation. "Why not? What's wrong with me?"

He turned back to stare at her in amazement, then roared with laughter. "Oh, Hillary, what a contradiction you are! One minute you're desperate because you think I've stolen your honor and the next you're insulted because I didn't."

"I don't find it very funny," she retorted. "You deliberately led me to believe that I, that we—"

"Slept together," Bret offered, casually sipping his coffee. "You deserved it. You drove me crazy all the way from the elevator to the bedroom." His smile widened at her rapid change of color. "You remember that well enough. Now remember this. Most men wouldn't have left a tempting morsel like you and slept on that miserable couch, so take care with your fruit punch from now on."

"I'm never going to take another drink as long as I live," Hillary vowed, rubbing her hands over her eyes. "I'm never going to look at a piece of fruit again. I need some tea or some of that horrible coffee, *something*." The sound of the doorbell shrilled through her head, and she swore with unaccustomed relish.

"I'll fix you some tea," Bret offered, grinning at her fumbling search for obscenities. "Go answer the door."

She answered the summons wearily, opening the door to find Charlene standing at the threshold, taking in her disheveled appearance with glacial eyes.

"Do come right in," Hillary said, shutting the door behind Charlene with a force that only added to her throbbing discomfort.

"I heard you made quite a spectacle of yourself last night."

"Good news travels fast, Charlene—I'm flattered you were so concerned."

"You don't concern me in the least." She brushed invisible lint from her vivid green jacket. "Bret does, however. You seem to make a habit of throwing yourself at him, and I have no intention of allowing it to continue."

*This is too much for anyone to take in my condition,* Hillary decided, feeling anger rising. Feigning a yawn, she assumed a bored expression. "Is th at all?"

"If you think I'm going to have a little nobody like you marring the reputation of the man I'm going to marry, you're very much mistaken."

For an instant, anger's heat was frozen in agony. The struggle to keep her face passive caused her head to pound with new intensity. "My congratulations to you, my condolences to Bret."

"I'll ruin you," Charlene began. "I'll see to it that your face is never photographed again."

"Hello, Charlene," Bret said casually as he entered the room, his shirt now more conventionally in place.

The redhead whirled, staring first at him, then at his jacket thrown carelessly over the back of the sofa. "What…what…are you doing here?"

"I should think that's fairly obvious," he answered, dropping to the sofa and slipping on his shoes. "If you didn't want to know, you shouldn't have taken it upon yourself to check up on me."

He's using me again, Hillary thought, banking down on shivering hurt and anger. Just using me to make her jealous.

Charlene turned on her, her bosom heaving with emotion. "You won't hold him! You're only a cheap one-night stand! He'll be bored with you within the week! He'll soon come back to me," she raved.

"Terrific," Hillary retorted, feeling her grip on her temper slipping. "You're welcome to him, I'm sure. I've had enough of both of you. Why don't you both leave? Now, at once!" She made a wild gesture at the door. "Out, out, out!"

"Just a minute," Bret broke in, buttoning up the last button of his shirt.

"You keep out of this," Hillary snapped, glaring at him. She turned back to Charlene. "I've had it up to the ears with you, but I'm in no mood for fighting at the moment. If you want to come back later, we'll see about it."

"I see no reason to speak to you again," Charlene announced with a toss of her head. "You're no problem to me. After all, what could Bret possibly see in a cheap little tramp like you?"

"Tramp," Hillary repeated in an ominously low voice. "Tramp?" she repeated, advancing.

"Hold on, Hillary." Bret jumped up, grabbing her around the waist. "Calm down."

"You really are a little savage, aren't you?" shot Charlene.

"Savage? I'll show you savage." Hillary struggled furiously against Bret.

"Be quiet, Charlene," he warned softly, "or I'll turn her loose on you."

He held the struggling Hillary until her struggles lost their force.

"Let me go. I won't touch her," she finally agreed. "Just get her out of here." She whirled on Bret. "And you get out too! I've had it with the pair of you. I won't be used this way. If you want to make her jealous, find someone else to dangle in front of her! I want you out— out of my life, out of my mind." She lifted her chin, heedless of the dampness that covered her cheeks. "I never want to see either of you again."

"Now you listen to me." Bret gripped her shoulders more firmly and gave her a brief but vigorous shake.

"No." She wrenched herself out of his grip. "I'm through listening to you. Through, finished—do you understand? Just get out of here, take your friend with you, and both of you leave me alone."

Picking up his jacket, Bret stared for a moment at flushed cheeks and swimming eyes. "All right, Hillary, I'll take her away. I'll give you a chance to pull yourself together, then I'll be back. We haven't nearly finished yet."

She stared at the door he closed behind him through a mist of angry tears. He could come back all right, she decided, brushing away drops of weakness. But she wouldn't be here.

Rushing into the bedroom, she pulled out her cases, throwing clothes into them in heaps. *I've had enough!*

she thought wildly, *enough of New York, enough of Charlene Mason, and especially enough of Bret Bardoff. I'm going home.*

In short order, she rapped on Lisa's door. Her friend's smile of greeting faded at the sight of Hillary's obvious distress.

"What in the world—" she began, but Hillary cut her off.

"I don't have time to explain, but I'm leaving. Here's my key." She thrust it into Lisa's hand. "There's food in the fridge and cupboards. You take it, and anything else you like. I won't be coming back."

"But, Hillary—"

"I'll make whatever arrangements have to be made about the furniture and the lease later. I'll write and explain as soon as I can."

"But, Hillary," Lisa called after her, "where are you going?"

"Home," she answered without turning back. "Home where I belong."

If Hillary's unexpected arrival surprised her parents, they asked no questions and made no demands. Soon she fell into the old, familiar pattern of days on the farm. A week drifted by, quiet and undemanding.

During this time it became Hillary's habit to spend quiet times on the open porch of the farmhouse. The interlude between dusk and sleep was the gentlest. It was the time that separated the busy hours of the day from the reflective hours of the night.

The porch swing creaked gently, disturbing the pure stillness of the evening, and she watched the easy movement of the moon, enjoying the scent of her father's pipe as he sat beside her.

"It's time we talked, Hillary," he said, draping his arm around her. "Why did you come back so suddenly?"

With a deep sigh, she rested her head against him. "A lot of reasons. Mostly because I was tired."

"Tired?"

"Yes, tired of being framed and glossed. Tired of seeing my own face. Tired of having to pull emotions and expressions out of my hat like a second-rate magician, tired of the noise, tired of the crowds." She made a helpless movement with her shoulders. "Just plain tired."

"We always thought you had what you wanted."

"I was wrong. It wasn't what I wanted. It wasn't all I wanted." She stood and leaned over the porch rail, staring into the curtain of night. "Now I don't know if I've accomplished anything."

"You accomplished a great deal. You worked hard and made a successful career on your own, and one that you can be proud of. We're all proud of you."

"I know I worked for what I got. I know I was good at my job." She moved away and perched on the porch rail. "When I left home, I wanted to see what I could do for myself by myself. I knew exactly what I wanted, where I was going. Everything was cataloged in neat little piles. First A, then B, and down the line. Now I've got something most women in my position would jump at, and I don't want it. I thought I did, but now, when all I have to do is reach out and take it, I don't want it. I'm tired of putting on the faces."

"All right, then it's time to stop. But I think there's more to your decision to come home than you're saying. Is there a man mixed up in all this?"

"That's all finished," Hillary said with a shrug. "I got in over my head, out of my class."

"Hillary Baxter, I'm ashamed to hear you talk that way."

"It's true." She managed a smile. "I never really fit into his world. He's rich and sophisticated, and I keep forgetting to be glamorous and do the most ridiculous things. Do you know, I still whistle for cabs? You just can't change what you are. No matter how many images you can slip on and off, you're still the same underneath." Shrugging again, she stared into space. "There was never really anything between us—at least not on his side."

"Then he must not have too many brains," her father commented, scowling at his pipe.

"Some might claim you're just a little prejudiced." Hillary gave him a quick hug. "I just needed to come home. I'm going up now. With the rest of the family coming over tomorrow, we'll have a lot to do."

The air was pure and sweet when Hillary mounted her buckskin gelding and set off on an early morning ride. She felt light and free, the wind blowing wildly through her hair, streaming it away from her face in a thick black carpet. In the joy of wind and speed, she forgot time and pain, and the clinging feeling of failure was lost. Reining in the horse, she contemplated the huge expanse of growing wheat.

It was endless, stretching into eternity—a golden ocean rippling under an impossibly blue sky. Somewhere a meadowlark heralded life. Hillary sighed with contentment. Lifting her face, she enjoyed the caressing fingers of sun on her skin, the surging scent of land bursting into life after its winter sleep.

Kansas in the spring, she mused. All the colors so real and vivid, the air so fresh and full of peace. *Why did I ever leave? What was I looking for?* She closed her eyes and let out a long breath. *I was looking for Hillary Baxter,* she thought, *and now that I've found her, I don't know what to do with her.*

"Time's what I need now, Cochise," she told her four-legged companion, and leaned forward to stroke his strong neck. "Just a little time to find all the scattered pieces and put them back together."

Turning the horse toward home, she set off in an easy, gentle lope, content with the soothing rhythm and the spring-softened landscape. As the farm and out-buildings came into view, however, Cochise pawed the ground, straining at the bit.

"All right, you devil." She tossed back her head and laughed, and with a touch of her heels sent the eager horse racing. The air vibrated with the sound of hooves on hard dirt. Hillary let her spirits fly as she gave the gelding his head. They cleared an old wooden jump in a fluid leap, touched earth, and streaked on, sending a flock of contented birds into a flurry of protesting activity.

As they drew nearer the house, her eyes narrowed as she spotted a man leaning on the paddock fence. She pulled back sharply on the reins, causing Cochise to rear in insult.

"Easy," she soothed, stroking his neck and murmuring soft words as he snorted in indignation. Her eyes were focused on the man. It appeared half a continent had not been big enough for a clean escape.

# Chapter 10

"Quite a performance." Bret straightened his lean form and strode toward them. "I couldn't tell where the horse left off and the woman began."

"What are you doing here?" she demanded.

"Just passing by—thought I'd drop in." He stroked the horse's muzzle.

Gritting her teeth, Hillary slipped to the ground.

"How did you know where to find me?" She stared up at him, wishing she had kept her advantage astride the horse.

"Lisa heard me pounding on your door. She told me you'd gone home." He spoke absently, appearing more interested in making the gelding's acquaintance than enlightening her. "This is a fine horse, Hillary." He turned his attention from horse to woman, gray eyes sweeping over windblown hair and flushed cheeks. "You certainly know how to ride him."

"He needs to be cooled off and rubbed down." She felt unreasonably annoyed that her horse seemed so taken with the long fingers caressing his neck. She turned to lead him away.

"Does your friend have a name?" He fell into step beside her.

"Cochise." Her answer was short. She barely suppressed the urge to slam the barn door in his face as Bret entered beside her.

"I wonder if you're aware how perfectly his coloring suits you." He made himself comfortable against the stall opening. Hillary began to groom the gelding with fierce dedication.

"I'd hardly choose a horse for such an impractical reason." She kept her attention centered on the buckskin's coat, her back firmly toward the man.

"How long have you had him?"

*This is ridiculous,* she fumed, wanting desperately to throw the curry comb at him. "I raised him from a foal."

"I suppose that explains why the two of you suit so well."

He began to poke idly about the barn while she completed her grooming. While her hands were busy, her mind whirled with dozens of questions she could not find the courage to form into words. The silence grew deep until she felt buried in it. Finally she was unable to prolong the gelding's brushing. She turned to abandon the barn.

"Why did you run away?" he asked as they were struck with the white flash of sunlight outside.

Her mind jumped like a startled rabbit. "I didn't run away." She improvised rapidly. "I wanted time to think over the offers I've had—it wouldn't do to make the wrong decision at this point in my career."

"I see."

Unsure whether the mockery in his voice was real or a figment of her imagination, she spoke dismissively. "I've got work to do. My mother needs me in the kitchen."

The fates, however, seemed to be against her as her mother opened the back door and stepped out to meet them.

"Why don't you show Bret around, Hillary? Everything's under control here."

"The pies." Hillary sent out rapid distress signals.

Ignoring the silent plea, Sarah merely patted her head. "There's plenty of time yet. I'm sure Bret would like a look around before supper."

"Your mother was kind enough to ask me to stay, Hillary." He smiled at her open astonishment before turning to her mother. "I'm looking forward to it, Sarah."

Fuming at the pleasant first-name exchange, Hillary spun around and muttered without enthusiasm, "Well, come on then." Halting a short distance away, she looked up at him with a honey-drenched smile. "Well, what would you care to see first? The chicken coop or the pig sty?"

"I'll leave that to you," he answered genially, her sarcasm floating over him.

Frowning, Hillary began their tour.

Instead of appearing bored as she had expected, Bret appeared uncommonly interested in the workings of the farm, from her mother's vegetable garden to her father's gigantic machinery.

He stopped her suddenly with a hand on her shoulder and gazed out at the fields of wheat. "I see what you meant, Hillary," he murmured at length. "They're magnificent. A golden ocean."

She made no response.

Turning to head back, his hand captured hers before she could protest.

"Ever seen a tornado?"

"You don't live in Kansas for twenty years and not see one," Hillary said briefly.

"Must be quite an experience."

"It is," she agreed. "I remember when I was about seven, we knew one was coming. Everyone was rushing around, securing animals and getting ready. I was standing right about here." She stopped, gazing into the distance at the memory. "I watched it coming, this enormous black funnel, blowing closer and closer. Everything was so incredibly still, you could feel the air weighing down on you. I was fascinated. My father picked me up, tossed me over his shoulder, and hauled me to the storm cellar. It was so quiet, almost like the world had died, then it was like a hundred planes thundering right over our heads."

He smiled down at her, and she felt the familiar tug at her heart. "Hillary." He lifted her hand to his lips briefly. "How incredibly sweet you are."

She began walking again, stuffing her hands strategically in her pockets. In silence, they rounded the side of the farmhouse, while she searched for the courage to ask him why he had come.

"You, ah, you have business in Kansas?"

"Business is one way to put it." His answer was hardly illuminating, and she attempted to match his easy manner.

"Why didn't you send one of your minions to do whatever you had in mind?"

"There are certain areas that I find more rewarding to deal with personally." His grin was mocking and obviously intended to annoy. Hillary shrugged as if she were indifferent to the entire conversation.

Hillary's parents seemed to take a liking to Bret, and Hillary found herself irritated that Bret fit into the scene so effortlessly. Seated next to her father, on a firm first-name basis, he chatted away like a long-lost friend. The numerous members of her family might have intimidated anyone else. However, Bret seemed undaunted. Within thirty minutes, he had charmed her two sisters-in-law, gained the respect of her two brothers, and the adoration of her younger sister. Muttering about pies, Hillary retreated to the kitchen.

A few minutes later, she heard: "Such domesticity."

Whirling around, she observed Bret's entrance into the room.

"You've flour on your nose." He wiped it away with his finger. Jerking away, she resumed her action with the rolling pin. "Pies, huh? What kind?" He leaned against the counter as though settling for a comfortable visit.

"Lemon meringue," she said shortly, giving him no encouragement.

"Ah, I'm rather partial to lemon meringue—tart and sweet at the same time." He paused and grinned at her averted face. "Reminds me of you." She cast him a withering glance that left him undaunted. "You do that very well," he observed as she began rolling out a second crust.

"I work better alone."

"Where's that famous country hospitality I've heard so much about?"

"You got yourself invited to dinner, didn't you?" She rolled the wooden pin over the dough as if it were the enemy. "Why did you come?" she demanded. "Did you want to get a look at my little farm? Make fun of my family and give Charlene a good laugh when you got back?"

"Stop it." He straightened from the counter and took her by the shoulders. "Do you think so little of those people out there that you can say that?" Her expression altered from anger to astonishment, and his fingers relaxed on her arms. "This farm is very impressive, and your family is full of warm, real people. I'm half in love with your mother already."

"I'm sorry," she murmured, turning back to her work. "That was a stupid thing to say."

He thrust his hands in the pockets of slim-fitting jeans and strolled to the screen door. "It appears baseball's in season."

The door slammed behind him, and Hillary walked over and looked out, watching as Bret was tossed a glove and greeted with open enthusiasm by various members of her family. The sound of shouting and laughter carried by the breeze floated to her. Hillary turned from the door and went back to work.

Her mother came into the kitchen and Hillary responded to her chattering with occasional murmurs. She felt annoyingly distracted by the activity outside.

"Better call them in to wash up." Sarah interrupted her thoughts, and Hillary moved automatically to the door, opening it and whistling shrilly. Her fingers retreated from her mouth in shock, and she cursed herself for again playing the fool in front of Bret. Stomping back into the kitchen, she slammed the screen behind her.

Hillary found herself seated beside Bret at dinner, and ignoring the bats waging war in her stomach, she gave herself over to the table chaos, unwilling for him or her family to see she was disturbed in any way.

As the family gravitated to the living room, Hillary saw Bret once more in discussion with her father, and pointedly gave her attention to her nephew, involving herself with his game of trucks on the floor. His small brother wandered over and climbed into Bret's lap, and she watched under the cover of her lashes as he bounced the boy idly on his knee.

"Do you live with Aunt Hillary in New York?" the child asked suddenly, and a small truck dropped from Hillary's hand with a clatter.

"Not exactly." He smiled slowly at Hillary's rising color. "But I do live in New York."

"Aunt Hillary's going to take me to the top of the Empire State Building," he announced with great pride. "I'm going to spit from a million feet in the air. You can come with us," he invited with childlike magnanimity.

"I can't think of anything I'd rather do." Lean fingers ruffled dark hair. "You'll have to let me know when you're going."

"We can't go on a windy day," the boy explained, meeting gray eyes with six-year-old wisdom. "Aunt Hillary says if you spit into the wind you get your face wet."

Laughter echoed through the room, and Hillary rose and picked up the boy bodily, marching toward the kitchen. "I think there's a piece of pie left. Let's go fill your mouth."

The light was muted and soft with dusk when Hillary's brothers and their families made their departure. A few traces of pink bleeding from the sinking sun traced the horizon. She remained alone on the porch for a time, watching twilight drifting toward darkness, the first stars blinking into life, the first crickets disturbing the silence.

Returning inside, the house seemed strangely quiet. Only the steady ticking of the old grandfather clock disturbed the hush. Curling into a chair, Hillary watched the progress of a chess game between Bret and her father. In spite of herself, she found herself enchanted by the movements of his long fingers over the carved pieces.

"Checkmate." She started at Bret's words, so complete had been her absorption.

Tom frowned at the board a moment, then stroked his chin. "I'll be darned, so it is." He grinned over at Bret and lit his pipe. "You play a fine game of chess, son. I enjoyed that."

"So did I." Bret leaned back in his chair, flicking his lighter at the end of a cigarette. "I hope we'll be able to play often. We should find the opportunity, since I intend to marry your daughter."

The statement was matter-of-factly given. As the words passed from Hillary's ear to brain, her mouth opened, but no sound emerged.

"As head of the family," Bret went on, not even glancing in her direction, "I should assure you that financially Hillary will be well cared for. The pursuit of her career is, of course, her choice, but she need only work for her own satisfaction."

Tom puffed on his pipe and nodded.

"I've thought this through very carefully," Bret continued, blowing out a lazy stream of smoke. "A man reaches a time when he requires a wife and wants children." His voice was low and serious, and Tom met laughing gray eyes equally. "Hillary suits my purposes quite nicely. She is undoubtedly stunning, and what man doesn't enjoy beauty? She's fairly intelligent, adequately strong, and is apparently not averse to children. She is a bit on the skinny side," he added with some regret, and Tom, who had been nodding in agreement to Hillary's virtues, looked apologetic.

"We've never been able to fatten her up any."

"There is also the matter of her temper," Bret deliberated, weighing pros and cons. "But," he concluded with a casual gesture of his hand, "I like a bit of spirit in a woman."

Hillary sprang to her feet, unable for several attempts to form a coherent sentence. "How dare you?" she managed at length. "How dare you sit there and discuss me as if I were a—a brood mare! And you," she chastised her father, "you just go along like you were pawning off the runt of the litter. My own father."

"I did mention her temper, didn't I?" Bret asked Tom, and he nodded sagely.

"You arrogant, conceited, son of a—"

"Careful, Hillary," Bret cautioned, stubbing out his cigarette and raising his brows. "You'll get your mouth washed out with soap again."

"If you think for one minute that I'm going to marry you, you're crazy! I wouldn't have you on a platter! So go back to New York, and…and print your magazines," she finished in a rush, and stormed from the house.

After her departure, Bret turned to Sarah. "I'm sure Hillary would want to have the wedding here. Any close friends can fly in easily enough, but since Hillary's family is here, perhaps I should leave the arrangements to you."

"All right, Bret. Did you have a date in mind?"

"Next weekend."

Sarah's eyes opened wide for a moment as she imagined the furor of arrangements, then tranquilly returned to her knitting. "Leave it to me."

He rose and grinned down at Tom. "She should have cooled off a bit now. I'll go look for her."

"In the barn," Tom informed him, tapping his pipe. "She always goes there when she's in a temper." Bret nodded and strode from the house. "Well, Sarah." With a light chuckle, Tom resumed puffing on his pipe. "Looks like Hillary has met her match."

The barn was dimly lit, and Hillary stomped around the shadows, enraged at both Bret and her father. *The two of them!* she fumed. *I'm surprised he didn't ask to examine my teeth.*

With a groan, the barn door swung open, and she spun around as Bret sauntered into the building.

"Hello, Hillary, ready to discuss wedding plans?"

"I'll never be ready to discuss anything with you!" Her angry voice vibrated in the large building.

Bret smiled into her mutinous face unconcernedly. The lack of reaction incensed her further and she began to shout, storming around the floor. "I'll never marry you—never, never, never. I'd rather marry a three-headed midget with warts."

"But you will marry me, Hillary," he returned with easy confidence. "If I have to drag you kicking and screaming all the way to the altar, you'll marry me."

"I said I won't." She halted her confused pacing in front of him. "You can't make me."

He grabbed her arms and surveyed her with laconic arrogance. "Oh, can't I?"

Pulling her close, he captured her mouth.

"You let go of me," she hissed, pulling away. "You let go of my arms."

"Sure." Obligingly, he relinquished his hold, sending her sprawling on her back in a pile of hay.

"You—bully!" she flung at him, and attempted to scramble to her feet, but his body neatly pinned her back into the sweet-smelling hay.

"I only did what I was told. Besides," he added with a crooked smile, "I always did prefer you horizontal." She pushed against him, averting her face as his mouth descended. He contented himself with the soft skin of her neck.

"You can't do this." Her struggles began to lose their force as his lips found new areas of exploration.

"Yes, I can," he murmured, finding her mouth at last. Slow and deep, the kiss battered at her senses until her lips softened and parted beneath his, her arms circled his neck. He drew back, rubbing her nose with his.

"Wretch!" she whispered, pulling him close until their lips merged again.

"Now are you going to marry me?" He smiled down at her, brushing hair from her cheek.

"I can't think," she murmured and shut her eyes. "I can't ever think when you kiss me."

"I don't want you to think." He busied his fingers loosening her buttons. "I just want you to say it." His hand took possession of her breast and gently caressed it. "Just say it, Hillary," he ordered, his mouth moving down from her throat, seeking her vulnerability. "Say it, and I'll give you time to think."

"All right," she moaned. "You win, I'll marry you."

"Good," he said simply, bringing his lips back to hers for a brief kiss.

She fought the fog of longing clouding her senses and attempted to escape. "You used unfair tactics."

He shrugged, holding her beneath him easily. "All's fair in love and war, my love." His eyes lost their laughter as he stared down at her. "I love you, Hillary. You're in every part of my mind. I can't get you out. I love every crazy, beautiful inch of you." His mouth crushed hers, and she felt the world slip from her grasp.

"Oh, Bret." She began kissing his face with wild abandon. "I love you so much. I love you so much I can't bear it. All this time I thought… When Charlene told me you'd been with her that night in the mountains, I—"

"Wait a minute." He halted her rapid kisses, cupping her face with his hands. "I want you to listen to me. First of all, what was between Charlene and me was over before I met you. She just wouldn't let go." He smiled and brushed her mouth with his. "I haven't been able to think of another woman since the first day I met you, and I was half in love with you even before that."

"How?"

"Your picture—your face haunted me."

"I never thought you were serious about me." Her fingers began to tangle in his hair.

"I thought at first it was just physical. I knew I wanted you as I'd never wanted another woman. That night in your apartment, when I found out you were innocent, that threw me a bit." He shook his head in wonder and buried his face in the lushness of her hair. "It didn't take long for me to realize what I felt for you was much more than a physical need."

"But you never indicated anything else."

"You seemed to shy away from relationships—you panicked every time I got too close—and I didn't want to scare you away. You needed time. I tried to give it to you. Hanging on in New York was difficult enough." He traced the hollow of her cheek with a finger. "But that day in my lodge, my control slipped. If Larry and June hadn't come when they did, things would have progressed differently. When you turned on me, telling me you were sick of being pawed, I nearly strangled you."

"Bret, I'm sorry, I didn't mean it. I thought—"

"I know what you thought," he interrupted. "I'm only sorry I didn't know then. I didn't know what Charlene had said to you. Then I began to think you wanted only your career, that you didn't want to make room in your life for anything or anyone else. In my office that day, you were so cool and detached, ticking off your choices, I wanted to toss you out the window."

"They were all lies," she whispered, rubbing her cheek against his. "I never wanted any of it, only you."

"When June finally told me about the scene with Charlene at the lodge, and I remembered your reaction, I began to put things together. I came looking for you at Bud's party." He pulled up his head and grinned. "I intended to talk things out, but you were hardly in any condition for declarations of love by the time I got there. I don't know how I stayed out of your bed that night, you were so soft and beautiful…and so smashed! You nearly drove me over the edge."

He lowered his head and kissed her, his control ebbing as his mouth conquered her. His hands began to mold her curves with an urgent hunger, and she clutched him closer, drowning in the pool of his desire.

"Good God, Hillary, we can't wait much longer." He removed his weight from her, rolling over on his back, but she went with him, closing her mouth over his. Drawing her firmly away, he let out a deep breath. "I don't think your father would think kindly of me taking his daughter in a pile of hay in his own barn."

He pushed her on her back, slipping his arm around her, cradling her head against his shoulder. "I can't give you Kansas, Hillary," he said quietly. She turned her head to look at him. "We can't live here—at least not now. I've obligations in New York that I simply can't deal with from here."

"Oh, Bret," she began, but he pulled her closer and continued.

"There's upper New York or Connecticut. There are plenty of places where commuting would be no problem. You can have a house in the country if that's what you want. A garden, horses, chickens, half a dozen kids. We'll come back here as often as we can, and go up to the lodge for long weekends, just the two of us." He looked down, alarmed at the tears spilling from wide eyes and over smooth cheeks. "Hillary, don't do that. I don't want you to be unhappy. I know this is home to you." He began to brush the drops from her face.

"Oh, Bret, I love you." She pulled his cheek against hers. "I'm not unhappy. I'm wonderfully, crazily happy that you care so much. Don't you know it doesn't matter where we are? Anyplace I can be with you is home."

He drew her away and regarded her with a frown. "Are you sure, love?"

She smiled and lifted her mouth, letting her kiss give him the answer.

* * * * *

# SEARCH FOR LOVE

## Chapter 1

The train ride seemed endless, and Serenity was tired. The argument the night before with Tony had not helped her disposition, plus the long flight from Washington to Paris, and now the arduous hours in the stuffy train had her gritting her teeth to hold back the groan. All in all, she decided miserably, she was a poor traveler.

The trip had been the excuse for the last, terminal battle between Serenity and Tony, their relationship having been strained and uneven for weeks. Her continued refusal to be pressured into marriage had provoked several minor tiffs, but Tony had wanted her, and his patience seemed inexhaustible. Not until her announcement of the intended trip had his forebearance cracked, and the war had begun.

"You can't go rushing off this way to France to see some supposed grandmother you never knew existed until a couple of weeks ago." Tony had paced, his agitation obvious by the way he allowed his hand to disturb his well-styled fair hair.

"Brittany," Serenity had elaborated. "And it doesn't matter when I found out she existed; I know now."

"This old lady writes you a letter, tells you she's your grandmother and wants to see you, and off you go, just like that." He had been totally exasperated. She knew his logical mind was unable to comprehend her impulse, and she had hung on to the threads of her own temper and had attempted to speak calmly.

"She's my mother's mother, Tony, the only family I have left, and I intend to see her. You know I've been making plans to go since her letter arrived."

"The old girl lets twenty-four years go by without a word, and now suddenly, this big summons." He had continued to pace the large, high-ceilinged room before whirling back to her. "Why in heaven's name did your parents never speak of her? Why did she wait until they were dead to contact you?"

Serenity had known he had not meant to be cruel; it was not in Tony's nature to be cruel, merely logical, his lawyer's mind dealing constantly in facts and figures. Even he could not know the slow, deadly ache that remained, lingering after two months, the time since her parents' sudden, unexpected deaths. Knowing that his words had not been intended to hurt did not prevent her from lashing out, and the argument had grown in proportion until Tony had stomped out and left her alone, seething and resentful.

Now, as the train chugged its way across Brittany, Serenity was forced to admit that she, too, had doubts.

Why had her grandmother, this unknown Comtesse Françoise de Kergallen, remained silent for nearly a quarter of a century? Why had her mother, her lovely, fragile, fascinatingly different mother, never mentioned a relative in far-off Brittany? Not even her father, as volatile, outspoken, and direct as he had been, had ever spoken of ties across the Atlantic.

They had been so close, Serenity mused with a sigh of memory. The three of them had done so much together. Even when she had been a child, her parents had included her when they visited senators, congressmen, and ambassadors.

Jonathan Smith had been a much-sought-after artist; a portrait created by his talented hand, a prized possession. Those in Washington society had clamored for his commissions for more than twenty years. He had been well liked and respected as a man as well as an artist, and the gentle charm and grace of Gaelle, his wife, had made the couple a highly esteemed addition to the capital set.

When Serenity had grown older, and her natural artistic abilities became apparent, her father's pride had known no bounds. They had sketched and painted together, first as tutor and pupil, then as man and woman, and they drew even closer with the shared joy of art.

The small family had shared an idyllic existence in the elegant rowhouse in Georgetown, a life full of love and laughter, until Serenity's world had crashed in around her, along with the plane which had been carrying her parents to California. It had been impossible to believe they were dead, and she still lived on. The high-ceilinged rooms would no longer echo with her father's booming voice or her mother's gentle laughter. The house was empty but for memories that lay like shadows in each corner.

For the first two weeks, Serenity could not bear the sight of a canvas or brush, or the thought of entering the third-floor studio where she and her father had spent so many hours, where her mother would enter and remind them that even artists had to eat.

When she had finally gathered up the courage to climb the stairs and enter the sun-filled room, she found, rather than unbearable grief, a strange, healing peace. The skylight showered the room with the sun's warmth, and the walls retained the love and laughter which had once existed there. She had begun to live again, paint again, and Tony had been kind and gentle, helping to fill the hollowness left by loss. Then, the letter had come.

Now she had left Georgetown and Tony behind in a quest for the part of her that belonged to Brittany and an unknown grandmother. The strange, formal letter which had brought her from the familiarity of Washington's crowded streets to the unaccustomed Breton countryside lay safely tucked in the smooth leather bag at her side. There had been no affection in the missive, merely facts and an invitation, more like a royal command, Serenity mused, half-annoyed, half-amused. But if her pride would have scoffed at the command, her curiosity, her desire to know more of her mother's family, had accepted. With her innate impulsiveness and organization, she had arranged her trip, closed up the beloved house in Georgetown, and burned her bridges with Tony.

The train groaned and screeched in protest as it dragged into the station at Lannion. Tingling excitement warred with jet lag as Serenity gathered her hand luggage and stepped onto the platform, taking her first attentive look at her mother's native country. She stared around her with an artist's eyes, lost for a moment in the simple beauty and soft, melding colors that were Brittany.

The man watched her concentration, the small smile playing on her parted lips, and his dark brow rose slightly in surprise. He took his time surveying her, a tall, willow-slim figure in a powder-blue traveling suit, the soft skirt floating around long, shapely legs. The soft breeze ran easy fingers through her sunlit hair, feathering it back to frame the delicate-boned, oval face. The eyes, he noted, were large and wide, the color of brandy, surrounded by thick lashes shades darker than her pale hair. Her skin looked incredibly soft, smooth like alabaster, and the combination lent an ethereal appearance: a delicate, fragile orchid. He would all too soon discover that appearances are often deceptive.

He approached her slowly, almost reluctantly. "You are Mademoiselle Serenity Smith?" he inquired in lightly accented English.

Serenity started at the sound of his voice, so absorbed in the countryside she had not noted his nearness. Brushing back a lock of hair, she turned her head and found herself looking up, much higher than was her habit, into dark, heavy-lidded brown eyes.

"Yes," she answered, wondering why those eyes made her feel so strange. "Are you from the Château Kergallen?"

The slow lifting of one dark brow was the only change in his expression. "*Oui,* I am Christophe de Kergallen. I have come to take you to the countess."

"De Kergallen?" she repeated with some surprise. "Not another mysterious relative?"

The brow remained lifted, and full, sensuous lips curved so slightly as to be imperceptible. "One could say, Mademoiselle, that we are, in an obscure manner, cousins."

"Cousins," she murmured as they studied each other, rather like two prizefighters sizing each other up before a bout.

Rich black hair fell thick and straight to his collar, and the dark eyes which continued to remain steady seemed nearly as black against his deep bronze skin. His features were sharp, hawklike, somewhat piratical, and he exuded a basic masculine aura which both attracted and repelled her. She immediately wished for her sketch pad, wondering if she could possibly capture his aristocratic virility with pencil and paper.

Her lengthy scrutiny left him unperturbed, and he held her gaze, his eyes cool and aloof. "Your trunks will be delivered to the château." He bent down, picking up the bags she had set on the platform. "If you will come with me, the countess is anxious to see you."

He led her to a gleaming black sedan, assisted her into the passenger's side, and stowed her bags in the back, his manner so cold and impersonal that Serenity felt both annoyed and curious. He began to drive in silence, and she turned in her seat and examined him with open boldness.

"And how," she demanded, "are we cousins?" *What*

*do I call him?* she wondered. *Monsieur? Christophe? Hey, you?*

"The countess's husband, your mother's father, died when your mother was a child." He began his explanation in polite, faintly bored tones, and she was tempted to tell him not to strain himself. "Several years later, the countess married my grandfather, the Comte de Kergallen, whose wife had died and left him with a son, my father." He turned his head and spared her a brief glance. "Your mother and my father were raised as brother and sister in the château. My grandfather died, my father married, lived long enough to see me born, and then promptly killed himself in a hunting accident. My mother pined for him for three years, then joined him in the family crypt."

The story had been recited in remote, unemotional tones, and the sympathy Serenity would have normally felt for the child left orphaned never materialized. She watched his hawk-like profile for another moment.

"So, that makes you the present Comte de Kergallen and my cousin through marriage."

Again, a brief, negligent glance. *"Oui."*

"I can't tell you how both facts thrill me," she stated, a definite edge of sarcasm in her tone. His brow rose once more as he turned to her, and she thought for an instant that she had detected laughter lighting the cool, dark eyes. She decided against it, positive that the man sitting next to her never laughed. "Did you know my mother?" she inquired when the silence grew.

*"Oui.* I was eight when she left the château."

"Why did she leave?" Serenity demanded, turning to him with direct amber eyes. He twisted his head and met them with equal directness, and she was assaulted by their power before he turned his attention back to the road.

"The countess will tell you what she wishes you to know."

"What she wishes?" Serenity sputtered, angered by the deliberate rebuff. "Let's understand each other, Cousin. I fully intend to find out exactly why my mother left Brittany, and why I've spent my life ignorant of my grandmother."

With slow, casual movements, Christophe lit a cheroot, expelling smoke lazily. "There is nothing I can tell you."

"You mean," she corrected, narrowing her eyes, "there is nothing you *will* tell me."

His broad shoulders moved in a purely Gallic shrug, and Serenity turned to stare out the front window, copying his movement with the American version, missing the slight smile which played on his mouth at her gesture.

They continued to drive in sporadic silence, with Serenity occasionally inquiring about the scenery, Christophe answering in polite monosyllables, making no effort to expand the conversation. Golden sun and pure sky might have been sufficient to soothe the disposition ruffled by the journey, but his continued coolness outbalanced nature's gift.

"For a count from Brittany," she observed with deceptive sweetness after being spared another two syllables, "you speak remarkably fine English."

Sarcasm rolled off him like a summer's breeze, and his response was lightly patronizing. "The countess also speaks English quite well, Mademoiselle. The servants, however, speak only French or Breton. If you find yourself in difficulty, you have only to ask the countess or myself for assistance."

Serenity tilted her chin and turned her rich golden eyes on him with haughty disdain. *"Ce n'est pas nécessaire,* Monsieur le Comte. *Je parle bien le français."*

One dark brow lifted in harmony with his lips. *"Bon,"* he replied in the same language. "That will make your visit less complicated."

"Is it much farther to the château?" she inquired, continuing to speak in French. She felt hot, crumpled, and tired. Due to the long trip and the time change, it seemed as if she had been in some kind of vehicle for days, and she longed for a stationary tub filled with hot, soapy water.

"We have been on Kergallen land for some time, Mademoiselle," he replied, his eyes remaining on the winding road. "The château is not much farther."

The car had been climbing slowly to a higher elevation. Serenity closed her eyes on the headache which had begun to throb in her left temple, and wished fervently that her mysterious grandmother lived in a less complicated place, like Idaho or New Jersey. When she opened her eyes again, all aches, fatigue, and complaints vanished like a mist in the hot sun.

"Stop!" she cried, reverting to English, unconsciously laying a hand on Christophe's arm.

The château stood high, proud, and solitary: an immense stone edifice from another century with drum towers and crenellated walls and a tiled conical roof glowing warm and gray against a cerulean-blue sky.

The windows were many, high and narrow, reflecting the diminishing sunlight with a myriad of colors. It was ancient, arrogant, confident, and Serenity fell immediately in love.

Christophe watched the surprise and pleasure register on her unguarded face, her hand still warm and light on his arm. A stray curl had fallen loose onto her forehead, and he reached out to brush it back, catching himself before he reached her and staring at his own hand in annoyance.

Serenity was too absorbed with the château to notice his movement, already planning what angles she would use for sketches, imagining the moat that might have encircled the château at one time in the past.

"It's fabulous," she said at last, turning to her companion. Hastily, she removed her hand from his arm, wondering how it could have gotten there. "It's like something out of a fairy tale. I can almost hear the sound of trumpets, see the knights in armor, and ladies in full, floating dresses and high, pointed hats. Is there a neighborhood dragon?" She smiled at him, her face illuminated and incredibly lovely.

"Not unless one counts Marie, the cook," he answered, lowering the cool, polite wall for a moment and allowing her a quick glimpse of the wide, disarming smile which made him seem younger and approachable.

So, *he's human, after all,* she concluded. But as her pulse leaped in response to the sudden smile, she realized that when human, he was infinitely more dangerous. As their eyes met and held, she had the strange sensation of being totally alone with him, the rest of the world only a backdrop as they sat alone in private, enchanted solitude, and Georgetown seemed a lifetime away.

The stiffly polite stranger soon replaced the charming escort, and Christophe resumed the drive in silence, all the more thick and cold after the brief friendly interlude.

*Watch it, Serenity,* she cautioned herself. *Your imagination's running rampant again. This man is most definitely not for you. For some unknown reason, he doesn't even like you, and one quick smile doesn't change him from a cold, condescending aristocrat.*

Christophe pulled the car to a halt in a large, circular drive bordered by a flagstone courtyard, its low stone walls spilling over with phlox. He alighted from the car with swift, agile grace, and Serenity copied him before he had rounded the hood to assist her, so enchanted by the storybook atmosphere that she failed to note the frown which creased his brow at her action.

Taking her arm, he led her up stone steps to a massive oaken door, and, pulling a gleaming brass handle, inclined his head in a slight bow and motioned her to enter.

The entrance hall was huge. The floors were buffed to a mirrorlike shine and scattered with exquisite hand-hooked rugs. The walls were paneled, hung with tapestries, wide and colorful and incredibly old. A large hall rack and hunt table, both oak and glowing with the patina of age, oaken chairs with hand-worked seats, and the scent of fresh flowers graced the room, which seemed oddly familiar to her. It was as if she had known what to expect when she had crossed the threshold into the château, and the room seemed to recognize her, and welcome her.

"Something is wrong?" Christophe asked, noting her expression of confusion.

She shook her head with a slight shiver. *"Déjà vu,"* she murmured, and turned to him. "It's very strange; I feel as though I've stood right here before." She caught herself with a jolt of shock before she added, "with you." Letting out a deep breath, she made a restless movement with her shoulders. "It's very odd."

"So, you have brought her, Christophe."

Serenity turned away from suddenly intense brown eyes to watch her grandmother approach.

La Comtesse de Kergallen was tall and nearly as slender as Serenity. Her hair was a pure, brilliant white, lying like clouds around a sharp, angular face that defied the network of wrinkles age had bestowed on it. The eyes were clear, a piercing blue under well-arched brows, and she carried herself regally, as one who knows that more than six decades had not dimmed her beauty.

*No Mother Hubbard, this,* Serenity thought quickly. *This lady is a countess right down to her fingertips.*

The eyes surveyed Serenity slowly, completely, and she observed a flicker of emotion cross the angular face before it once again became impassive and guarded. The countess extended a well-shaped, ringed hand.

"Welcome to the Château Kergallen, Serenity Smith. I am Madame la Comtesse Françoise de Kergallen."

Serenity accepted the offered hand in her own, wondering whimsically if she should kiss it and curtsy. The clasp was brief and formal—no affectionate embrace, no smile of welcome. She swallowed disappointment and spoke with equal formality.

"Thank you, Madame. I am pleased to be here."

"You must be tired after your journey," the countess stated. "I will show you to your room myself. You will wish to rest before you change for dinner."

She moved to a large, curving staircase, and Serenity followed. Pausing on the landing, she glanced back to find Christophe watching her, his face creased in a brooding frown. He made no effort to smooth it away or remove his eyes from hers, and Serenity found herself turning swiftly and hurrying after the countess's retreating back.

They walked down a long, narrow corridor with brass lights set at intervals into the walls, replacing, she imagined, what would have once been torches. When the countess stopped at a door, she turned once more to Serenity, and after giving her another quick study, she opened the door and motioned her to enter.

The room was large and open, yet somehow retained an air of delicate grace. The furniture was glossy cherry, and a large four-poster canopied bed dominated the room, its silk coverlet embroidered with time-consuming stitches. A stone fireplace was set in the wall opposite the foot of the bed, its mantle carved and ornate, a collection of Dresden figures reflecting in the large framed mirror over it. One end of the room was curved and glassed, an upholstered windowseat inviting one to sit and ponder the breathtaking view.

Serenity felt the uncontrollable pull of the room, an aura of love and happiness, the gentle elegance well remembered. "This was my mother's room."

Again, the quick play of emotion flickered, like a candle caught in a draft. "*Oui.* Gaelle decorated it herself when she was sixteen."

"Thank you for giving it to me, Madame." Even the cool reply could not dispel the warmth the room brought her, and she smiled. "I shall feel very close to her during my stay."

The countess merely nodded and pressed a small button next to the bed. "Bridget will draw your bath. Your trunks will arrive shortly, and she will see to your unpacking. We dine at eight, unless you would care for some refreshment now."

"No, thank you, Countess," Serenity replied, beginning to feel like a boarder in a very well-run hotel. "Eight will be fine."

The countess moved to the doorway. "Bridget will show you to the drawing room after you have rested. We have cocktails at seven-thirty. If there is anything you require, you have only to ring."

The door closed behind her, and Serenity took a deep breath and sat heavily on the bed.

*Why did I come?* she asked herself, closing her eyes on a sudden surge of loneliness. *I should have stayed in Georgetown, stayed with Tony, stayed with what I could understand. What am I searching for here?* Taking a long breath, she fought the encompassing depression and surveyed her room again. *My mother's room,* she reminded herself and felt the soothing hands of comfort. *This is something I can understand.*

Moving to the window, Serenity watched day soften into twilight, the sun flashing with final, brilliant fire before surrendering to slumber. A breeze stirred the air, and the few scattered clouds moved with it, rolling lazily across the darkening sky.

A château on a hill in Brittany. Shaking her head at the thought, she knelt on the windowseat and watched evening's nativity. *Where does Serenity Smith fit into this?* Somewhere. She frowned at the knowledge which sprang from her heart. *Somehow I belong here, or a part of me does. I felt it the moment I saw those incredible stone walls, and again when I walked into the hall.* Pushing the feeling to the depths of her brain, she concentrated on her grandmother.

She certainly wasn't overwhelmed by the reunion, Serenity decided with a rueful smile. Or perhaps it was just the European formality that made her seem so cold and distant. *It hardly seems reasonable that she would ask me to come if she hadn't wanted to see me. I suppose I expected more because I wanted more.* Lifting her shoulders, she allowed them to fall slowly. *Patience has never been one of my virtues, but I suppose I'd better develop it. Perhaps if my greeting at the station had been a bit more welcoming...* Her frown appeared again as she replayed Christophe's attitude.

*I could swear he would have liked to bundle me back on the train the minute he set eyes on me.* Then, that infuriating conversation in the car. Frown deepened into scowl, and she ceased to focus on the quiet dimness of dusk. *That is a very frustrating man,* and she added, her scowl softening into thoughtfulness, *the very epitome of a Breton count. Perhaps that's why he affected me so strongly.* Resting her chin on her palm, she recalled the awareness which had shimmered between them as they had sat alone in the lengthening shadow of the château. *He's unlike any man I've ever known: elegant and vital at the same time. There's a potency there, a virility wrapped inside the sophistication.* Power. The word flashed into her brain, drawing her brows close. *Yes,* she admitted with a reluctance she could not quite understand, *there's power there, and an essence of self-assurance.*

*From an artist's standpoint, he's a remarkable study. He attracts me as an artist,* she told herself, *certainly not as a woman. A woman would have to be mad to get tangled up with a man like that. Absolutely mad,* she repeated to herself firmly.

## Chapter 2

The oval, free-standing gilt-framed mirror reflected a slim, fair-haired woman. The flowing, high-necked gown in a muted "ashes of roses" shade lent a glow to the creamy skin, leaving arms and shoulders bare. Serenity met the reflection's amber eyes, held them, and sighed. It was nearly time to go down and again meet her grandmother—the regal, reserved countess—and her cousin, the formal, oddly hostile count.

Her trunks had arrived while she was enjoying the bath drawn by the small, dark Breton maid. Bridget had unpacked and put away her clothes, shyly at first, then chattering and exclaiming over the articles as she hung them in the large wardrobe or folded them in the antique bureau. The simple friendliness had been a marked contrast to the attitude of those who were her family.

Serenity's attempts to rest between the cool linen

sheets of the great canopied bed had been futile, all her emotions in turmoil. The strange awareness she had experienced upon entering the château, the stiff, formal welcome of her grandmother, and the strong, physical response to the remote count had all banded together to make her unaccustomedly nervous and unsure of herself. She found herself wishing again she had allowed Tony to sway her, and had remained among the things and people she knew and understood.

Letting out a deep breath, she straightened her shoulders and lifted her chin. She was not a naïve schoolgirl to be awed by castles and overdone formality, she reminded herself. She was Serenity Smith, Jonathan and Gaelle Smith's daughter, and she would hold her head up and deal with counts and countesses.

Bridget knocked softly at her door, and Serenity followed her down the narrow corridor and began her descent down the curved staircase, cloaked in confidence.

"*Bonsoir,* Mademoiselle Smith." Christophe greeted her with his usual formality as she reached the bottom landing, and Bridget made a quick, unobtrusive exit.

"*Bonsoir,* Monsieur le Comte," Serenity returned, equally ritualistic, as they once more surveyed each other closely.

The black dinner suit lent a certain Satanic appearance to his aquiline features, the dark eyes glistening to near jet-black, the skin against the black and stark white of his shirt gleaming dusky-bronze. If there were pirates in his lineage, Serenity decided, they were elegant ones—and, she concluded further, as his eyes lingered on her, probably highly successful in all aspects of piratical pursuits.

"The countess awaits us in the drawing room," he announced when he had looked his fill, and with unexpected charm, he offered her his arm.

The countess watched as they entered the room, the tall, haughty man and the slim, golden-haired woman, a perfect foil at his side. A remarkably handsome couple, she reflected, one that would cause heads to turn wherever they went. "*Bonsoir,* Serenity, Christophe." She greeted them, regally resplendent in a gown of sapphire-blue, diamonds shooting fire from her throat. "*Mon apéritif,* Christophe, *s'il te plaît.* And for you, Serenity?"

"Vermouth, thank you, Madame," she replied, the practiced social smile on her lips.

"You rested well, I hope," the older woman inquired as Christophe handed her the small crystal glass.

"Yes, very well, Madame." She turned to accept the offered wine. "I..." The inane words she was about to utter stuck in her throat as the portrait caught her eye, and she turned around fully and faced it.

A cream-skinned, pale-haired woman looked back at her, the face the mirror image of her own. But for the length of the light gold mist of hair, falling to the shoulders, and the eyes that shone deep blue rather than amber, the portrait was Serenity: the oval face, delicate, with interesting hollows, the full, shapely mouth, the fragile, elusive beauty of her mother, reproduced in oil a quarter of a century earlier.

Her father's work—Serenity knew this immediately and unmistakably. The brush strokes, the use of color, the individual technique that shouted Jonathan Smith as surely as if she had read the small signature in the bottom corner. Her eyes filled, and she blinked back the threatening mist. Seeing the portrait had brought her parents close for a moment, and she was saturated with a deep sense of warmth and belonging that she had just been learning to live without.

She continued to study the painting, allowing herself to take in the details of her father's work, the folds of the oyster-white gown which seemed to float on a hidden breeze, the rubies at her mother's ears, a sharp contrast of color, the stone repeated in the ring on her finger. During the survey, something nagged at the back of her mind, some small detail out of place which refused to bring itself out of her consciousness, and she let it fade and merely experienced.

"Your mother was a very beautiful woman," the countess remarked after a time, and Serenity answered absently, still absorbed by the glowing look of love and happiness in her mother's eyes.

"Yes, she was. It's amazing how little she changed since my father painted this. How old was she?"

"Barely twenty," the countess replied, cultured tones edging with curtness. "You recognized your father's work quickly."

"Of course," Serenity agreed, not noticing the tones, and turning, she smiled with honest warmth. "As his daughter and a fellow artist, I recognize his work as quickly as his handwriting." Facing the portrait again, she gestured with a slim, long-fingered hand. "That was painted twenty-five years ago, and it still breathes with life, almost as if they were both right here in this room."

"Your resemblance to her is very strong," Christophe observed as he sipped his wine from his place by the mantel, capturing her attention as completely as if he had put his hands on her. "I was quite struck by it when you stepped from the train."

"But for the eyes," the countess pronounced before Serenity could form a suitable comment. "The eyes are his."

There was no mistaking the bitterness which vibrated in her voice, and narrowing the eyes under discussion, Serenity spun around, the skirt of her gown following lazily. "Yes, Madame, I have my father's eyes. Does that displease you?"

Elegant shoulders moved in dismissal, and the countess lifted her glass and sipped.

"Did my parents meet here, in the château?" Serenity demanded, patience straining. "Why did they leave and never come back? Why did they never speak to me of you?" Glancing from her grandmother to Christophe, she met two cool, expressionless faces. The countess had lifted a shield, and Serenity knew Christophe would help her maintain it. He would tell her nothing; any answers must come from the woman. She opened her mouth to speak again when she was cut off with a wave of a ringed hand.

"We will speak of it soon enough." The words were spoken like a royal decree as the countess rose from her chair. "Now, we will go in to dinner."

The dining room was massive, but Serenity had decided everything was massive in the château. High-beamed ceilings towered like those in a cathedral, and the dark wainscotted walls were broken by high windows framed with rich velvet drapes, the color of blood. A fireplace large enough to stand in commanded an entire wall, and she thought, when lit, it must be an awesome sight. A heavy chandelier gave the room its lights, its crystals trembling in a glistening rainbow of colors on the suite of dark majestic oak.

The meal began with an onion soup, thick, rich, and very French, and the trio maintained a polite conversation throughout the course. Serenity glanced at Christophe, intrigued against her will by his darkly handsome looks and haughty bearing.

*He certainly doesn't like me,* she concluded with a puzzled frown. *He didn't like me the moment he set eyes on me. I wonder why.* With a mental shrug, she began to eat her creamed salmon. *Perhaps he doesn't like women in general.* Looking over, his eyes met hers with a force that rivaled an electric storm, and her heart leaped suddenly, as if seeking to escape from behind her ribs. *No,* she amended quickly, tearing her eyes from his and studying the clear white wine in her glass, *he's no woman hater; those eyes are full of knowledge and experience. Tony never made me react like this.* Lifting her glass, she sipped with determination. *No one ever made me react like this.*

"Stevan," the countess commanded, *"du vin pour* Mademoiselle."

The countess's order to the hovering servant brought Serenity back from her contemplations. *"Mais non, merci. C'est bien."*

"You speak French very well for an American, Serenity," the dowager observed. "I am grateful your education was complete, even in that barbarous country."

The disdain in the last few words was so blatant that Serenity was unsure whether to be insulted or amused by the slight on her nationality. "That 'barbarous' country, Madame," she said dryly, "is called America, and it's nearly civilized these days. Why, we go virtually weeks between Indian attacks."

The proud head lifted imperiously. "There is no need for impudence, young woman."

"Really?" Serenity asked with a guileless smile. "Strange, I was sure there was." Lifting her wineglass, she saw, to her surprise, Christophe's teeth flash white against his dark skin in a wide, quick grin.

"You may have your mother's gentle looks," the countess observed, "but you have your father's tongue."

"Thank you." She met the clear blue eyes with an acknowledging nod. "On both counts."

The meal concluded, the conversation was allowed to drift back into generalities. And if the interlude took on the aspect of a truce, Serenity was still floundering as to the reason for the war. They adjourned once more to the main drawing room, Christophe lounging idly in an overstuffed chair swirling his after-dinner brandy while the countess and Serenity sipped coffee from fragile china cups.

"Jean-Paul le Goff, Gaelle's fiancé, met Jonathan Smith in Paris." The countess began to speak without preamble, and Serenity's cup halted on its journey to her lips, her eyes flying to the angular face. "He was quite taken with your father's talent and commissioned him to paint Gaelle's portrait as a wedding gift."

"My mother was engaged to another man before she married my father?" Serenity asked, setting down her cup with a great deal of care.

"*Oui*. The betrothal had been understood between

the families for years; Gaelle was content with the arrangement. Jean-Paul was a good man, of good background."

"It was to be an arranged marriage, then?"

The countess waved away Serenity's sense of distaste with a gesture of her hand. "It is an old custom, and as I said, Gaelle was content. Jonathan Smith's arrival at the château changed everything. Had I been more alert, I would have recognized the danger, the looks which passed between them, the blushes which rose to Gaelle's cheeks when his name was spoken."

Françoise de Kergallen sighed deeply and gazed up at the portrait of her daughter. "Never did I imagine Gaelle would break her word, disgrace the family honor. Always she was a sweet, obedient child, but your father blinded her to her duty." The blue eyes shifted from the portrait to the living image. "I had no knowledge of what had passed between them. She did not, as she had always done before, confide in me, seek my advice. The day the portrait was completed, Gaelle fainted in the garden. When I insisted on summoning a doctor, she told me there was no need—she was not ill, but with child."

The countess stopped speaking, and the silence spread like a heavy cloak through the room. "Madame," Serenity said, breaking the silence in clear, even tones, "if you are attempting to shock my sensibilities by telling me I was conceived before my parents were married, I must disappoint you. I find it irrelevant. The days of stone-throwing and branding have passed, in my country at least. My parents loved each other; whether they expressed that love before or after they exchanged vows does not concern me."

The countess sat back in her chair, laced her fingers, and studied Serenity intently. "You are very outspoken, *n'est-ce pas?*"

"Yes, I am." She gave the woman a level look. "However, I try to prevent my honesty from causing injury."

*"Touché,"* Christophe murmured, and the arched white brows rose fractionally before the countess gave her attention back to Serenity.

"Your mother had been married a month before you were conceived." The statement was given without a change of expression. "They were married in secret in a small chapel in another village, intending to keep the knowledge to themselves until your father was able to take Gaelle to America with him."

"I see." Serenity sat back with a slight smile. "My existence brought matters into the open a bit sooner than expected. And what did you do, Madame, when you discovered your daughter married and carrying the child of an obscure artist?"

"I disowned her, told them both to leave my home. From that day, I had no daughter." The words were spoken quickly, as if to throw off a burden no longer tolerable.

A small sound of anguish escaped Serenity, and her eyes flew to Christophe only to meet a blank, brooding wall. She rose slowly, a deep ache assailing her, and turning her back on her grandmother, she faced the gentle smile in her mother's portrait.

"I'm not surprised they put you out of their lives and kept you out of mine." Whirling back, she confronted the countess, whose face remained impassive, the pallor of her cheeks the only evidence of emotion. "I'm sorry for you, Madame. You robbed yourself of great happiness. It is you who have been isolated and alone. My parents shared a deep, encompassing love, and you cloistered yourself with pride and bruised honor. She would have forgiven you; if you knew her at all, then you know that. My father would have forgiven you for her sake, for he could deny her nothing."

"Forgive me?" High color replaced the pallor, and rage shook the cultured voice. "What need I with the forgiveness of a common thief and a daughter who betrayed her heritage?"

Amber eyes grew hot, like golden flames against flushed cheeks, and Serenity shrouded her fury in frigidity. "Thief? Madame, do you say my father stole from you?"

"*Oui,* he stole from me." The answering voice was hard and steady, matching the eyes. "He was not content to steal my child, a daughter I loved more than life. He added to his loot the Raphael Madonna which had belonged to my family for generations. Both priceless, both irreplaceable, both lost to a man I foolishly welcomed into my home and trusted."

"A Raphael?" Serenity repeated, lifting a hand to her temple in confusion. "You're implying my father stole a Raphael? You must be mad."

"I imply nothing," the countess corrected, lifting her head like a queen about to pronounce sentence. "I am stating that Jonathan Smith took both Gaelle and the Madonna. He was very clever. He knew it was my intention to donate the painting to the Louvre and he offered to clean it. I trusted him." The angular face was once more a grim mask of composure. "He exploited my trust, blinded my daughter to her duty, and left the château with both my treasures."

"It's a lie!" Serenity raged, anger welling up inside her with a force of a tidal wave. "My father would never steal—never! If you lost your daughter, it was because of your own pride, your own blindness."

"And the Raphael?" The question was spoken softly, but it rang in the room and echoed from the walls.

"I have no idea what became of your Raphael." She looked from the rigid woman to the impassive man and felt very much alone. "My father didn't take it; he was not a thief. He never did one dishonest thing in his life." She began to pace the room, battling the urge to shout and shatter their wall of composure. "If you were so sure he had your precious painting, why didn't you have him arrested? Why didn't you prove it?"

"As I said, your father was very clever," the countess rejoined. "He knew I would not involve Gaelle in such a scandal, no matter how she had betrayed me. With or without my consent, he was her husband, the father of the child she carried. He was secure."

Stopping her furious pacing, Serenity turned, her face incredulous. "Do you think he married her for security? You have no conception of what they had. He loved her more than his life, more than a hundred Raphaels."

"When I found the Raphael missing," the dowager continued, as if Serenity had not spoken, "I went to your father and demanded an explanation. They were already preparing to leave. When I accused him of taking the Raphael, I saw the look which passed between them—this man I had trusted, and my own daughter. I saw that he had taken the painting, and Gaelle knew him to be a thief but would stand with him against me. She betrayed herself, her family, and her country." The speech ended on a weary whisper, a brief spasm of pain appearing on the tightly controlled face.

"You have talked of it enough tonight," Christophe stated and rose to pour a brandy from a decanter, bringing the countess the glass with a murmur in Breton.

"They did not take it." Serenity took a step closer to the countess, only to be intercepted by Christophe's hand on her arm.

"We will speak of it no more at this time."

Jerking her arm away from his hold, she emptied her fury on him. "You won't tell me when I will speak! I will not tolerate my father being branded a thief! Tell me, Monsieur le Comte, if he had taken it, where is it? What did he do with it?"

Christophe's brow lifted, and his eyes held hers, the meaning in his look all too clear. Serenity's color ebbed, then flowed back in a rush, her mouth opening helplessly, before she swallowed and spoke in calm, distinct tones.

"If I were a man, you would pay for insulting both my parents and me."

"*Alors,* Mademoiselle," he returned with a small nod, "it is my good fortune you are not."

Serenity turned from the mockery in his tone and addressed the countess, who sat watching their exchange in silence. "Madame, if you sent for me because you believed I might know of the whereabouts of your Raphael, you will be disappointed. I know nothing. In turn, I have my own disappointment, because I came to you thinking to find a family tie, another bond with my mother. We must both learn to live with our disappointments."

Turning, she left the room without so much as a backward glance.

Giving the door to her bedroom a satisfactory slam, Serenity dragged her cases from the wardrobe and dropped them onto the bed. Mind whirling in near-incoherent fury, she began pulling neatly hung clothing from its sanctuary and tossing it into the mouth of the open suitcases in a colorful jumble of confusion.

"Go away!" she called out with distinct rudeness as a knock sounded on her door, then turned and spared Christophe a lethal glare as he ignored the command.

He gave her packing technique a raised-brow study before closing the door quietly behind him. "So, Mademoiselle, you are leaving."

"Perfect deduction." She tossed a pale pink blouse atop the vivid mountain on her bed and proceeded to ignore him.

"A wise decision," he stated as she pointedly kept her back to him. "It would have been better if you had not come."

"Better?" she repeated, turning to face him as the slow, simmering rage began to boil. "Better for whom?"

"For the countess."

She advanced on him slowly, eyes narrowing as one prepared for battle, giving one brief mental oath on his advantage of height. "The countess invited me to come. Summoned," she corrected, allowing her tone to edge.

"Summoned is more accurate. How dare you stand there and speak to me as if I had trampled on sacred ground! I never even knew the woman existed until her letter came, and I was blissfully happy in my ignorance."

"It would have been more prudent if the countess had left you to your bliss."

"That, Monsieur le Comte, is a brilliant example of understatement. I'm glad you understand I could have struggled through life without ever knowing any of my Breton connections." Turning in dismissal, Serenity vented her anger on innocent clothing.

"Perhaps you will find the struggle remains simple since the acquaintance will be brief."

"You want me out, don't you?" Spinning, she felt the last thread of dignity snap. "The quicker the better. Let me tell you something, Monsieur le Comte de Kergallen, I'd rather camp on the side of the road than accept your gracious hospitality. Here." She tossed a flowing flowered skirt in his general direction. "Why don't you help me pack?"

Stooping, he retrieved the skirt and laid it on a graceful upholstered chair, his cool, composed manner infuriating Serenity all the more. "I will send Bridget to you." The astringent politeness of his tone caused Serenity to glance quickly for something more solid to hurl at him. "You do seem to require assistance."

"Don't you dare send anyone!" she shouted as he turned for the door, and he faced her again, inclining his head at the order.

"As you wish, Mademoiselle. The state of your attire is your own concern."

Detesting his unblemished formality, Serenity found

herself forced to provoke him. "I'll see to my own packing, Cousin, when I decide to leave." Deliberately, she turned and lifted a garment from the heap. "Perhaps I'll change my mind and stay for a day or two, after all. I've heard the Breton countryside has much charm."

"It is your privilege to remain, Mademoiselle." Catching the faint tint of annoyance in his tone, Serenity found it imperative to smile in victory. "I would, however, not recommend it under the circumstances."

"Wouldn't you?" Her shoulders moved in a small, elegant shrug, and she tilted her face to his in provocation. "That is yet another inducement for remaining." She saw both her words and actions had touched a chord of response as his eyes darkened with anger. His expression, however, remained calm and composed, and she wondered what form his temper would take when and if he unleashed it.

"You must do as you wish, Mademoiselle." He surprised her by closing the distance between them and capturing the back of her neck with strong fingers. At the touch, she realized his temper was not as far below the surface as she had imagined. "You may, however, find your visit not as comfortable as you might like."

"I'm well able to deal with discomfort." Attempting to pull away, she found the hand held her stationary with little effort.

"Perhaps, but discomfort is not something sought by a person of intelligence." The politeness of Christophe's smile was more arrogant than a sneer, and Serenity stiffened and endeavored to draw away again. "I would have said you possessed intelligence, Mademoiselle, if not wisdom."

Determined not to surrender to slowly growing fear, Serenity kept both eyes and voice level. "My decision to go or stay is not something I need to discuss with you. I will sleep on it and make the suitable arrangements in the morning. Of course, you can always chain me to a wall in the dungeon."

"An interesting alternative." His smile became both mocking and amused, his fingers squeezing lightly before they finally released her. "I will sleep on it." He moved to the door, giving her a brief bow as he turned the knob. "And make the suitable arrangements in the morning."

Frustrated by being outmaneuvered, Serenity hurled a shoe at the panel which closed behind him.

## Chapter 3

The quiet awoke Serenity. Opening her eyes, she stared without comprehension at the sun-filled room before she remembered where she was. She sat up in bed and listened. Silence, the deep, rich quality of silence, broken only by the occasional music of a bird. A quiet lacking the bustling, throbbing city noises she had known all of her life, and she decided she liked it.

The small, ornate clock on the cherry writing desk told her it was barely six, so she lay back for a moment in the luxury of elegant pillows and sheets and wallowed in laziness. Though her mind had been crowded with the facts and accusations her grandmother had disclosed, the fatigue from the long journey had taken precedence, and she had slept instantly and deeply, oddly at peace in the bed which had once been her mother's.

Now, she stared up at the ceiling and ran through the previous evening again in her mind.

The countess was bitter. All the layers of practiced composure could not disguise the bitterness, or, Serenity admitted, the pain. Even through her own anger she had glimpsed the pain. Though she had banished the daughter, she had kept the portrait, and perhaps, Serenity concluded, the contradiction meant the heart was not as hard as the pride.

Christophe's attitude, however, still left her simmering. It seemed he had stood towering over her like a biased judge, ready to condemn without trial. *Well,* she determined, *I have my own share of pride, and I won't cower and shrink while my father's name is muddied, and my head put on the block. I can play the game of cold politeness, as well. I'm not running home like a wounded puppy; I'm going to stay right here.*

Gazing at the streaming sunlight, she gave a deep sigh. *"C'est un nouveau jour,* Maman," she said aloud. And, slipping from the bed, she walked over to the window. The garden spread out below her like a precious gift. "I'll go for a walk in your garden, Maman, and later I'll sketch your home." Sighing, she reached for her robe. "Then perhaps the countess and I can come to terms."

She washed and dressed quickly, choosing a pastel-printed sundress which left her arms and shoulders bare. The château remained in tranquil silence as she made her way to the main floor and stepped out into the warmth of the summer morning.

Strange, she mused, turning in a large circle. How strange not to see another building or cars or even another human being. The air was fresh and mildly scented, and she took a deep breath, consuming it before she began to circle the château on her way to the garden.

It was even more astonishing at close range than it had been from her window. Lush blooms exploded in an incredible profusion of colors, scents mixing and mingling into one exotic fragrance, at once tangy and sweet. There were a variety of paths cutting through the well-tended arrangements, smooth flagstones catching the morning sun and holding it glistening on their surface. Choosing one path at random, she strolled in idle contentment, enjoying the solitude, the artist in her reveling in the riot of hues and shapes.

"*Bonjour,* Mademoiselle." A deep voice broke the quiet, and Serenity whirled around, startled at the intrusion on her solitary contemplations. Christophe approached her slowly, tall and lean, his movements reminding her of an arrogant Russian dancer she had met at a Washington party. Graceful, confident, and very male.

"*Bonjour,* Monsieur le Comte." She did not waste a smile, but greeted him with careful cordiality. He was casually dressed in a buff-colored shirt and sleek-fitting brown jeans, and if she had felt the breeze of the buccaneer before, she was now caught in the storm.

He reached her and stared down with his habitual thorough survey. "You are an early riser. I trust you slept well."

"Very well, thank you," she returned, angry at having to battle not only animosity, but also attraction. "Your gardens are beautiful and very appealing."

"I have a fondness for what is beautiful and appealing." His eyes were direct, the dark brown smothering the amber, until she felt unable to breathe, dropping her eyes from the power of his.

"Oh, well, hello." They had been speaking in French, but at the sight of the dog at Christophe's heels, Serenity reverted back to English. "What's his name?" She crouched down to ruffle the thick, soft fur.

"Korrigan," he told her, looking down at her bent head as the sun streamed down, making a halo of pale curls.

"Korrigan," she repeated, enchanted by the dog and forgetting her annoyance with his master. "What breed is he?"

"Brittany spaniel."

Korrigan began to reciprocate her affection with tender licks on smooth cheeks. Before Christophe could command the dog to stop, Serenity laughed and buried her face against the animal's soft neck.

"I should have known. I had a dog once; it followed me home." Glancing up, she grinned as Korrigan continued to love her with a moist tongue. "Actually, I gave him a great deal of encouragement. I named him Leonardo, but my father called him Horrible, and that's the name that stuck. No amount of washing or brushing ever improved his inherent scruffiness."

As she went to rise, Christophe extended his hand to assist her to her feet, his grasp firm and disturbing. Checking the urge to jerk away from him, she disengaged herself casually and continued her walk. Both master and dog fell into step beside her.

"Your temper has cooled, I see. I found it surprising that such a dangerous temper exists inside such a fragile shell."

"I'm afraid you're mistaken." She twisted her head, giving him a brief but level glance. "Not about the temper, but the fragility. I'm really quite sturdy and not easily dented."

"Perhaps you have not yet been dropped," he countered, and she gave her attention to a bush pregnant with roses. "You have decided to stay for a time?"

"Yes, I have," she admitted and turned to face him directly, "although I get the distinct impression you'd rather I didn't."

His shoulders moved in an eloquent shrug. "*Mais, non,* Mademoiselle. You are welcome to remain as long as it pleases you to do so."

"Your enthusiasm overwhelms me," muttered Serenity.

"*Pardon?*"

"Nothing." Letting out a quick breath, she tilted her head and gave him a bold stare. "Tell me, Monsieur, do you dislike me because you think my father was a thief, or is it just me personally?"

The cool, set expression did not alter as he met her stare. "I regret to have given you such an impression. Mademoiselle, my manners must be at fault. I will attempt to be more polite."

"You're so infernally polite at times it borders on rudeness," she snapped, losing control and stomping her foot in exasperation.

"Perhaps you would find rudeness more to your taste?" His brow lifted as he regarded her temper with total nonchalance.

"Oh!" Turning away, she reached out angrily to pluck a rose. "You infuriate me! Darn!" she swore as a thorn pricked her thumb. "Now look what you made me do." Lifting her thumb to her mouth, she glared.

"My apologies," Christophe returned, a mocking light in his eyes. "That was most unkind of me."

"You are arrogant, patronizing, and stuffy," Serenity accused, tossing her curls.

"And you are bad-tempered, spoiled, and stubborn," he rejoined, narrowing his gaze and folding his arms across his chest. They stared at each other for a moment, his polite veneer slipping, allowing her a glimpse of the ruthless and exciting man beneath the coolly detached covering.

"Well, we seem to hold high opinions of each other after so short an acquaintance," she observed, smoothing back displaced curls. "If we know each other much longer, we'll be madly in love."

"An interesting conclusion, Mademoiselle." With a slight bow, he turned and headed back toward the château. Serenity felt an unexpected but tangible loss.

"Christophe," she called on impulse, wanting inexplicably to clear the air between them. He turned back, brow lifted in question, and she took a step toward him. "Can't we just be friends?"

He held her eyes for a long moment, so deep and intense a look that she felt he stripped her to the soul. "No, Serenity, I am afraid we will never just be friends."

She watched his tall, lithe figure stride away, the spaniel once more at his heels.

An hour later, Serenity joined her grandmother and Christophe at breakfast, with the countess making the usual inquiries as to how she had spent her night. The conversation was correct, if uninspired, and Serenity felt the older woman was making an effort to ease the tension brought on by the previous evening's confrontation. Perhaps, Serenity decided, it was not considered proper to squabble over croissants. *How amazingly civilized we are!* Suppressing an ironical smile, she mirrored the attitude of her companions.

"You will wish to explore the château, Serenity, *n'est-ce pas?*" Lifting her eyes as she set down the creamer, the countess stirred her coffee with a perfectly manicured hand.

"Yes, Madame, I would enjoy that," Serenity agreed with the expected smile. "I should like to make some sketches from the outside later, but I would love to see the inside first."

"*Mais, oui.* Christophe," she said, addressing the dark man who was idly sipping his coffee, "we must escort Serenity through the château this morning."

"Nothing would give me greater pleasure, Grandmère," he agreed, placing his cup back in its china saucer. "But I regret I shall be occupied this morning. The new bull we imported is due to arrive, and I must supervise its transport."

"Ah, the cattle," the countess sighed and moved her shoulders. "You think too much about the cattle."

It was the first spontaneous statement Serenity had noted, and she picked it up automatically. "Do you raise cattle, then?"

"Yes," Christophe confirmed, meeting her inquiring gaze. "The raising of cattle is the château's business."

"Really?" she countered with exaggerated surprise.

"I didn't think the de Kergallens bothered with such mundane matters. I imagined they just sat back and counted their serfs."

His lips curved slightly and he gave a small nod. "Only once a month. Serfs do tend to be highly prolific."

She found herself laughing into his eyes. Then as his quick, answering grin pounded a warning in her brain, she gave her attention to her own coffee.

In the end, the countess herself escorted Serenity on her tour of the rambling château, explaining some of its history as they moved from one astonishing room to another.

The château had been built in the late seventeenth century, and being in existence for just slightly less than three hundred years, it was not considered old by Breton standards. The château itself and the estates which belonged to it had been handed down from generation to generation to the oldest son, and although some modernizations had been made, it remained basically the same as it had been when the first Comte de Kergallen brought his bride over the drawbridge. To Serenity it was the essence of a lost and timeless charm, and the immediate affection and enchantment she had felt at first sight only grew with the explorations.

In the portrait gallery, she saw Christophe's dark fascination reproduced over the centuries. Though varied from generation to generation, the inveterate pride remained, the aristocratic bearing, the elusive air of mystery. She paused in front of one eighteenth-century ancestor whose resemblance was so striking that she took a step nearer to make a closer study.

"You find Jean-Claud interesting, Serenity?" the

countess questioned, following her gaze. "Christophe is much like him in looks, *n'est-ce pas?*"

"Yes, it's remarkable." The eyes, she decided, were much too assured, and much too alive, and unless she were very much mistaken, the mouth had known a great many women.

"He is reputed to have been a bit, uh, *sauvage,*" she continued with a hint of admiration. "It is said smuggling was his pastime; he was a man of the sea. The story is told that once when in England, he fell enamored of a woman of that country, and not having the patience for a long, formal, old-fashioned courtship, he kidnapped her and brought her to the château. He married her, of course; she is there." She pointed to a portrait of a rose-and-cream-fleshed English girl of about twenty. "She does not look unhappy."

With this comment, she strolled down the corridor, leaving Serenity staring up at the smiling face of a kidnapped bride.

The ballroom was huge, the far wall being opened with lead-paned windows adding to the space. Another wall was entirely mirrored, reflecting the brilliant prisms of the trio of chandeliers which would throw their sparkling light like silent stars from the high-beamed ceiling. Stiff-backed Regency chairs with elegant tapestry seats were strategically arranged for those who merely wished to look on as couples whirled across the highly polished floor. She wondered if Jean-Claud had given a wedding ball for his Sabine wife, and decided he undoubtedly had.

The countess led Serenity down another narrow corridor to a set of steep stone steps, winding spiral-like to the topmost tower. Although the room they entered was bare, Serenity immediately gave a cry of pleasure, moving to its center and gazing about as though it had been filled with treasures. It was large and airy and completely circular, and the high windows which encompassed it allowed the streaming sunlight to kiss every inch of space. Without effort, she pictured herself painting here for hours in blissful solitude.

"Your father used this room as his studio," the countess informed her, the stiffness returning to her voice, and Serenity broke off her fantasies and turned to confront her grandmother.

"Madame, if it is your wish that I remain here for a time, we must come to an understanding. If we cannot, I will have no choice but to leave." She kept her voice firm and controlled and astringently polite, but the eyes betrayed the struggle with temper. "I loved my father very much, as I did my mother. I will not tolerate the tone you use when you speak of him."

"Is it customary in your country for a young woman to address her elders in such a manner?" The regal head was held high, temper equally apparent.

"I can speak only for myself, Madame," she returned, standing straight and tall in the glow of sunlight. "And I am not of the opinion that age always equates with wisdom. Nor am I hypocrite enough to pay you lip service while you insult a man I loved and respected above all others."

"Perhaps it would be wiser if we refrained from discussing your father while you are with us." The request was an unmistakable command, and Serenity bristled with anger.

"I intend to mention him, Madame. I intend to discover precisely what became of the Raphael Madonna and clear the black mark you have put on his name."

"And how do you intend to accomplish this?"

"I don't know," she tossed back, "but I will." Pacing the room, she spread her hands unconsciously in a completely French gesture. "Maybe it's hidden in the château; maybe someone else took it." She whirled on the other woman with sudden fury. "Maybe you sold it and placed the blame on my father."

"You are insulting!" the countess returned, blue eyes leaping with fire.

"You brand my father a thief, and you say that *I* am insulting?" Serenity retorted, meeting her fire for fire. "I knew Jonathan Smith, Countess, and he was no thief, but I do not know you."

The countess regarded the furious young woman silently for several moments, blue flames dying, replaced by consideration. "That is true," she acknowledged with a nod. "You do not know me, and I do not know you. And if we are strangers, I cannot place the blame on your head. Nor can I blame you for what happened before you were born."

Moving to a window, she stared out silently. "I have not changed my opinion of your father," she said at length, and turning, she held up a hand to silence Serenity's automatic retort. "But I have not been just where his daughter is concerned. You come to my home, a stranger, at my request, and I have greeted you badly. For this much, I apologize." Her lips curved in a small smile. "If you are agreeable, we will not speak of the past until we know each other."

"Very well, Madame," Serenity agreed, sensing both request and apology were an olive branch of sorts.

"You have a soft heart to go with a strong spirit," the dowager observed, a faint hint of approval in her tone. "It is a good match. But you also have a swift temper, *n'est-ce pas?*"

"*Évidemment,*" Serenity acknowledged.

"Christophe is also given to quick outbursts of temper and black moods," the countess informed her in a sudden change of topic. "He is strong and stubborn and requires a wife of equal strength, but with a heart that is soft."

Serenity stared in confusion at her grandmother's ambiguous statement. "She has my sympathy," she began, then narrowed her eyes as a small seed of doubt began to sprout. "Madame, what have Christophe's needs to do with me?"

"He has reached the age when a man requires a wife," the countess stated simply. "And you are past the age when most Breton women are well married and raising a family."

"I am only half-Breton," she asserted, distracted for a moment. Her eyes widened in amazement. "Surely you don't…you aren't thinking that Christophe and I…? Oh, how beautifully ridiculous!" She laughed outright, a full, rich sound that echoed in the empty room. "Madame, I am sorry to disappoint you, but the count does not care for me. He didn't like me the moment he set eyes on me, and I'm forced to admit that I'm not overly fond of him, either."

"What has liking to do with it?" the countess demanded, her hands waving the words away.

Serenity's laughter stilled, and she shook her head in disbelief even as realization seeped through. "You've spoken to him of this already?"

*"Oui, d'accord,"* the countess agreed easily.

Serenity shut her eyes, nearly swamped with humiliation and fury. "No wonder he resented me on sight—between this and thinking what he does of my father!" She turned away from her grandmother, then back again full of righteous indignation. "You overreach your bounds, Comtesse. The time of arranged marriages has long since passed."

"Poof!" It was a dismissive exclamation. "Christophe is too much his own man to agree to anything arranged by another, and I see you are too headstrong to do so. But—" a slow smile creased the angular face as Serenity looked on with wide, incredulous eyes—"you are very lovely, and Christophe is an attractive and virile man. Perhaps nature will—what is it? Take its course."

Serenity could only gape open-mouthed into the calm, inscrutable face.

"Come." The countess moved easily toward the door. "There is more for you to see."

# Chapter 4

The afternoon was warm, and Serenity was simmering. Indignation had spread from her grandmother to encompass Christophe, and the more she simmered, the more it became directed at him.

*Insufferable, conceited aristocrat!* she fumed. Her pencil ran violently across her pad as she sketched the drum towers of the château. *I'd rather marry Attila the Hun than be bound to that stiff-necked boor!* She broke the midday hush with a short burst of laughter. *Madame is probably picturing dozens of miniature counts and countesses playing formal little games in the courtyard and growing up to carry on the imperial line in the best Breton style!*

What a lovely place to raise children, she thought, pencil pausing, and eyes softening. *It's so clean and quiet and beautiful.* A deep sigh filled the air, and she started. Then realizing that it had emitted from her own lips, she frowned furiously. *La Comtesse Serenity de Kergallen,* she said silently and frowned with more feeling. *That'll be the day!*

A movement caught her attention, and she twisted her head, squinting against the sun to watch Christophe approach. His strides were long and sure, and he crossed the lawn with an effortless rhythm of limbs and muscles. *He walks as if he owns the world,* she observed, part in admiration, part in resentment. By the time he reached her, resentment had emerged victorious.

"You!" she spat without preamble, rising from the soft tuft of grass and standing like a slender, avenging angel, gold and glowing.

His gaze narrowed at her tone, but his voice remained cool and controlled. "Something disturbs you, Mademoiselle?"

The ice in his voice only fanned the fire of anger, and dignity was abandoned. "Yes, I'm disturbed! You know very well I'm disturbed! Why in heaven's name didn't you tell me about this ludicrous idea of the countess's?"

"Ah." Brows rose, and lips curved in a sardonic smile. "*Alors,* Grandmère has informed you of the plans for our marital bliss. And when, my beloved, shall we have the banns announced?"

"You conceited…" she sputtered, unable to dream up an appropriately insulting term. "You know what you can do with your banns! I wouldn't have you on a bet!"

"*Bon,*" he replied with a nod. "Then we are at last in full agreement. I have no desire to tie myself to a wasp-tongued brat. Whoever christened you Serenity had very little foresight."

"You're the most detestable man I have ever met!" she raged, her temper a direct contrast to his cool composure. "I can't abide the sight of you."

"Then you have decided to cut your visit short and return to America?"

She tilted her chin and shook her head slowly. "Oh, no, Monsieur le Comte, I shall remain right here. I have inducements for staying which outweigh my feelings for you."

The dark eyes narrowed into slits as he studied her face. "It would appear the countess has added a few francs to make you more agreeable."

Serenity stared at him in puzzlement until his meaning slowly seeped through, draining her color and darkening her eyes. Her hand swung out and struck him with full force in a loud, stinging slap, and then she spun on her heel and began to run toward the château. Hard hands dug into her shoulders and whirled her around, crushing her against the firm length of his body as his lips descended on hers in a brutal, punishing kiss.

The shock was electric, like a brilliant light flashed on, then extinguished. For a moment, she was limp against him, unable to surface from a darkness teeming with heat and demand. Her breath was no longer her own; she realized suddenly he was stealing even that, and she began to push at his chest, then pound with helpless, impotent fists, terrified she would be captured forever in the swirling, simmering darkness.

His arms banded around her, molding her soft slenderness to the hard, unyielding lines of his body, merging them into one passionate form. His hand slid up to cup the back of her neck with firm fingers, forcing her head to remain still, his other arm encircling her waist, maintaining absolute possession.

Her struggles slipped off him as though they were not taking place, emphasizing his superior strength and the violence which bubbled just beneath the surface. Her lips were forced apart as his mouth continued its assault, exploring hers with an intimacy without mercy or compassion. The musky scent of his maleness was assailing her senses, numbing both brain and will, and dimly she heard her grandmother describing the long-dead count with Christophe's face. *Sauvage,* she had said. *Sauvage.*

He gave her mouth its freedom, his grip returning to her shoulders as he looked down into clouded, confused eyes. For a moment, the silence hung like a shimmering wall of heat.

"Who gave you permission to do that?" she demanded unevenly, a hand reaching to her head to halt its spinning.

"It was either that or return your slap, Mademoiselle," he informed her, and from his tone and expression, she could see he had not yet completed the transformation from pirate to aristocrat. "Unfortunately, I have a reluctance to strike a woman, no matter how richly she may deserve it."

Serenity jerked away from his restraint, feeling the treacherous tears stinging, demanding release. "Next time, slap me. I'd prefer it."

"If you ever raise your hand to me again, my dear cousin, rest assured I will bruise more than your pride," he promised.

"You had it coming," she tossed back, but the temerity of her words was spoiled by wide eyes shimmering like golden pools of light. "How dare you accuse me of accepting money to stay here? Did it ever occur to you that I might *want* to know the grandmother I was denied all my life? Did you ever think that I might *want* to know the place where my parents met and fell in love? That I need to stay and prove my father's innocence?" Tears escaped and rolled down smooth cheeks, and Serenity despised each separate drop of weakness. "I only wish I could have hit you harder. What would you have done if someone had accused *you* of being bought like a side of beef?"

He watched the journey of a tear as it spilled from her eye and clung to satin skin, and a small smile tilted one corner of his mouth. "I would have beat them soundly, but I believe your tears are a more effective punishment than fists."

"I don't use tears as a weapon." She wiped at them with the back of her hand, wishing she could have stemmed the flow.

"No; they are therefore all the more potent." A long bronzed finger brushed a drop from ivory skin, the contrast of colors lending her a delicate, vulnerable appearance, and he removed his hand quickly, addressing her in a casual tone. "My words were unjust, and I apologize. We have both received our punishment, so now we are—how do you say?—quits."

He gave her his rare, charming smile, and she stared at him, drawn by its power and enchanted by the positive change it lent to his appearance. Her own smile answered, the sudden shining of the sun through a veil of rain. He made a small, impatient sound, as though he regretted the momentary lapse, and nodding, he turned on his heel and strode away, leaving Serenity staring after him.

During the evening meal, the conversation was once more strictly conventional, as if the astonishing conversation in the tower room and the tempestuous encounter on the château grounds had not taken place. Serenity marveled at the composure of her companions as they carried on a light umbrella of table talk over *langoustes à la crème*. If it had not been for the fact that her lips still felt the imprint, she would have sworn she had imagined the stormy, breathtaking kiss Christophe had planted there. It had been a kiss which had stirred some deep inner feeling of response and had jolted her cool detachment more than she cared to admit.

It meant nothing, she insisted silently and applied herself to the succulent lobster on her plate. She'd been kissed before and she would be kissed again. She would not allow any moody tyrant to give her one more moment's concern. Deciding to resume her role in the game of casual formality, she sipped from her glass and made a comment on the character of the wine.

"You find it agreeable?" Christophe picked up the trend of conversation in an equally light tone. "It is the château's own Muscadet. We produce a small quantity each year for our own enjoyment and for the immediate vicinity."

"I find it very agreeable," Serenity commented. "How exciting to enjoy wine made from your own vineyards. I've never tasted anything quite like it."

"The Muscadet is the only wine produced in Brittany," the countess informed Serenity with a smile. "We are primarily a province of the sea and lace."

Serenity ran a finger over the snowy-white cloth that adorned the oak table. "Brittany lace, it's exquisite. It looks so fragile, yet years only increase the beauty."

"Like a woman," Christophe murmured, and Serenity lifted her eyes to meet his dark regard.

"But then, there are also the cattle." She grabbed at the topic to cover momentary confusion.

"Ah, the cattle." His lips curved, and Serenity had the uncomfortable impression that he was well aware of his effect on her.

"Having lived in the city all my life, I'm totally ignorant when it comes to cattle." She floundered on, more and more disconcerted by the directness of his eyes. "I'm sure they make quite a picture grazing in the fields."

"We must introduce you to the Breton countryside," the countess declared, drawing Serenity's attention. "Perhaps you would care to ride out tomorrow and view the estate?"

"I would enjoy that, Madame. I'm sure it will be a pleasant change from sidewalks and government buildings."

"I would be pleased to escort you, Serenity," Christophe offered, surprising her. Turning back to him, her expression mirrored her thoughts. He smiled and inclined his head. "Do you have the suitable attire?"

"Suitable attire?" she repeated, surprise melting into confusion.

"But yes." He appeared to be enjoying her changing expressions, and his smile spread. "Your taste in clothing is impeccable, but you would find it difficult to ride a horse in a gown like that."

Her gaze lowered to the gently flowing lines of her willow-green dress before rising to his amused glance. "Horse?" she said, frowning.

"You cannot tour the estate in an automobile, *ma petite.* The horse is more adaptable."

At his laughing eyes, she straightened and drew out her dignity. "I'm afraid I don't ride."

*"C'est impossible!"* the countess exclaimed in disbelief. "Gaelle was a marvelous horsewoman."

"Perhaps equestrian abilities are not genetic, Madame," Serenity suggested, amused by her grandmother's incredulous expression. "I am no horsewoman at all. I can't control a merry-go-round pony."

"I will teach you." Christophe's words were a statement rather than a request, and she turned to him, amusement fading into hauteur.

"How kind of you to offer, Monsieur, but I have no desire to learn. Do not trouble yourself."

"Nevertheless," he stated and lifted his wineglass, "you shall. You will be ready at nine o'clock, *n'est-ce pas?* You will have your first lesson."

She glared at him, astonished by his arbitrary dismissal of her refusal. "I just told you…"

"Try to be punctual, *chérie,*" he warned with deceptive laziness as he rose from the table. "You will find it more comfortable to walk to the stables than to be dragged by your golden hair." He smiled as if the latter prospect held great appeal for him. *"Bonne nuit,* Grandmère," he added with affection before he disappeared from the room, leaving Serenity fuming, and his grandmother unashamedly pleased.

"Of all the insufferable nerve!" she sputtered when she located her voice. Turning angry eyes on the other woman, she added defiantly, "If he thinks I'm going to meekly obey and…"

"You would be wise to obey, meekly or otherwise," the dowager interrupted. "Once Christophe has set his mind…" With a small, meaningful shrug, she left the rest of the sentence to Serenity's imagination. "You have slacks, I presume. Bridget will bring you a pair of your mother's riding boots in the morning."

"Madame," Serenity began slowly, as if attempting to make each word understood, "I have no intention of getting on a horse in the morning."

"Do not be foolish, child." A slender, ringed hand reached negligently for a wineglass. "He is more than capable of carrying out his threat. Christophe is a very stubborn man." She smiled, and for the first time Serenity felt genuine warmth. "Perhaps even more stubborn than you."

Muttering strong oaths, Serenity pulled on the sturdy boots that had been her mother's. They had been cleaned and polished to a glossy black shine and fit her small feet as if custom-made for them.

*It seems even you are conspiring against me, Maman,* she silently chided her mother in despair. Then she called out a casual *"Entrez"* as a knock sounded on her door. It was not the little maid, Bridget, who opened the door, however, but Christophe, dressed with insouciant elegance in fawn riding breeches and a white linen shirt.

"What do you want?" she asked with a scowl, pulling on the second boot with a firm tug.

"Merely to see if you are indeed punctual, Serenity," he returned with an easy smile, his eyes roaming over her mutinous face and the slim, supple body clad in a silkscreen-printed T-shirt and French tailored jeans.

Wishing he would not always look at her as if memorizing each feature, she rose in defense. "I'm ready, Captain Bligh, but I'm afraid you won't find me a very apt pupil."

"That remains to be seen, *ma chérie.*" His eyes swept over her again, as if considering. "You seem to be quite capable of following a few simple instructions."

Her eyes narrowed into jeweled slits, and she struggled with the temper he had a habit of provoking. "I am reasonably intelligent, thank you, but I don't like being bulldozed."

*"Pardon?"* His blank expression brought out a smug smile.

"I shall have to recall a great many colloquialisms, Cousin. Perhaps I can slowly drive you mad."

Serenity accompanied Christophe to the stables in haughty silence, determinedly lengthening her strides to match his gait and preventing the necessity of trailing after him like an obedient puppy. When they reached the outbuilding, a groom emerged leading two horses, bridled and saddled in anticipation. One was full black and gleaming, the other a creamy buckskin, and to Serenity's apprehensive eyes, both were impossibly large.

She halted suddenly and eyed the pair with a dubious frown. *He wouldn't really drag me by the hair,* she thought carefully. "If I just turned around and walked away, what would you do about it?" Serenity inquired aloud.

"I would only bring you back, *ma petite.*" The dark brow rose at her deepening frown, revealing he had already anticipated her question.

"The black is obviously yours, Comte," she concluded in a light voice, struggling to control a mounting panic. "I can already picture you galloping over the countryside in the light of a full moon, the gleam of a saber at your hip."

"You are very astute, Mademoiselle." He nodded, and taking the buckskin's reins from the groom, he walked the mount toward her. She took an involuntary step back and swallowed.

"I suppose you want me to get on him."

"Her," he corrected, mouth curving.

She flashed at him, angry and nervous and disgusted with her own apprehension. "I'm not really concerned about its sex." Looking over the quiet horse, she swallowed again. "She's…she's very large." Her voice was fathoms weaker than she had hoped.

"Babette is as gentle as Korrigan," Christophe assured her in unexpectedly patient tones. "You like dogs, *n'est-ce pas?*"

"Yes, but…"

"She is soft, no?" He took her hand and lifted it to Babette's smooth cheek. "She has a good heart and wishes only to please."

Her hand was captured between the smooth flesh of the horse and the hard insistence of Christophe's palm, and she found the combination oddly enjoyable. Relaxing, she allowed him to guide her hand over the mare and twisted her head, smiling over her shoulder.

"She feels nice," she began, but as the mare blew from wide nostrils, she jumped nervously and stumbled back against Christophe's chest.

"Relax, *chérie*." He chuckled softly, his arms encircling her waist to steady her. "She is only telling you that she likes you."

"It just startled me," Serenity returned in defense, disgusted with herself, and decided it was now or never. She turned to tell him she was ready to begin, but found herself staring wordlessly into dark, enigmatic eyes as his arms remained around her.

She felt her heart stop its steady rhythm, remaining motionless for a stifling moment, then race sporadically at a wild pace. For an instant, she believed he would kiss her again, and to her own astonishment and confusion, she realized she wanted to feel his lips on hers above all else. A frown creased his brow suddenly, and he released her in a sharp gesture.

"We will begin." Cool and controlled, he stepped effortlessly into the role of instructor.

Pride took over, and Serenity became determined to be a star pupil. Swallowing her anxiety, she allowed Christophe to assist her in mounting. With some surprise, she noted that the ground was not as far away as she had anticipated, and she gave her full attention to Christophe's instructions. She did as he bade, concentrating on following his directions precisely, determined not to make a fool of herself again.

Serenity watched Christophe mount his stallion with

a fluid grace and economy of movement she envied. The spirited black suited the dark, haughty man to perfection, and she reflected, with some distress, that not even Tony at his most ardent had ever affected her the way this strange, remote man did with his enveloping stares.

She couldn't be attracted to him, she argued fiercely. He was much too unpredictable, and she realized, with a flash of insight, that he could hurt her as no man had been able to hurt her before. *Besides,* she thought, frowning at the buckskin's mane, *I don't like his superior, dominating attitude.*

"Have you decided to take a short nap, Serenity?" Christophe's mocking voice brought her back with a snap, and meeting his laughing eyes, she felt herself flush to her undying consternation. *"Allons-y, chérie."* Her deepening color was noted with a curve of his lips, as he directed his horse away from the stables and proceeded at a slow walk.

They moved side by side, and after several moments Serenity found herself relaxing in the saddle. She passed Christophe's instructions on to the mare, which responded with smooth obedience. Confidence grew, and she allowed herself to view the scenery, enjoying the caress of the sun on her face and the gentle rhythm of the horse under her.

*"Maintenant,* we trot," Christophe commanded suddenly, and Serenity twisted her head to regard him seriously.

"Perhaps my French is not as good as I supposed. Did you say trot?"

"Your French is fine, Serenity."

"I'm quite content to amble along," she returned with a careless shrug. "I'm in no hurry at all."

"You must move with the jogging of the horse," he instructed, ignoring her statement. "Rise with every other jog. Press gently with your heels."

"Now, listen…"

"Afraid?" he taunted, his brow lifting high in mockery. Before common sense could overtake pride, Serenity tossed her head and pressed her heels against the horse's side.

*This must be what it feels like to operate one of those damnable jackhammers they're forever tearing up the streets with,* she thought breathlessly, bouncing without grace on the trotting mare.

"Rise with every other jog," Christophe reminded her, and she was too preoccupied with her own predicament to observe the wide grin which accompanied his words. After a few more awkward moments, she caught onto the timing.

*"Comment ça va?"* he inquired as they moved side by side along the dirt path.

"Well, now that my bones have stopped rattling, it's not so bad. Actually"—she turned and smiled at him—"it's fun."

*"Bon.* Now we canter," he said simply, and she sent him a withering glance.

"Really, Christophe, if you want to murder me, why not try something simpler like poison, or a nice clean stab in the back?"

He threw back his head and laughed, a full, rich sound that filled the quiet morning, echoing on the breeze. When he turned his head and smiled at her,

Serenity felt the world tilt, and her heart, ignoring the warnings of her brain, was lost.

*"Allons, ma brave."* His voice was light, carefree, and contagious. "Press in your heels, and I will teach you to fly."

Her feet obeyed automatically, and the mare responded, quickening her gate to a smooth, easy canter. The wind played with Serenity's hair and brushed her cheeks with cool fingers. She felt as though she were riding on a cloud, unsure whether the lightness was a result of the rush of wind or the dizziness of love. Enthralled with the novelty of both, she did not care.

At Christophe's command, she drew back on the reins, slowing the mare from a canter to a trot to a walk before finally coming to a halt. Lifting her face to the sky, she gave a deep sigh of pleasure before turning to her companion. The wind and excitement had whipped a rose blush onto her cheeks, her eyes were wide, golden, and bright, and her hair was tousled, an unruly halo around her happiness.

"You enjoyed yourself, Mademoiselle?"

She flashed him a brilliant smile, still intoxicated with love's potent wine. "Go ahead; say 'I told you so.' It's perfectly all right."

*"Mais non, chérie,* it is merely a pleasure to see one's pupil progress with such speed and ability." He returned her smile, the invisible barrier between them vanishing. "You move naturally in the saddle; perhaps the talent is genetic, after all."

"Oh, Monsieur." She fluttered her lashes over a gleam of mischief. "I must give the credit to my teacher."

"Your French blood is showing, Serenity, but your technique needs practice."

"Not so good, huh?" Pushing back disheveled hair, she gave a deep sigh. "I suppose I'll never get it right. Too much American Puritan from my father's ancestors."

"Puritan?" Christophe's full laugh once more disturbed the quiet morning. "*Chérie,* no Puritan was ever so full of fire."

"I shall take that as a compliment, though I sincerely doubt it was intended as one." Turning her head, she looked down from the hilltop to the spreading valley below. "Oh, how beautiful."

A scene from a postcard slumbered in the distance, gentle hills dotted with grazing cattle against a backdrop of neat cottages. Farther in the distance, she observed a tiny village, a small toy town set down by a giant hand, dominated by a white church, its spire reaching heavenward.

"It's perfect," she decided. "Like slipping back in time." Her eyes roamed back to the grazing cattle. "Those are yours?" she asked, gesturing with her hand.

"*Oui,*" he asserted.

"This is all your property, then?" she asked again, feeling a sudden sinking sensation.

"This is part of the estates." He answered with a careless movement of his shoulders.

*We've been riding for so long,* she thought with a frown, *and we're still on his land. Lord knows how far it spreads in other directions. Why can't he be an ordinary man?* Turning her head, she studied his hawklike profile. *But he is not an ordinary man,* she reminded herself. *He is the Comte de Kergallen, master of all he surveys, and I must remember that.* Her gaze moved back to the valley, her frown deepening. *I don't want to be in love with him.* Swallowing the sudden dryness of her throat, she used her words as a defense against her heart.

"How wonderful to possess so much beauty."

He turned to her, brow raising at her tone. "One cannot possess beauty, Serenity, merely care for and cherish it."

She fought against the warmth his soft words aroused, keeping her eyes glued to the valley. "Really? I was under the impression that young aristocrats took such things for granted." She made a wide, sweeping gesture. "After all, this is only your due."

"You have no liking for aristocracy, Serenity, but you have aristocratic blood, as well." Her blank look brought a slow smile to his chiseled features, and his tone was cool. "Yes, your mother's father was a count, though his estates were ravaged during the war. The Raphael was one of the few treasures your grandmother salvaged when she escaped."

*The damnable Raphael again!* Serenity thought dismally. He was angry; she determined this from the hard light in his eyes, and she found herself oddly pleased. It would be easier to control her feelings for him if they remained at odds with each other.

"So, that makes me half-peasant, half-aristocrat," she retorted, moving her slim shoulders in dismissal. "Well, *mon cher cousin,* I much prefer the peasant half myself. I'll leave the blue blood in the family to you."

"You would do well to remember there is no blood

between us, Mademoiselle." Christophe's voice was low, and meeting his narrowed eyes, Serenity felt a trickle of fear. "The de Kergallens are notorious for taking what they want, and I am no exception. Take care how you use your brandy eyes."

"The warning is unnecessary, Monsieur. I can take care of myself."

He smiled, a slow, confident smile, more unnerving than a furious retort, and turned his mount back toward the château.

The return ride was accomplished in silence, broken only by Christophe's occasional instructions. They had crossed swords again, and Serenity was forced to admit he had parried her thrust easily.

When they reached the stables, Christophe dismounted with his usual grace, handing the reins to a groom and moving to assist her before she could copy his action.

Defiantly, she ignored the stiffness in her limbs as she eased herself from the mare's back and Christophe's hands encircled her waist. They remained around her for a moment, and he brooded down at her before releasing the hold that seemed to burn through the light material of her shirt.

"Go have a hot bath," he ordered. "It will ease the stiffness you are undoubtedly feeling."

"You have an amazing capacity for issuing orders, Monsieur."

His eyes narrowed before his arm went around her with incredible speed, pulling her close and crushing her lips in a hard, thorough kiss that left no time for

struggle or protest, but drew a response as easily as a
hand turning a water tap.

For an eternity he kept her the prisoner of his will,
plunging her deeper and deeper into the kiss. Its bruising intensity released a new and primitive need in her,
and abandoning pride for love, she surrendered to demands she could not conquer. The world evaporated,
the soft Breton landscape melting like a watercolor left
out in the rain, leaving nothing but warm flesh and lips
which sought her surrender. His hand ran over the slim
curve of her hip, then up her spine with sure authority, crushing her against him with a force which would
have cracked her bones had they not already dissolved
in the heat.

Love. Her mind whirled with the word. Love was
walks in soft rain, a quiet evening beside a crackling
fire. How could it be a throbbing, turbulent storm which
left you weak and breathless and vulnerable? How could
it be that one would crave the weakness as much as life
itself? Was this how it had been for Maman? Was this
what put the dreamy mists of knowledge in her eyes?
*Will he never set me free?* she wondered desperately,
and her arms encircled his neck, body contradicting
will.

"Mademoiselle," he murmured with soft mockery,
keeping his mouth a breath from hers, his fingers teasing the nape of her neck, "you have an amazing capacity
for provoking punishment. I find the need to discipline
you imperative."

Releasing her, he turned and strode carelessly away,
stopping to acknowledge the greeting of Korrigan, who
trotted faithfully at his heels.

# *Chapter 5*

Serenity and the countess shared their lunch on the terrace, surrounded by sweet-smelling blossoms. Refusing the offered wine, Serenity requested coffee instead, enduring the raised white brow with tranquil indifference.

*I suppose this makes me an undoubted Philistine,* she concluded, suppressing a smile as she enjoyed the strong black liquid along with the elegant shrimp bisque.

"I trust you found your ride enjoyable," the countess stated after they had exchanged comments on the food and weather.

"To my utter amazement, Madame," Serenity admitted, "I did. I only wished I had learned long ago. Your Breton scenery is magnificent."

"Christophe is justifiably proud of his land," the countess asserted, studying the pale wine in her glass. "He loves it as a man loves a woman, an intense sort of passion. And though the land is eternal, a man needs a wife. The earth is a cold lover."

Serenity's brows rose at her grandmother's frankness, the sudden abandonment of formality. Her shoulders moved in a faintly Gallic gesture. "I'm sure Christophe has little trouble finding warm ones." *He probably merely snaps his fingers and dozens tumble into his arms,* she added silently, almost wincing at the fierce stab of jealousy.

*"Naturellement,"* the countess agreed, a glimmer of amusement lighting up her eyes. "How could it be otherwise?" Serenity digested this with a scowl, and the dowager lifted her wineglass. "But men like Christophe require constancy rather than variety after a time. Ah, but he is so like his grandfather." Looking over quickly, Serenity saw the soft expression transform the angular face. "They are wild, these Kergallen men, dominant and arrogantly masculine. The women who are given their love are blessed with both heaven and hell." Blue eyes focused on amber once more and smiled. "Their women must be strong or be trampled beneath them, and they must be wise enough to know when to be weak."

Serenity had been listening to her grandmother's words as if under a spell. Shaking herself, she pushed back the plate of shrimp for which her appetite had fled. "Madame," she began, determined to make her position clear, "I have no intention of entering into the competition for the present count. As I see it, we are incredibly ill matched." She recalled suddenly the feel of his lips against hers, the demanding pressure of his hard body, and she trembled. Raising her eyes to her grandmother's, she shook her head in fierce denial. "No." She did not stop to reason if she was speaking to her heart or the woman across from her, but stood and hurried back into the château.

The full moon had risen high in the star-studded sky, its silver light streaming through the high windows as Serenity awoke, miserable, sore, and disgusted. Though she had retired early, latching onto the inspiration of a fictitious headache to separate herself from the man who clouded her thoughts, sleep had not come easily. Now, just a few short hours since she had captured it, it had escaped. Turning in the oversized bed, she moaned aloud at her body's revolt.

*I'm paying the price for this morning's little adventure.* She winced and sat up with a deep sigh. *Perhaps I need another hot bath,* she decided with dim hope. *Lord knows it couldn't make me any stiffer.* She eased herself from the mattress, legs and shoulders protesting violently. Ignoring the robe at the foot of the bed, she made her way across the dimly lit room toward the adjoining bath, banging her shin smartly against an elegant Louis XVI chair.

She swore, torn between anger and pain. Still muttering, she nursed her leg, pulling the chair back into position and leaning on it. "What?" she called out rudely as a knock sounded on her door.

It swung open, and Christophe, dressed casually in a robe of royal-blue silk, stood observing her. "Have you injured yourself, Serenity?" It was not necessary to see his expression to be aware of his mockery.

"Just a broken leg," she snapped. "Pray, don't trouble yourself."

"May one inquire as to why you are groping about in the dark?" He leaned against the doorframe, cool, calm, and in total command, his arrogance all the catalyst Serenity's mercurial temper required.

"I'll tell you why I'm groping about in the dark, you smug, self-assured beast!" she began, her voice a furious whisper. "I was going to drown myself in the tub to put myself out of the misery you inflicted on me today!"

"I?" he said innocently, his eyes roaming over her, slim and golden in the shimmering moonlight, her long, shapely legs and pure alabaster-toned skin exposed by the briefness of her flimsy nightdress. She was too angry to be aware of her dishabille or his appreciation, oblivious to the moonlight which seeped through the sheerness of her gown and left her curves delectably shadowed.

"Yes, you!" she shot back at him. "It was you who got me up on that horse this morning, wasn't it? And now each individual muscle in my body despises me." Groaning, she rubbed her palm against the small of her back. "I may never walk properly again."

"Ah."

"Oh, what a wealth of meaning in a single syllable." She glared at him, doing her best to stand with some dignity. "Could you do it again?"

*"Ma pauvre petite,"* he murmured in exaggerated sympathy. *"Je suis désolé."* He straightened and began to move toward her. Then, suddenly recalling her state of dress, her eyes grew wide.

"Christophe, I…" she began as his hands descended

on her bare shoulders, but the words ended in a sigh as his fingers massaged the strain.

"You have discovered new muscles, yes? And they are not being agreeable. It will not be so difficult the next time." He led her to the bed and pressed her shoulders so that she sat, unresisting, savoring the firm movements on her neck and shoulders. Easing down behind her, his long fingers continued down her back, kneading away the ache as if by magic.

She sighed again, unconsciously moving against him. "You have wonderful hands," she murmured, a blessed lethargy seeping into her as the soreness disappeared and a warm contentment took its place. "Marvelous strong fingers; I'll be purring any minute."

She was not aware when the transition occurred, when the gentle relaxation became a slow kindling in her stomach, his objective massage an insistent caress, but she felt her head suddenly spinning with the heat.

"That's better, much better," she faltered and made to move away, but his hands went quickly to her waist, holding her immobile as his lips sought the soft vulnerability of her neck in a gentle feather of a kiss. She trembled, then started like a frightened doe, but before she could escape, he had twisted her to face him, his lips descending in possession on hers, stilling all protests.

Struggle died before it became a reality, the kindling erupting into a burst of flame, and her arms encircled his neck as she was pressed against the mattress. His mouth seemed to devour hers, hard and assured, and his hands followed the curves of her body as if he had made love to her countless times. Impatiently, he pushed aside the thin strap on her shoulder, seeking and finding the satin smoothness of her breast, his touch inciting a tempest of desire, and she began to move under him. His demands became more urgent, his hands more insistent as they moved down the whisper of silk, his lips leaving hers to assault her neck with an insatiable hunger.

"Christophe," she moaned, knowing she was incapable of combating both him and her own weakness. "Christophe, please, I can't fight you here. I could never win."

"Do not fight me, *ma belle,*" he whispered into her neck. "And we shall both win."

His mouth took hers again, soft and lingering, causing desire to swell, then soar. Slowly, his lips explored her face, brushing along the hollows of her cheeks, teasing the vulnerability of parted lips before moving on to other conquests. A hand cupped her breast in lazy possession, fingers tracing its curve, tarrying over the nipple until a dull, throbbing ache spread through her. The sweet, weakening pain brought a moan, and her hands began to seek the rippling muscles of his back, as if to accentuate his power over her.

His lazy explorations altered to urgency once more, as if her submission had fanned the fires of his own passions. Hands bruised soft flesh, and her mouth was savaged by his, the teeth which had nibbled along her bottom lip replaced by a mouth which ravaged her senses, and demanded more than surrender, but equal passion.

The hand left her breast to run down her side, pausing over her hip before he continued on, claiming the smooth, fresh skin of her thigh, and her breath came only in shuddering sighs as his lips moved lower along her throat to taste the warm hollow between her breasts.

With one final flash of lucidity, she knew she stood on the edge of a precipice, and one more step would plunge her into an everlasting void.

"Christophe, please." She began to tremble, though nearly suffocating with the heat. "Please, you frighten me, I frighten me. I've never… I've never been with a man before."

His movements stopped, and the silence became thick as he lifted his face and stared down at her. Slivers of moonlight slept on her pale hair, tousled on the snowy pillow, her eyes smoky with awakened passion and fear.

With a short, harsh sound, he lifted his weight from her. "Your timing, Serenity, is incredible."

"I'm sorry," she began, sitting up.

"For what do you apologize?" he demanded, anger just below the surface of icy calm. "For your innocence, or for allowing me to come very close to claiming it?"

"That's a rotten thing to say!" she snapped, fighting to steady her breathing. "This happened so quickly, I couldn't think. If I had been prepared, you would never have come so close."

"You think not?" He dragged her up until she was kneeling on the surface of the bed, once more molded against him. "You are prepared now. Do you think I could not take you this minute with you more than willing to allow it?"

He glared down at her, the air around him tingling with assurance and fury, and she could say nothing, knowing she was helpless against his authority and her own surging need. Her eyes were huge in her pale face, fear and innocence shining like beacons, and he swore and pushed her away.

"*Nom de Dieu!* You look at me with the eyes of a child. Your body disguises your innocence well; it is a dangerous masquerade." Moving to the door, he turned back to survey the lightly clad form made small by the vastness of the bed. "Sleep well, *mignonne,*" he said with a touch of mockery. "The next time you choose to run into the furniture, it would be wise if you lock your door; I will not walk away again."

Serenity's cool greeting to Christophe over breakfast was returned in kind, his eyes meeting hers briefly, showing no trace of the passion or anger they had held the previous night. Perversely, she was annoyed at his lack of reaction as he chatted with the countess, addressing Serenity only when necessary, and then with a strict politeness which could be detected only by the most sensitive ear.

"You have not forgotten Geneviève and Yves are dining with us this evening?" the countess asked Christophe.

"*Mais non,* Grandmère," he assured her, replacing his cup in its saucer. "It is always a pleasure to see them."

"I believe you will find them pleasant company, Serenity." The countess turned her clear blue eyes on her granddaughter. "Geneviève is very close to your age, perhaps a year younger, a very sweet, well-mannered young woman. Her brother, Yves, is very charming and quite attractive." A smile was born on her lips.

"You will find his company, uh, *diverting*. Do you not agree, Christophe?"

"I am sure Serenity will find Yves highly entertaining."

Serenity glanced over quickly at Christophe. Was there a touch of briskness to his tone? He was sipping his coffee calmly, and she decided she had been mistaken.

"The Dejots are old family friends," the countess went on, drawing Serenity's attention back to her. "I am sure you will find it pleasant to have company near your own age, *n'est-ce pas?* Geneviève is often a visitor to the château. As a child she trotted after Christophe like a faithful puppy. *Bien sûr,* she is not a child any longer." She threw a meaningful glance at the man at the head of the long oak table, and Serenity used great willpower not to wrinkle her nose in disdain.

"Geneviève grew from an awkward pigtailed child into an elegant, lovely woman," Christophe replied, and the affection in his voice was unmistakable.

*Good for her,* Serenity thought, struggling to keep an interested smile in place.

"She will make a marvelous wife," the countess predicted. "She has a quiet beauty and natural grace. We must persuade her to play for you, Serenity. She is a highly skilled pianist."

*Chalk up one more for the paragon of virtue,* Serenity brooded to herself silently, miserably jealous of the absent Geneviève's relationship with Christophe. Aloud, she said, "I shall look forward to meeting your friends, Madame." Silently, she assured herself that she would dislike the perfect Geneviève on sight.

The golden morning passed quietly, a lazy mid-morning hush falling over the garden as Serenity sketched. She had exchanged a few words with the gardener before they had both settled down to their respective tasks. Finding him an interesting study, she sketched him as he bent over the bushes, trimming the overblown blossoms and chattering, scolding and praising his colorful, scented friends.

His face was timeless, weathered and lined with character, unexpectedly bright blue eyes shining against a ruddy complexion. The hat covering his shock of steel-gray hair was black, a wide, flat-brimmed cap with velvet ribbons streaming down the back. He wore a sleeveless vest and aged knickers, and she marveled at his agility in the wooden *sabots*.

So deep was her concentration on capturing his Old World aura with her pencil that she failed to hear the footsteps on the flagstones behind her. Christophe watched her for some moments as she bent over her work, the graceful curve of her neck calling to his mind an image of a proud white swan floating on a cool, clear lake. Only when she tucked her pencil behind her ear and brushed an absent hand through her hair did he make his presence known.

"You have captured Jacques admirably, Serenity." His brow rose in amusement at the startled jump she made and the hand that flew to her heart.

"I didn't know you were there," she said, cursing the breathlessness of her voice and the pounding of her pulse.

"You were deep in your work," he explained, casually sitting next to her on the white marble bench. "I did not wish to disturb you."

*Ho,* she amended silently, *you'd disturb me if you were a thousand miles away.* Aloud, she spoke politely: "*Merci.* You are most considerate." In defense, she turned her attention to the spaniel at their feet. "Ah, Korrigan, *comment ça va?*" She scratched behind his ear, and he licked her hand with loving kisses.

"Korrigan is quite taken with you," Christophe remarked, watching the long, tapering fingers being bathed. "He is normally much more reserved, but it appears you have captured his heart." Korrigan collapsed in an adoring heap over her feet.

"A very sloppy lover," she remarked, holding out her hand.

"A small price to pay, *ma belle,* for such devotion."

He drew a handkerchief from his pocket, captured her hand, and began to dry it. The effect on Serenity was violent. Sharp currents vibrated from the tips of her fingers and up her arm, spreading a tingling heat through her body.

"That's not necessary. I have a rag right here." She indicated her case of chalks and pencils and attempted to pull her hand away from his.

His eyes narrowed, his grip increasing, and she found herself outmatched in the short, silent struggle. With a sigh of angry exasperation, she allowed her hand to lay limp in his.

"Do you always get your own way?" she demanded, eyes darkening with suppressed fury.

*"Bien sûr,"* he replied with irritating confidence, releasing her now-dry hand and giving her a long, mea-

suring look. "I feel you are also used to having your own way, Serenity Smith. Will it not be interesting to see who, how do you say, 'comes out on top' during your visit?"

"Perhaps we should put up a scoreboard," she suggested, retreating behind the armor of frigidity. "Then there would be no doubt as to who comes out on top."

He gave her a slow, lazy smile. "There will be no doubt, *cousine*."

Her retort was cut off by the appearance of the countess, and Serenity automatically smoothed her features into relaxed lines to avoid the other woman's speculation.

"Good morning, my children." The countess greeted them with a maternal smile that surprised her grand-daughter. "You are enjoying the beauty of the garden. I find it at its most peaceful at this time of day."

"It's lovely, Madame," Serenity concurred. "One feels there is no other world beyond the colors and scents of this one solitary spot."

"I have often felt that way." The angular lines softened. "The hours I have spent here over the years are uncountable." She seated herself on a bench across from the dark man and fair-skinned woman and sighed. "What have you drawn?" Serenity offered her pad, and the countess studied the drawing before raising her eyes to study the woman in turn. "You have your father's talent." At the grudging admission, Serenity's eyes sharpened, and her mouth opened to retort. "Your father was a very talented artist," the countess continued. "And I begin to see he had some quality of goodness to have earned Gaelle's love and your loyalty."

"Yes, Madame," Serenity replied, realizing she had been awarded a difficult concession. "He was a very good man, both a constant loving father and husband."

She resisted the urge to bring up the Raphael, unwilling to break the tenuous threads of understanding being woven. The countess nodded. Then, turning to Christophe, she made a comment about the evening's dinner party.

Picking up drawing paper and chalks Serenity began idly to draw her grandmother. The voices hummed around her, soothing, peaceful sounds suited to the garden's atmosphere. She did not attempt to follow the conversation, merely allowing the murmuring voices to wash over her as she began to concentrate on her work with more intensity.

In duplicating the fine-boned face and the surprisingly vulnerable mouth, she saw more clearly the countess's resemblance to her mother, and so, in fact, to herself. The countess's expression was relaxed, an ageless beauty that instinctively held itself proud. But somehow now, Serenity saw a glimpse of her mother's softness and fragility, the face of a woman who would love deeply—and therefore be hurt deeply. For the first time since she had received the formal letter from her unknown grandmother, Serenity felt a stirring of kinship, the first trickle of love for the woman who had borne her mother, and so had been responsible for her own existence.

Serenity was unaware of the variety of expressions flitting across her face, or of the man who sat beside her, observing the metamorphosis while he carried on his conversation. When she had finished, she lay down her chalks and wiped her hands absently, starting when she turned her head and encountered Christophe's direct stare. His eyes dropped to the portrait in her lap before coming back to her bemused eyes.

"You have a rare gift, *ma chérie,*" he murmured. And she frowned in puzzlement, unsure from his tone whether he was speaking of her work or something entirely different.

"What have you drawn?" the countess inquired. Serenity tore her eyes from his compelling regard and handed her grandmother the portrait.

The countess studied it for several moments, the first expression of surprise fading into something Serenity could not comprehend. When the eyes rose and rested on her, the face altered with a smile.

"I am honored and flattered. If you would permit me, I would like to purchase this." The smile increased. "Partly for my vanity, but also because I would like a sample of your work."

Serenity watched her for a moment, hovering on the line between pride and love. "I'm sorry, Madame." She shook her head and took the drawing. "I cannot sell it." She glanced down at the paper in her hand before handing it back and meeting the blue eyes. "It is a gift for you, Grandmère." She watched the play of emotion move both mouth and eyes before speaking again. "Do you accept?"

"*Oui.*" The word came on a sigh. "I shall treasure your gift, and this"—she looked down once more at the chalk portrait— "shall be my reminder that one should never allow pride to stand in the way of love." She rose and touched her lips to Serenity's cheeks before she moved down the flagstone path toward the château.

Standing, Serenity moved away from the bench. "You have a natural ability to invite love," Christophe observed, and she rounded on him, her emotions highly tuned.

"She's my grandmother, too."

He noted the veil of tears shimmering in her eyes and rose to his feet in an easy movement. "My statement was a compliment."

"Really? I thought it a condemnation." Despising the mist in her eyes, she wanted both to be alone and to lean against his broad shoulder.

"You are always on the defensive with me, are you not, Serenity?" His eyes narrowed as they did when he was angry, but she was too involved with battling her own emotions to care.

"You've given me plenty of cause," she tossed back. "From the moment I stepped off the train, you made your feelings clear. You'd condemned both my father and me. You're cold and autocratic and without a bit of compassion or understanding. I wish you'd go away and leave me alone. Go flog some peasants or something; it suits you."

He moved so quickly that she had no chance to back away, his arms nearly splitting her in two as they banded around her. "Are you afraid?" he demanded, and his lips crushed hers before she could answer, and all reason was blotted out.

She moaned against the pain and pleasure his mouth inflicted, going limp as his hold increased, conquering even her breath.

*How is it possible to hate and love at the same time?*
her heart demanded of her numbed brain, but the answer
was lost in a flood of turbulent, triumphant passion.
Fingers tangled ruthlessly in her hair, pulling her head
back to expose the creamy length of her neck, and he
claimed the vulnerable skin with a mouth hot and hungry. The thinness of her blouse was no defense against
the sultry heat of his body, but he disposed of the brief
barrier, his hand sliding under, then up along her flesh
to claim the swell of her breast with a consummate and
absolute possession.

His mouth returned to ravage hers, bruising softness
with a demand she could not deny. No longer did she
question the complexity of her love, but yielded like a
willow in a storm to the entreatment of her own needs.

He lifted his face, and his eyes were dark, the fires
of anger and passion burning them to black. He wanted
her, and her eyes grew wide and terrified at the knowledge. No one had ever wanted her this intensely, and no
one had ever possessed the power to take her this effortlessly. For even without his love, she knew she would
submit, and even without her submission, he would take.

He read the fear in her eyes, and his voice was low
and dangerous. "*Oui, petite cousine,* you have cause
to be afraid, for you know what will be. You are safe
for the moment, but take care how and where you provoke me again."

Releasing her, he walked easily up the path his
grandmother had chosen, and Korrigan bounded up,
sent Serenity an apologetic glance, and then followed
close on his master's heels.

# *Chapter 6*

Serenity dressed with great care for dinner that evening, using the time to put her feelings in order and decide on a plan of action. No amount of arguments or reasoning could alter the fact that she had plunged headlong into love with a man she had known only a few days, a man who was as terrifying as he was exciting.

An arrogant, domineering, audaciously stubborn man, she added, pulling up the zipper at the back of her dress. And one who had condemned her father as a thief. *How could I let this happen?* she berated herself. *How could I have prevented it?* she reflected with a sigh. *My heart may have deserted me, but my head is still on my shoulders, and I'm going to have to use it. I refuse to allow Christophe to see that I've fallen in love with him and subject myself to his mockery.*

Seated at the cherrywood vanity, she ran a brush

through soft curls and touched up her light application
of makeup. War paint, she decided, and grinned at the
reflection. *It fits; I'd rather be at war with him than in
love. Besides*—the grin turned into a frown—*there is
also Mademoiselle Dejot to contend with tonight.*

Standing, she surveyed her full reflection in the free-
standing mirror. The amber silk echoed the color of her
eyes and added a warm glow to her creamy skin. Thin
straps revealed smooth shoulders, and the low, rounded
bodice teased the subtle curve of breast. The knife-
pleated skirt floated gently to her ankles, the filminess
and muted color adding to her fragile, ethereal beauty.

She frowned at the effect, seeing fragility when she
had desired poise and sophistication. The clock informed her that there was no time to alter gowns, so
slipping on shoes and spraying a cloud of scent around
her, she hurried from the room.

The murmur of voices emitting from the main drawing room made Serenity realize, to her irritation, that
the dinner guests had already arrived. Her artist's eye
immediately sketched the tableau which greeted her
as she entered the room: the gleaming floor and warm
polished paneling, the high, lead-paned windows, the
immense stone fireplace with the carved mantel—all
set the perfect backdrop for the elegant inhabitants of
the château's drawing room, with the countess the un-
disputed queen in regal red silk.

The severe black of Christophe's dinner suit threw
the snow-white of his shirt into relief and accented the
tawny color of his skin. Yves Dejot was also in black,
his skin more gold than bronze, his hair an unexpected
chestnut. But it was the woman between the two dark

men who caught both Serenity's eye and reluctant admiration. If her grandmother was the queen, here was the crown princess. Jet-black hair framed a small, elfin face of poignant beauty. Almond-shaped eyes of pansy-brown dominated the engaging face, and the gown of forest-green glowed against the rich golden skin.

Both men rose as she entered the room, and Serenity gave her attention to the stranger, all too aware of Christophe's habitual all-encompassing survey. As introductions were made, she found herself looking into chestnut eyes, the same shade as his hair, which held undeniable masculine approval and an unmistakable light of mischief.

"You did not tell me, *mon ami,* that your cousin was a golden goddess." He bent over Serenity's fingers, brushing them with his lips. "I shall have to visit the château more often, Mademoiselle, during your stay."

She smiled with honest enjoyment, summing up Yves Dejot as both charming and harmless. "I am sure my stay will be all the more enjoyable with that prospect in mind, Monsieur," she responded, matching his tone, and she was rewarded with a flashing smile.

Christophe continued his introductions, and Serenity's hand was clasped in a small, hesitant grip. "I am so happy to meet you at last, Mademoiselle Smith." Geneviève greeted her with a warm smile. "You are so like your mother's portrait, it is like seeing the painting come to life."

The voice was sincere, and Serenity concluded that no matter how hard she tried, it would be impossible to dislike the pixielike woman who gazed at her with the liquid eyes of a cocker spaniel.

The conversation continued light and pleasant throughout *apéritifs* and dinner, delectable oysters in champagne setting the mood for an elegantly prepared and served meal. The Dejots were curious about America and Serenity's life in its capital, and she attempted to describe the city of contrasts as the small group enjoyed *le ris de veau au Chablis.*

She began to draw a picture with words of stately old government buildings, the graceful lines and columns of the White House. "Unfortunately, there has been a great deal of modernization, with huge steel and glass monstrosities replacing some of the old buildings. Neat, vast, and charmless. But there are dozens of theatres, from Ford's, where Lincoln was assassinated, to the Kennedy Center."

Continuing, she took them from the stunning elegance of Embassy Row to the slums and tenements outside the federal enclave, through museums and galleries and the bustle of Capitol Hill.

"But we lived in Georgetown, and this is a world apart from the rest of Washington. Most of the homes are row houses or semi-detached, two or three stories, with small bricked-in yards edged with azaleas and flowerbeds. Some of the side streets are still cobblestoned, and it still retains a rather old-fashioned charm."

"Such an exciting city," Geneviève commented. "You must find our life here very quiet. Do you miss the animation, the activity of your home?"

Serenity frowned into her wineglass, then shook her head. "No," she answered, somewhat surprised by her own admission. "That's strange, I suppose." She met the brown eyes across from her. "I spent my entire life there, and I was very happy, but I don't miss it at all. I had the strangest feeling of affinity when I first walked into the château, a feeling of recognition. I've been very content here."

Glancing over, she found Christophe's eyes on her, brooding and penetrating, and she felt a quick surge of panic. "Of course, it's a relief not to enter into the daily contest for a parking space," she added with a smile, attempting to shake off the mood of seriousness. "Parking spaces are more precious than gold in Washington, and behind the wheel even the most mild-mannered person would commit murder and mayhem to obtain one."

"Have you resorted to such tactics, *ma chérie?*" Christophe asked. Raising his wineglass, he kept his eyes on her.

"I shudder to think of my crimes," she answered, relieved by the light turn of topic. "I dare not confess what lengths I've gone to in order to secure a few feet of empty space. I can be terribly aggressive."

"It is not possible to believe that aggression is a quality of such a delicate willow," Yves declared, blanketing her in his charming smile.

"You would be surprised, *mon ami,*" Christophe commented with an inclination of his head. "The willow has many unexpected qualities."

Serenity continued to frown at him as the countess skillfully changed the subject.

The drawing room was gently lit, lending an air of intimacy to the vast room. As the group enjoyed after-dinner coffee and brandy, Yves seated himself next to Serenity and began dispensing his abundant supply of Gallic charm. She noted, with a great deal of discomfort around her heart, which she was forced to recognize as pure, honest jealousy, that Christophe devoted himself to entertaining Geneviève. They spoke of her parents, who were touring the Greek islands, of mutual acquaintances and old friends. He listened attentively as Geneviève related an anecdote, flattered, laughed, teased, his attitude being one of overall gentleness, a softness Serenity had not seen in him before. Their relationship was so obviously special, so close and long standing, that Serenity felt a swift pang of despair.

*He treats her as though she were made of fine, delicate crystal, small and precious, and he treats me as though I were made of stone, sturdy, strong, and dull.*

It would have been infinitely easier if Serenity could have disliked the other woman, but natural friendliness overcame jealousy, and as time went by, she found herself liking both Dejots more and more.

Geneviève consented, after some gentle prompting by the countess, to play a few selections on the piano. The music floated through the room as sweet and fragile as its mistress.

*I suppose she's perfect for him,* Serenity concluded dismally. *They have so much in common, and she brings out a tenderness in him that will keep him from hurting her.* She glanced over to where Christophe sat, relaxed against the cushions of the sofa, his dark, fascinating eyes fixed on the woman at the piano. A swift variety of emotions ran through her—longing, despair, resentment, settling into a hopeless fog of depression as she realized no matter how perfect Geneviève might be for him, she could never happily watch Christophe court another woman.

"As an artist, Mademoiselle," Yves began as the music ended and conversation resumed, "you require inspiration, *n'est-ce pas?*"

"Of one kind or another," she agreed and smiled at him.

"The gardens of the château are immensely inspirational in the moonlight," he pointed out with an answering smile.

"I am in the mood for inspiration," she decided on quick impulse. "Perhaps I could impose on you to escort me."

"Mademoiselle," he answered happily, "I would be honored."

Yves informed the rest of the party of their intention, and Serenity accepted his proffered arm without seeing the dark look thrown at her by the remaining male member.

The garden was indeed an inspiration, the brilliance of colors muted in the silver shimmer of moonlight. The scents intertwined into a heady perfume, mellowing the warm summer evening into a night for lovers. She sighed as her thoughts strayed back to the man in the château's drawing room.

"You sigh from pleasure, Mademoiselle?" Yves questioned as they strolled down a winding path.

*"Bien sûr,"* she answered lightly, shaking off her somber mood and granting her escort one of her best smiles. "I'm overcome by the overwhelming beauty."

"Ah, Mademoiselle." He lifted her hand to his lips and kissed it with much feeling. "The beauty of each blossom pales before yours. What rose could compare with such lips, or gardenia with such skin?"

"How do French men learn to make love with words?"

"It is taught from the cradle, Mademoiselle," he informed her with suspicious sobriety.

"How difficult for a woman to resist such a setting." Serenity took a deep, consuming breath. "A moonlit garden outside a Breton château, the air filled with perfume, a handsome man with poetry on his lips."

*"Hélas!"* Yves gave a heavy sigh. "I fear you will find the strength to do so."

She shook her head with mock sorrow. "I am unfortunately extremely strong, and you," she added with a grin, "are a charming Breton wolf."

His laughter broke the night's stillness. "Ah, already you know me too well. If it were not for the feeling I had when we met that we were destined to be friends and not lovers, I would pursue my campaign with more feeling. But, we Bretons are great believers in destiny."

"And it is so difficult to be both friends and lovers."

*"Mais, oui."*

"Then friends it shall be," Serenity stated, extending her hand. "I shall call you Yves, and you shall call me Serenity."

He accepted her hand and held it a moment. "*C'est extraordinaire* that I should be content with friendship with one like you. You possess an elusive beauty that locks into a man's mind and keeps him constantly aware of you." His shoulders moved in a Gallic shrug which said more than a three-hour speech. "Well, such is life," he remarked fatalistically. Serenity was still laughing when they re-entered the château.

The following morning, Serenity accompanied her grandmother and Christophe to Mass in the village she had viewed from the hilltop. A light, insistent rain had begun during the pre-dawn hours, its soft hissing against her window awakening her until its steady rhythm had lulled her back to sleep.

The rain continued as they drove to the village, drenching leaves and causing flowers in the cottage's neat garden to droop heavy-headed, lending them an air of a colorful congregation at prayer. She had noticed, with some puzzlement, that Christophe had maintained a strange silence since the previous evening. The Dejots had departed soon after Serenity and Yves had rejoined the group in the drawing room, and though Christophe's farewells to his guests were faultlessly charming, he had avoided addressing Serenity directly. The only communication between them had been a brief—and, she had imagined—forbidding glance, quickly veiled.

Now, he spoke almost exclusively to the countess, with occasional comments or replies made directly to Serenity, polite, with a barely discernible hostility which she decided to ignore.

The focal point of the small village was the chapel, a tiny white structure with its neatly trimmed grounds an almost humorous contrast to its slightly apologetic, crumbling state. The roof had had more than one recent repair, and the single oak door at the entrance was weathered and battered from age and constant use.

"Christophe has offered to have a new chapel built," the countess commented. "But the villagers will not have it. This is where their fathers and grandfathers have worshipped for centuries, and they will continue to worship here until it crumbles about their ears."

"It's charming," Serenity decided, for somehow the

tiny chapel's faintly dilapidated air gave it a certain
steadfast dignity, a sense of pride at having witnessed
generations of christenings, weddings, and funerals.

The door groaned in apology as Christophe opened
it, allowing the two women to precede him. The interior was dark and quiet, the high-beamed ceiling adding an illusion of space. The countess glided to the front
pew, taking her place in the seats which had been reserved for the Château Kergallen for nearly three centuries. Spying Yves and Geneviève across the narrow
aisle, Serenity threw them both a full smile and was
rewarded with an answering one from Geneviève and
a barely discernible wink from Yves.

"This is hardly the proper setting for your flirta-
tions, Serenity," Christophe whispered in her ear as he
assisted her out of her damp trenchcoat.

Her color rose, making her feel like a child caught
giggling in the sacristy, and she turned her head to retort as the priest, who seemed as old as the chapel, approached the altar, and the service began.

A feeling of peace drifted over her like a soft, down-
filled quilt. The rain insulated the congregation from
the outside, its soft whispering on the roof adding to
the quiet rather than detracting from it. The low drone
of Breton from the ancient priest, and the light rumble
of response, an occasional whimper from an infant, a
muffled cough, the dark stained glass with rivulets of
rain running down its surface—all combined into a quiet
timelessness. Sitting in the well-worn pew, Serenity felt
the chapel's magic and understood the villagers' refusal
to give up the crumbling building for a more substantial
structure, for here was peace, and the serenity for which

she had been named. A continuity with the past, and a link with the future.

As the service ended, so did the rain, and a vague beam of sunlight filtered through the stained glass, introducing a subtle, elusive glow. When they emerged outside, the air was fresh, sparkling from the clean scent of rain. Drops still clung to the newly washed leaves, glistening like tears against the bright green surfaces.

Yves greeted Serenity with a courtly bow and a lingering kiss on the fingers. "You have brought out the sun, Serenity."

*"Mais, oui,"* she agreed, smiling into his eyes. "I have ordered all my days in Brittany to be bright and sunny."

Removing her hand, she smiled at Geneviève, who resembled a dainty primrose in a cool yellow dress and narrow-brimmed hat. Greetings were exchanged, and Yves leaned down toward Serenity like a conspirator.

"Perhaps you would care to take advantage of the sunshine, *chérie,* and come for a drive with me. The countryside is exquisite after a rain."

"I'm afraid Serenity will be occupied today," Christophe answered before she could accept or decline, and she glared at him. "Your second lesson," he said smoothly, ignoring the battle lights in her amber eyes.

"Lesson?" Yves repeated with a crooked smile. "What are you teaching your lovely cousin, Christophe?"

"Horsemanship," he responded with a like smile, "at the moment."

"Ah, you could not find a finer instructor," Geneviève observed with a light touch on Christophe's arm. "Christophe taught me to ride when Yves and my father had given me up as hopelessly inadequate. You are so patient." Her cocker spaniel eyes gazed up at the lean man, and Serenity stifled an incredulous laugh.

*Patient* was the last word she would use to describe Christophe. Arrogant, demanding, autocratic, overconfident—she began silently listing qualities she attributed to the man at her side. Cynical and overbearing, also. Her attention wandered from the conversation, her gaze lighting on a small girl sitting on a patch of grass with a frisky black puppy. The dog was alternately bathing the child's face with enthusiastic kisses and running in frantic circles around her as the child's high, sweet laughter floated on the air. It was such a relaxing, innocent picture that it took Serenity a few extra seconds to react to what happened next.

The dog suddenly darted across the grass toward the road, and the child scrambled up, dashing after it, calling the dog's name in stern disapproval. Serenity watched without reaction as a car approached. Then a cold draft of fear overtook her as she observed the child's continuing flight toward the road.

Without thought, she streaked in pursuit, frantically calling in Breton for the child to stop, but the girl's attention was riveted on her pet, and she rushed over the grass, stepping out in the path of the oncoming car.

Serenity heard the squeal of brakes as her arms wrapped around the child, and she felt the rush of wind and slight bump of the fender against her side as she hurled both herself and the girl across the road, landing in a tangled heap on its surface. There was absolute silence for a split-second, and then pandemonium broke loose as the puppy, which Serenity was now sitting on rather heavily, yelped in rude objection, and the child's loud wails for her mother joined the animal's indignation.

Suddenly, excited voices in a mixture of languages joined the wailing and yelping, adding to Serenity's dazed, befuddled state. She could find no strength to remove her weight from the errant puppy, and the girl struggled from her now-limp grasp and ran into the arms of her pale, tearful mother.

Strong, hard arms lifted Serenity to her feet, holding her shoulders and tilting back her head so that she met Christophe's dark, stormy eyes. "Are you hurt?" When she shook her head, he continued in a tight, angry voice: *"Nom de Dieu!* You must be mad!" He shook her slightly, increasing the dizziness. "You could have been killed! How you missed being struck is a miracle."

"They were playing so sweetly," she recalled in a vague voice. "Then that silly dog goes tearing off into the street. Oh, I wonder if I hurt it; I sat right on it. I don't think the poor animal liked it."

"Serenity." Christophe's furious voice and the vigorous shaking brought her attention back to him. *"Mon Dieu!* I begin to believe you really are mad!"

"Sorry," she murmured, feeling empty and lightheaded. "Silly to think of the dog first and the child later. Is she all right?"

He let out a soft stream of curses on a long breath. *"Oui,* she is with her mother. You moved like a cheetah; otherwise, both of you would not be standing up babbling now."

"Adrenaline," she muttered and swayed. "It's gone now."

His grip increased on her shoulders as he surveyed

her face. "You are going to faint?" The question was accompanied by a deep frown.

"Certainly not," she replied, attempting to sound firm and dignified, but succeeding in a rather wavering denial.

"Serenity." Geneviève reached her, taking her hand and abandoning formality. "That was so brave." Tears swam in the brown eyes, and she kissed both of Serenity's pale cheeks.

"Are you hurt?" Yves echoed Christophe's question, his eyes concerned rather than angry.

"No, no, I'm fine," she assured him, unconsciously leaning on Christophe for support. "The puppy got the worst of it when I landed on it." *I just want to sit down,* she thought wearily, *until the world stops spinning.*

Suddenly, she found herself being addressed in rapid, tearful Breton by the child's mother. The words were slurred with emotion, and the dialect was so thick she had difficulty following the stream of conversation. The woman continually wiped brimming eyes with a wrinkled ball of handkerchief, and Serenity made what she hoped were the correct responses, feeling incredibly tired and faintly embarrassed as the mother's hands grabbed and kissed with fervent gratitude. At a low order from Christophe, they were relinquished, and she retreated, gathering up her child and melting away into the crowd.

"Come." He slipped an arm around Serenity's waist, and the mass of people parted like the waves of the Red Sea as he led her back toward the chapel. "I think both you and the mongrel should be put on a short leash."

"How kind of you to lump us together," she muttered,

then caught sight of her grandmother sitting on a small stone bench, looking pale and suddenly old.

"I thought you would be killed," the countess stated in a thick voice, and Serenity knelt in front of her.

"I'm quite indestructible, Grandmère," she claimed with a confident smile. "I inherited it from both sides of my family."

The thin, bony hand gripped Serenity's tightly. "You are very impudent and stubborn," the countess declared in a firmer voice. "And I love you very much."

"I love you, too," Serenity said simply.

## Chapter 7

Serenity insisted on receiving her riding lesson after the midday meal, vetoing both the suggested prescription of a long rest and the prospect of summoning a doctor.

"I don't need a doctor, Grandmère, and I don't need a rest. I'm perfectly all right." She shrugged aside the morning's incident. "A few bumps and bruises; I told you I'm indestructible."

"You are stubborn," the countess corrected, and Serenity merely smiled and shrugged again.

"You have had a frightening experience," Christophe inserted, studying her with critical eyes. "A less strenuous activity would be more suitable."

"For heaven's sake, not you, too!" She pushed away her coffee impatiently. "I'm not some mid-Victorian weakling who subsides into fits of vapors and needs to be coddled. If you don't want to take me riding, I'll call Yves and accept his invitation for the drive which you refused for me." Her fine-boned face was set, and her chin lifted. "I am not going to go to bed in the middle of the day like a child."

"Very well." Christophe's eyes darkened. "You will have your ride, though perhaps your lesson will not be as stimulating as what Yves intended."

She stared at him for a moment in bewilderment before color seeped into her cheeks. "Oh, really, what a ridiculous thing to say."

"I will meet you at the stables in half an hour." He interrupted her protestations, rose from the table, and strode from the room before she could formulate a suitable rebuttal.

Turning to her grandmother, her face was a picture of indignation. "Why is he so insufferably rude to me?"

The countess's slim shoulders moved expressively, and she looked wise. "Men are complicated creatures, *chérie*."

"One day," Serenity predicted with an ominous frown, "one day he's not going to walk away until I've had my say."

Serenity met Christophe at the appointed time, determined to focus every ounce of energy into developing the proper riding technique. She mounted the mare with concentrated confidence, then followed her silent instructor as he pointed his horse in the opposite direction from that which they had taken on their last outing. When he broke into a light canter, she copied his action, and she experienced the same intoxicating freedom as she had before. There was, however, no sudden, exciting flash of smile on his features, no laughter or teasing words, and she told herself she was better off without them. He called out an occasional instruction, and she obeyed immediately, needing to prove both to him and herself that she was capable. So, she contented herself with the task of riding and an infrequent glance at his dark, hawklike profile.

*Lord help me,* she sighed in defeat, taking her eyes from him and staring straight ahead. *He's going to haunt me for the rest of my life. I'll end up a crotchety old maid, comparing every man I see to the one I couldn't have. I wish to God I'd never laid eyes on him.*

*"Pardon?"* Christophe's voice broke into her silent meditations, and she started, realizing she must have muttered something aloud.

"Nothing," she stammered, "it was nothing." Taking a deep breath, she frowned. "I could swear I smell the sea." He slowed his mount to a walk, and she reined in beside him as a faint rumble broke the silence. "Is that thunder?" She gazed up into a clear blue sky, but the rumble continued. "It *is* the sea!" she exclaimed, all animosity forgotten. "Are we near it? Will I be able to see it?" He merely halted his horse and dismounted. "Christophe, for heaven's sake!" She watched in exasperation as he tied his mount's reins to a tree. "Christophe!" she repeated, struggling from the saddle with more speed than grace. He took her arm as she landed awkwardly and tied her mount beside his before leading her farther down the path. "Choose whatever language you like," she invited magnanimously, "but talk to me before I go crazy!"

He stopped, turned, and drew her close, covering her mouth with a brief, distracting kiss. "You talk too much," he stated simply and continued on his way.

"Really," she began, but subsided when he turned and looked down at her again. Satisfied with her silence, he led her on, the distant rumbling growing nearer and more insistent. When he stopped again, Serenity caught her breath at the scene below.

The sea stretched as far as she could see, the sun's rays dancing on its deep green surface. The surf rolled in to caress the rocks, its foam resembling frothy lace on a deep velvet gown. Teasingly, it flowed back from the shore, only to roll back like a coquettish lover.

"It's marvelous," she sighed, reveling in the sharp salt-sprayed air and the breeze which ruffled her hair. "I suppose you must be used to this by now; I doubt I ever could be."

"I always enjoy looking at the sea," he answered, his eyes focused on the distant horizon, where the clear blue sky kissed the deep green. "It has many moods; perhaps that is why the fishermen call it a woman. Today she is calm and gentle, but when she is angry, her temper is a magnificent thing to see."

His hand slid down her arm to clasp her in a simple, intimate gesture she had not expected from him, and her heart did a series of somersaults. "When I was a boy, I thought to run away to the sea, live my life on the water, and sail with her moods." His thumb rubbed against the tender skin of her palm, and she swallowed before she could speak.

"Why didn't you?"

His shoulders moved, and she wondered for a moment if he remembered she was there. "I discovered that the land has its own magic—vivid-colored grass, rich soil, purple grapes, and grazing cattle. Riding a horse over the long stretches of land is as exciting as sailing over the waves of the sea. The land is my duty, my pleasure, and my destiny."

He looked down into the amber eyes, fixed wide and open on his face, and something passed between them, shimmering and expanding until Serenity felt submerged by its power. Then, she was crushed against him, the wind swirling around them like ribbons to bind them closer as his mouth demanded an absolute surrender. She clung to him as the roar of the sea swelled to a deafening pitch, and suddenly she was straining against him and demanding more.

If the mood of the sea was calm and gentle, his did not mirror it. Helpless against her own need, she reveled in the savage possession of his mouth, the urgent insistence of the hands which claimed her, as if by right. Trembling, not with fear, but with the longing to give, she pressed yet closer, willing him to take what she offered.

His mouth lifted once, briefly, and she shook her head against the liberation, pulling his face back to hers, lips begging for the merging. Her fingers dug into the flesh of his shoulders at the force of the new embrace, his mouth seeking hers with a new hunger, as if he would taste her or starve. His hand slipped under the silk of her blouse to claim the breast which ached for his touch, the warmth of his fingers searing like glowing embers against her skin, and though her mouth was conquered, his tongue demanding the intimacy of velvet moisture, her mind murmured his name over and over until there was nothing else.

Arms banded around her again, hands abandoning their explorations, and breath flew away and was forgotten in the new, crushing power. Soft breasts pressed against the hard leanness of his chest, thigh straining against thigh, heart pounding against heart, and Serenity knew she had taken the step from the precipice and would never return to the solidity of earth.

He released her so abruptly, she would have stumbled had his hand not gripped her arm to steady her. "We must go back," he stated as if the moment had never been. "It grows late."

Her hands reached up to push the tumbled curls from her face, her eyes lifting to his, wide and full of confused pleading. "Christophe." She said his name on a whisper, unable to form any other sound, and he stared down at her, the brooding look familiar and, as always, unfathomable.

"It grows late, Serenity," he repeated, and the underlying anger in his tone brought only more bewilderment.

Suddenly cold, her arms wrapped around her body to ward off the chill. "Christophe, why are you angry with me? I haven't done anything wrong."

"Haven't you?" His eyes narrowed and darkened with familiar temper, and through the ache of rejection, her own rose to meet it.

"No. What could I do to you? You're so infuriatingly superior, up there on your little golden throne. A partial aristocrat like myself could hardly climb up to your level to cause any damage."

"Your tongue will cause you endless trouble, Serenity, unless you learn to control it." His voice was precise and much too controlled, but Serenity found discretion buried under a growing mountain of fury.

"Well, until I choose to do so, perhaps I'll use it to tell you precisely what I think about your arrogant, autocratic, domineering, and infuriating attitude toward life in general, and myself in particular."

"A woman," he began, in a voice she noted was entirely too soft and too silky, "with your temperament, *ma petite cousine,* must be continually shown there is only one master." He took her arm in a firm hold and turned away from the sea. "I said we will go."

"*You,* Monsieur," she returned, holding her ground and sending him a look of smoldering amber, "can go whenever you want."

Her exit of furious dignity took her three feet before her shoulders were captured in a viselike grip, then whirled around to face a fury which made her own temper seem tranquil. "You cause me to think again about the wisdom of beating a woman." His mouth took hers swiftly, hard and more punishing than a fist, and Serenity felt a quick surge of pain, tasting only anger on his lips, and no desire. Fingers dug into her shoulders, but she allowed herself neither struggle nor response, remaining passive in his arms as courage fled into hopelessness.

Set free, she stared up at him, detesting the veil of moistness which clouded her eyes. "You have the advantage, Christophe, and will always win a physical battle." Her voice was calm and carefully toned, and she watched his brows draw close, as if her reaction puzzled him. His hand lifted to brush at a drop which had escaped to flow down her cheek, and she jerked away, wiping it away herself and blinking the rest back.

"I've had my quota of humiliations for one day, and I will not dissolve into a pool of tears for your benefit." Her voice became firmer as she gained control, and her shoulders straightened as Christophe watched the transformation in silence. "As you said, it's getting late." Turning, she walked back up the path to where the horses waited.

The days passed quietly, soft summer days filled with the sun and the sweet perfume of flowers. Serenity devoted most of the daylight hours to painting, reproducing the proud, indomitable lines of the château on canvas. She had noted, at first with despair and then with increasing anger, Christophe's calculated avoidance of her. Since the afternoon when they had stood on the cliff above the sea, he had barely spoken to her, and then only with astringent politeness. Pride soon covered her hurt like a bandage over an open wound, and painting became a refuge against longing.

The countess never mentioned the Raphael, and Serenity was content for the time to drift, wanting to strengthen the bond between them before delving further into its disappearance and the accusation against her father.

She was immersed in her work, clad in faded jeans and a paint-splattered smock, her hair disheveled by her own hand, when she spotted Geneviève approaching across the smooth carpet of lawn. A beautiful Breton fairy, Serenity imagined, small and lovely in a buff-colored riding jacket and dark brown breeches.

"*Bonjour,* Serenity," she called out when Serenity raised a slim hand in greeting. "I hope I am not disturbing you."

"Of course not. It's good to see you." The words came easily because she meant them, and she smiled and put down her brush.

"Oh, but I have made you stop," Geneviève began in apology.

"You've given me a marvelous excuse to stop," she corrected.

"May I see?" Geneviève requested. "Or do you not like your work viewed before it is finished?"

"Of course you may see. Tell me what you think."

She moved around to stand beside Serenity. The background was completed: the azure sky, lamb's-wool clouds, vivid green grass, and stately trees. The château itself was taking shape gradually: the gray walls glowing pearly in the sunlight, high glistening windows, the drum towers. There was much left to complete, but even in its infancy, the painting captured the fairy-tale aura Serenity had envisioned.

"I have always loved the château," Geneviève stated, her eyes still on the canvas. "Now I see you do, as well." Pansy eyes lifted from the half-completed painting and sought Serenity's. "You have captured its warmth, as well as its arrogance. I am glad to know you see it as I do."

"I fell in love with it the first moment I saw it," Serenity admitted. "The longer I stay, the more hopelessly I'm lost." She sighed, knowing her words described the man, as well as his home.

"You are lucky to have such a gift. I hope you will not think less of me if I confess something."

"No, of course not," Serenity assured her, both surprised and intrigued.

"I am terribly envious of you," she blurted out quickly, as if courage might fail her.

Serenity stared down at the lovely face incredulously. "You, envious of me?"

*"Oui."* Geneviève hesitated for a moment, and then began to speak in a rush. "Not only of your talent as an artist, but of your confidence, your independence." Serenity continued to gape, her mouth wide open in astonishment. "There is something about you which draws people to you—an openness, a warmth in your eyes that makes one want to confide, feeling somehow you will understand."

"How extraordinary," Serenity murmured, astonished. "But, Geneviève," she began in a lighter tone, "you're so lovely and warm, how could you envy anyone, least of all me? You make me feel like a veritable Amazon."

"Men treat you as a woman," she explained, her voice faintly desperate. "They admire you not only for the way you look, but for what you are." She turned away, then back again quickly, a hand brushing at her hair. "What would you do if you loved a man, had loved him all of your life, loved with a woman's heart, but he saw you only as an amusing child?"

Serenity felt a cloud of despair envelop her heart. *Christophe,* she concluded. *Dear Lord, she wants my advice about Christophe.* She stifled the urge to give a shout of hysterical laughter. *I'm supposed to give her pointers on the man I love. Would she seek me out if she knew what he thinks of me...of my father?* Her eyes met Geneviève's dark ones, filled with hope and trust. She sighed.

"If I were in love with such a man, I would take great pains to let him know I was a woman, and that was how I wanted him to see me."

"But how?" Geneviève's hand spread in a helpless gesture. "I am such a coward. Perhaps I would lose even his friendship."

"If you really love him, you'll have to risk it or face the rest of your life as only his friend. You must tell... your man, the next time he treats you as a child, that you are a woman. You must tell him so that there is no doubt in his mind what you mean. Then, the move is his."

Geneviève took a deep breath and squared her shoulders. "I will think about what you have said." She turned her warm eyes on Serenity's amber ones once more. "Thank you for listening, for being a friend."

Serenity watched the small, graceful figure retreat across the grass. *You're a real martyr,* Serenity, she told herself. *I thought self-sacrifice was supposed to make one glow with inner warmth; I just feel cold and miserable.* She began packing up her paints, no longer finding pleasure in the sunshine. *I think I'll give up martyrdom and take up foreclosing on widows and orphans; it couldn't make me feel any worse.*

Depressed, Serenity wandered up to her room to store her canvas and paints. With what she considered a herculean effort, she managed to produce a smile for the maid, who was busily folding freshly laundered lingerie into the bureau drawer.

"*Bonjour,* Mademoiselle." Bridget greeted Serenity with a dazzling smile of her own, and amber eyes blinked at the power.

"*Bonjour,* Bridget. You seem in remarkably good spirits." Glancing at the shafts of sunlight which flowed triumphantly through the windows, Serenity sighed and shrugged. "I suppose it is a beautiful day."

"*Oui,* Mademoiselle. *Quel jour!*" She gestured toward the sky with a hand filled with filmy silk. "I think I have never seen the sun smile more sweetly."

Unable to cling to depression under the attack of blatant good humor, Serenity plopped into a chair and grinned at the small maid's glowing face. "Unless I read the signs incorrectly, I would say it's love which is smiling sweetly."

Heightened color only added more appeal to the young face as Bridget paused in her duties to beam yet another smile over Serenity. "*Oui,* Mademoiselle, I am very much in love."

"And I gather from the look of you"—Serenity continued battling a sweet surge of envy of the youthful confidence—"that you are very much loved."

"*Oui,* Mademoiselle." Sunlight and happiness formed an aura around her. "On Saturday, Jean-Paul and I will be married."

"Married?" Serenity repeated, faintly astonished as she studied the tiny form facing her. "How old are you, Bridget?"

"Seventeen," she stated with a sage nod for her vast collection of years.

*Seventeen,* Serenity mused with an unconscious sigh. "Suddenly, I feel ninety-two."

"We will be married in the village," Bridget continued, warming to Serenity's interest. "Then everyone will come back to the château, and there will be singing and dancing in the garden. The count is very kind and very generous. He says we will have champagne." Serenity watched as joy turned to awe.

"Kind," she murmured, turning the adjective over in her mind. *Kindness is not a quality I would have attributed to Christophe.* Letting out a long breath, she recalled his gentle attitude toward Geneviève. *Obviously, I simply don't bring it out in him.*

"Mademoiselle has so many lovely things." Glancing up, Serenity saw Bridget fondling a flowing white negligée, her eyes soft and dreamy.

"Do you like it?" Rising, she fingered the hem, remembering the silky texture against her skin, then let it drift like a pure fall of snow to the floor.

"It's yours," Serenity declared impulsively, and the maid turned back, soft eyes now as wide as dark saucers.

"*Pardon,* Mademoiselle?"

"It's yours," she repeated, smiling into astonishment. "A wedding present."

"Oh, *mais non,* I could not…it is too lovely." Her voice faltered to a whisper as she gazed at the gown with wistful desire, then turned back to Serenity. "Mademoiselle could not bear to part with it."

"Of course I can," Serenity corrected. "It's a gift, and it would please me to know you were enjoying it." Studying the simple white silk which Bridget clutched to her breast, she sighed with a mixture of envy and hopelessness. "It was made for a bride, and you will look beautiful in it for your Jean-Paul."

"Oh, Mademoiselle!" Bridget breathed, blinking back tears of gratitude. "I will treasure it always." She followed this declaration with a joyful stream of Breton thanks, the simple words lifting Serenity's spirits. She left the future bride gazing into the mirror, negligée spread over apron as she dreamed of her wedding night.

The sun again smiled sweetly on Bridget's wedding day, the sky a cerulean-blue touched with a few friendly white wisps of clouds.

As the days had passed, Serenity's depression had altered to a frigid resentment. Christophe's aloof demeanor fanned the fires of temper, but determinedly, she had buried them under equally haughty ice. As a result, their conversations had been limited to a few stony, formally polite sentences.

She stood, flanked by him and the countess on the tiny lawn of the village church awaiting the bridal procession. The raw-silk suit she had chosen deliberately for its cool, untouchable appearance had been categorically dismissed by a wave of her grandmother's regal hand. Instead, she had been presented with an outfit of her mother's, the scent of lavender still clinging, as fresh as yesterday. Instead of appearing sophisticated and distant, she now appeared like a young girl awaiting a party.

The full gathered skirt just brushed bare calves, its brilliant vertical stripes of red and white topped with a short white apron. The peasant scoop-necked blouse was tucked into the tiny waist, its short puffed sleeves leaving arms bare to the sun. A black sleeveless vest fitted trimly over the subtle curve of breast, her pale halo of curls topped with a beribboned straw hat.

Christophe had made no comment on her appearance, merely inclining his head when she had descended the stairs, and now Serenity continued the silent war by addressing all her conversation exclusively to her grandmother.

"They will come from the house of the bride," the countess informed her, and though Serenity was uncomfortably aware of the dark man who stood behind her, she gave the appearance of polite attentiveness. "All of her family will walk with her on her last journey as a maiden. Then, she will meet the groom and enter the chapel to become a wife."

"She's so young," Serenity murmured in a sigh, "hardly more than a child."

"*Alors,* she is old enough to be a woman, my aged one." With a light laugh, the countess patted Serenity's hand. "I was little more when I married your grandfather. Age has little to do with love. Do you not agree, Christophe?"

Serenity felt, rather than saw, his shrug. "So it would seem, Grandmère. Before she is twenty, our Bridget will have a little one tugging on her apron and another under it."

"*Hélas!*" the countess sighed with suspicious wistfulness, and Serenity turned to regard her with careful curiosity. "It appears neither of my grandchildren see fit to provide me with little ones to spoil." She gave Serenity a sad, guileless smile. "It is difficult to be patient when one grows old."

"But it becomes simpler to be shrewd," Christophe commented in a dry voice, and Serenity could not prevent herself from glancing up at him. He gave her a brief, raised-brow look, and she met it steadily, determined not to falter under its spell.

"To be wise, Christophe," the countess corrected, unperturbed and faintly smug. "This is a truer statement. *Voilà!*" she announced before any comment could be made. "They come!"

Soft new flower petals floated and danced to earth as small children tossed them from wicker baskets. They laid a carpet of love for the bride's feet. Innocent petals, wild from the meadow and forest, and the children danced in circles as they offered them to the air. Surrounded by her family, the bride walked like a small, exquisite doll. Her dress was traditional, and obviously old, and Serenity knew she had never seen a bride more radiant or a dress more perfect.

Aged white, the full, pleated skirt flowed from the waist to dance an inch from the petal-strewn road. The neck was high and trimmed with lace, and the bodice was fitted and snug, touched with delicate embroidery. She wore no veil, but instead had on a round white cap topped with a stiff lace headdress which lent the tiny dark form an exotic and ageless beauty.

The groom joined her, and Serenity noted, with a near-maternal relief, that Jean-Paul looked both kind and nearly as innocent as Bridget herself. He, too, was attired traditionally: white knickers tucked into soft boots, and a deep blue double-breasted jacket over an embroidered white shirt. The narrow-brimmed Breton

cap with its velvet ribbons accentuated his youth, and
Serenity surmised he was little older than his bride.

Shining young love glowed around them, pure and
sweet as the morning sky, and the sudden, unexpected
pang of longing caused Serenity to draw in her breath,
then clutch her hands together tightly to combat a con-
vulsive shudder. *Just once,* she thought, and swallowed
against the dryness of her throat, *just once I would have
Christophe look at me that way, and I could live on it
for the rest of my life.*

Starting as a hand touched her arm, she looked up
to find his eyes on her, faintly mocking and altogether
cool. Tilting her chin, she allowed him to lead her inside the chapel.

The château's garden was a perfect world in which
to celebrate a new marriage, vivid and fresh and alive
with scents and hues. The terrace was laden with white-
clothed tables brimming over with food and drink. The
château had laid on its finest for the village wedding,
silver and crystal gleaming with the pride of age in the
glory of sunlight. And the village, Serenity observed,
accepted it as their due. As they belonged to the château, so it belonged to them. Music rose over the mixture of voices and laughter: the sweet, lilting strain of
violins and the softly nasal call of bagpipes.

Serenity watched from the terrace as bride and
groom performed their first dance as man and wife, a
folk dance, full of charm and saucy movements, and
Bridget flirted with her husband with tossing head
and teasing eyes, much to the approval of the audience. Dancing continued, growing livelier, and Serenity

found herself being pulled into the crowd by a charmingly determined Yves.

"But I don't know how," she protested, unable to prevent the laugh his persistence provoked.

"I will teach you," he returned simply, taking both her hands in his. "Christophe is not the only one with the ability to instruct." He inclined his head in acknowledgment of her frown. "Ah-ha! I thought as much." Her frown deepened at the ambiguity, but he merely smiled, lifted one hand to his lips briefly, and continued. "*Maintenant,* first we step to the right."

Caught up first in her lesson, then in the pleasure of the simple music and movements, Serenity found the tensions of the past days drifting away. Yves was attentive and charming, taking her through the steps of the dances and bringing her glasses of champagne. Once seeing Christophe dancing with a small, graceful Geneviève, a cloud of despair threatened her sun, and she turned away quickly, unwilling to fall back into the well of depression.

"You see, *chérie,* you take to the dance naturally." Yves smiled down at her as the music paused.

"Assuredly, my Breton genes have come to the fore to sustain me."

"So," he said in mock censure, "will you not give credit to your instructor?"

"*Mais, oui.*" She gave him a teasing smile and a small curtsy. "My instructor is both charming and brilliant."

"True," he agreed, chestnut eyes twinkling against the gravity of his tone. "And my student is both beautiful and enchanting."

"True," she agreed in turn, and laughing, she linked her arm through his.

"Ah, Christophe." Her laughter froze as she saw Yves's gaze travel above her head. "I have usurped your role as tutor."

"It appears you are both enjoying the transition." Hearing the icy politeness in his voice, Serenity turned to him warily. He looked entirely too much like the seafaring count in the portrait gallery for her comfort. The white silk shirt opened carelessly to reveal the strong, dark column of throat, the sleeveless black vest a startling contrast. The matching black pants were mated to soft leather boots, and Serenity decided he looked more dangerous than elegant.

"A delightful student, *mon ami,* as I am sure you agree." Yves's hand rested lightly on Serenity's shoulder as he smiled into the set, impassive face. "Perhaps you would care to test the quality of my instructions for yourself."

*"Bien sûr."* Christophe acknowledged the offer with a slight inclination of his head. Then, with a graceful, rather old-fashioned gesture, he held out his hand, palm up for Serenity's acquiescence.

She hesitated, both fearing and longing for the contact of flesh. Then seeing the challenge in his dark eyes, she placed her palm in his with aristocratic grace.

Serenity moved with the music, the steps of the old, flirting dance coming easily. Swaying, circling, joining briefly, the dance began as a confrontation, a formalized contest between man and woman. Their eyes held, his bold and confident, hers defiant, and they moved in alternating circles, palms touching. As his arm slipped lightly around her waist, she tossed her head back to keep the gaze unbroken, ignoring the sudden thrill as their hips brushed.

Steps quickened with the music, the melody growing more demanding, the ancient choreography growing more enticing, the contact of bodies lengthening. She kept her chin tilted insolently, her eyes challenging, but she felt the heat begin its insistent rise as his arm became more possessive of her waist, drawing her closer with each turn. What had begun as a duel was now a seduction, and she felt his silent power taking command of her will as surely as if his lips had claimed hers. Drawing on one last shred of control, she stepped back, seeking the safety of distance. His arm pulled her against him, and helplessly, her eyes sought the mouth which hovered dangerously over hers. Her lips parted, half in protest, half in invitation, and his lowered until she could taste his breath on her tongue.

The silence when the music ended was like a thunderclap, and she watched wide-eyed as he drew the promise of his mouth away with a smile of pure triumph.

"Your teacher is to be commended, Mademoiselle." His hands dropped from her waist, and with a small bow, he turned and left her.

The more remote and taciturn Christophe became, the more open and expansive became the countess, as though sensing his mood and seeking to provoke him.

"You seem preoccupied, Christophe," the countess stated artlessly as they dined at the large oak table.

"Are your cattle giving you trouble, or perhaps an *affaire de coeur?*"

Determinedly, Serenity kept her eyes on the wine she swirled in her glass, patently fascinated by the gently moving color.

"I am merely enjoying the excellent meal, Grandmère," Christophe returned, not rising to the bait. "Neither cattle nor women disturb me at the moment."

"Ah." The countess breathed life into the syllable. "Perhaps you group both together."

Broad shoulders moved in a typical gesture. "They both demand attention and a strong hand, *n'est-ce pas?*"

Serenity swallowed a bit of *canard à l'orange* before it choked her.

"Have you left many broken hearts behind in America, Serenity?" The countess spoke before Serenity could voice the murderous thoughts forming in her brain.

"Dozens," she returned, aiming a deadly glance at Christophe. "I have found that some men lack the intelligence of cattle, more often having the arms, if not the brains, of an octopus."

"Perhaps you have been dealing with the wrong men," Christophe suggested, his voice cool.

This time it was Serenity's shoulders which moved. "Men are men," she said in dismissal, seeking to annoy him with her own generalization. "They either want a warm body for groping in corners, or a piece of Dresden to sit on a shelf."

"And how, in your opinion, does a woman wish to be treated?" he demanded as the countess sat back and enjoyed the fruits of her instigation.

"As a human being with intellect, emotions, rights, needs." Her hands moved expressively. "Not as a happy convenience for a man's pleasure to be tucked away until the mood strikes him, or a child to be petted and amused."

"You seem to have a low opinion of men, *ma chérie*," Christophe intimated, neither of them aware they were speaking more in this conversation than they had in days.

"Only of antiquated ideas and prejudice," she contradicted. "My father always treated my mother as a partner; they shared everything."

"Do you look for your father in the men you meet, Serenity?" he asked suddenly, and her eyes widened, surprised and disconcerted.

"Why, no, at least I don't think so," she faltered, trying to see into her own heart. "Perhaps I look for his strength and his kindness, but not a replica. I think I look for a man who could love me as completely as he loved my mother—someone who could take me with all my faults and imperfections and love me for what I am, not what he might want me to be."

"And when you find such a man," Christophe asked, giving her an unfathomable stare, "what will you do?"

"Be content," she murmured, and made an effort to give her attention to the food on her plate.

Serenity continued her painting the following day. She had slept poorly, disturbed by the admission she had made to Christophe's unexpected question. She had spoken spontaneously, the words the fruit of a feeling she had not been aware of possessing. Now with the warmth of the sun at her back and brush and pallet in hand, she endeavored to lose her discomfort in the love of painting.

She found it difficult to concentrate, Christophe's lean features invading her mind and blurring the sharp lines of the château. Rubbing her forehead, she finally threw down her brush in disgust and began to pack her equipment, mentally cursing the man who insisted on interfering with both her work and her life. The sound of a car cut into her eloquent swearing, and she turned, her hand shading her eyes from the sun, to watch the approaching vehicle wind down the long drive.

It halted a few yards from where she stood, and her mouth dropped open in amazement as a tall, fair man got out and began walking toward her.

"Tony!" she cried in surprise and pleasure, rushing across the grass to meet him.

His arms gripped her waist, and his lips covered hers in a brief but thorough kiss.

"What are you doing here?"

"I could say I was just in the neighborhood." He grinned down at her. "But I don't think you'd buy that." He paused and studied her face. "You look terrific," he decided, and bent to kiss her again, but she eluded him.

"Tony, you haven't answered me."

"The firm had some business to conduct in Paris," he explained. "So I flew over, and when I set things straight, I drove out here to see you."

"Two birds with one stone," she concluded wryly, feeling a vague disappointment. *It would have been nice,* she reflected, *if he had dropped his business and charged across the Atlantic because he couldn't bear to be parted from me.* But not Tony! She studied his good-looking, clear-cut features. *Tony's much too methodical for impulses, and that's been part of the problem.*

He brushed her brow with a casual kiss. "I missed you."

"Did you?"

He looked slightly taken aback. "Well, of course I did, Serenity." His arm slipped around her shoulders as he began walking toward her painting apparatus. "I'm hoping you'll come back with me."

"I'm not ready to go yet, Tony. I have commitments here. There are things I have to clear up before I can even think about going back."

"What things?" he asked with a frown.

"I can't explain, Tony," she evaded, unwilling to take him into her confidence. "But I've barely had time to know my grandmother; there are so many lost years to make up for."

"You can't expect to stay here for twenty-five years and make up for lost time." His voice was filled with exasperation. "You have friends back in Washington, a home, a career." He stopped and took her by the shoulders. "You know I want to marry you, Serenity. You've been putting me off for months."

"Tony, I never made any promises to you."

"Don't I know it." Releasing her, he stared around in abstraction. With a pang of guilt, she tried harder to make him understand.

"I've found part of myself here. My mother grew up here; her mother still lives here." She turned and faced the château, making a wide, sweeping gesture.

"Just look at it, Tony. Have you ever seen anything to compare with it?"

He followed her gaze and studied the large stone structure with another frown. "Very impressive," he stated without enthusiasm. "It's also huge, rambling, and, more than likely, drafty. Give me a brick house on P Street any day."

She sighed, deflated, then turning to her companion, smiled with affection. "Yes, you're right, you don't belong here."

"And you do?" The frown deepened.

"I don't know," she murmured, her eyes roaming over the conical roof and down to the courtyard. "I just don't know."

He studied her profile a moment, then strategically changed the subject. "Old Barkley had some papers for you." He referred to the attorney who had handled her parents' affairs and for whom he worked as a junior partner. "So instead of trusting them to the mail, I'm delivering them in person."

"Papers?"

"Yes, very confidential." He grinned in his familiar way. "Wouldn't give me a clue as to what they were about; just said it was important that you get them as soon as possible."

"I'll look at them later," she said in dismissal, having had enough of papers and technical forms since her parents' deaths. "You must come inside and meet my grandmother."

If Tony had been unimpressed with the château, he was overwhelmed by the countess. Serenity hid her smile as she introduced Tony to her grandmother, noting the widening of his eyes as he accepted the offered hand. She was, Serenity thought with silent satisfaction, magnificent. Leading Tony into the main drawing room, the countess ordered refreshments and proceeded to pump Tony in the most charming way for every ounce of information about himself. Serenity sat back and observed the maneuver, proud of her straight face.

*He doesn't stand a chance,* she decided as she poured tea from the elegant silver pot. Handing the dainty china cup to her grandmother, their eyes met. The unexpected mischief in the blue eyes almost caused a burst of laughter to escape, so she busied herself with the pouring of more tea with intense concentration.

*The old schemer!* she thought, surprised that she was not offended. *She's determining if Tony's a worthy candidate for her granddaughter's hand, and poor Tony is so awed by her magnificence, he doesn't see what's going on.*

At the end of an hour's conversation, the countess had learned Tony's life history: his family background, education, hobbies, career, politics, many details of which Serenity had been ignorant herself. The inquisition had been skillful, so subtly accomplished that Serenity suppressed the urge to stand and applaud when it was completed.

"When do you have to get back?" she asked, feeling she should save Tony from disclosing his bank balance.

"I have to leave first thing in the morning," he told her, relaxed and totally oblivious to the gentle third degree to which he had been subjected. "I wish I could stay longer, but…" He shrugged.

*"Bien sûr,* your work comes first," the countess fin-

ished for him, looking understanding. "You must dine with us tonight, Monsieur Rollins, and stay with us until morning."

"I couldn't impose on your hospitality, Madame," he objected, perhaps halfheartedly.

"Impose? Nonsense!" His objection was dismissed with a regal wave of the hand. "A friend of Serenity's from so far away—I would be deeply offended if you would refuse to stay with us."

"You are very kind. I'm grateful."

"It is my pleasure," the countess stated as she rose. "You must show your friend around the grounds, and I will see that a room is prepared for him." Turning to Tony, she extended her hand once more. "We have cocktails at seven-thirty, Monsieur Rollins. I will look forward to seeing you then."

# Chapter 8

Serenity stood in front of the full-length mirror without seeing the reflection. The tall, slender woman in the amethyst gown, soft waves of crepe flowing like a jeweled breeze, might not have stared back from the highly polished glass. Serenity's mind was playing back the afternoon's events, her emotions running from pleasure, irritation, and disappointment to amusement.

After the countess had left them alone, Serenity had conducted Tony on a brief tour of the grounds. He had been vaguely complimentary about the garden, taking in its surface beauty, his logical, matter-of-fact mind unable to see beyond the roses and geraniums to the romance of hues and textures and scents. He was lightly amused by the appearance of the ancient gardener and slightly uncomfortable with the overwhelming spaciousness of the view from the terrace. He preferred, in his words, a few houses or at least a traffic light. Serenity had shaken her head at this in indulgent affection, but had realized how little she had in common with the man with whom she had spent so many months.

He was, however, completely overawed by the château's châtelaine. Anyone less like a grandmother, he had stated with great respect, he had never encountered. She was incredible, he had said, to which Serenity silently agreed, though perhaps for different reasons. She looked as if she belonged on a throne, indulgently granting audiences, and she had been so gracious, so interested in everything he had said. *Oh, yes,* Serenity had concurred silently, trying and failing to be indignant. *Oh yes, dear, gullible Tony, she had been vastly interested.* But what was the purpose of the game she was playing?

When Tony was settled in his room, strategically placed, Serenity noted, at the farthest end of the hall from herself, she had sought out her grandmother with the excuse of thanking her for inviting Tony to stay.

Seated in her room at an elegant Regency writing desk penning correspondence on heavy-crested stationery, the countess had greeted Serenity with an innocent smile, which somehow resembled the cat who swallowed the canary.

*"Alors."* She had put down her pen and gestured to a low brocade divan. "I hope your friend has found his room agreeable."

*"Oui,* Grandmère, I am very grateful to you for inviting Tony to stay for the night."

*"Pas de quoi, ma chérie."* The slender hand had ges-

tured vaguely. "You must think of the château as your home, as well as mine."

"*Merci,* Grandmère," Serenity had said demurely, leaving the next move to the older woman.

"A very polite young man."

"*Oui,* Madame."

"Quite attractive..."—a slight pause—"...in an ordinary sort of way."

"*Oui,* Madame," Serenity had agreed conversationally, tossing the ball into her grandmother's court. The ball was received and returned.

"I have always preferred more unusual looks in a man, more strength and vitality. Perhaps"—a slight teasing curve of the lips—"more of the buccaneer, if you know what I mean."

"Ah, *oui,* Grandmère." Serenity had nodded, keeping a guileless open gaze on the countess. "I understand very well."

"*Bien.*" The slim shoulders had moved. "Some prefer a tamer male."

"So it would seem."

"Monsieur Rollins is a very intelligent, well-mannered man, very logical and earnest."

*And dull.* Serenity had added the unspoken remark before speaking aloud in annoyance. "He helps little old ladies across the street twice a day."

"Ah, a credit to his parents, I am sure," the countess had decided, either unaware or unperturbed by Serenity's mockery. "I am sure Christophe will be most pleased to meet him."

A faint glimmer of uneasiness had been born in Serenity's brain. "I'm sure he will."

*"Mais, oui."* The countess smiled. "Christophe will be very interested to meet such a close friend of yours." The emphasis on "close" had been unmistakable, and Serenity's senses had sharpened as her uneasiness had grown.

"I fail to see why Christophe should be overly interested in Tony, Grandmère."

"Ah, *ma chérie,* I am sure Christophe will be fascinated by your Monsieur Rollins."

"Tony is not *my* Monsieur Rollins," Serenity had corrected, rising from the divan and advancing on her grandmother. "And I really don't see anything they have in common."

"No?" the countess asked with such irritating innocence that Serenity fought with amusement.

"You are a devious minx, Grandmère. What are you up to?"

Blue eyes met amber with the innocence of sweet childhood. "Serenity, *ma chérie,* I have no idea what you are talking about." As Serenity had opened her mouth to retort, the countess once more cloaked herself in her royalty. "I must finish my correspondence. I will see you this evening."

The command had been crystal clear, and Serenity had been forced to leave the room unsatisfied. The closing of the door with undue force had been her only concession to her rising temper.

Serenity's thoughts returned to the present. Slowly, her slim form, draped in amethyst, came into focus in the mirror. She smoothed her blond curls absently and erased the frown from her face. *We're going to play this very cool,* she informed herself as she fastened on pearl earrings. *Unless I am very much mistaken, my aristocratic grandmother would like to stir up some fireworks this evening, but she won't set off any sparks in this corner.*

She knocked on the door of Tony's room. "It's Serenity, Tony. If you're ready, I'll walk down with you." Tony's call bade her to enter, and she opened the door to see the tall, fair man struggling with a cufflink. "Having trouble?" she inquired with a wide grin.

"Very funny." He looked up from his task with a scowl. "I can't do anything lefthanded."

"Neither could my father," she stated with a quick, warm feeling of remembrance. "But he used to curse beautifully. It's amazing how many adjectives he used to describe a small pair of cufflinks." She moved to him and took his wrist in her hand. "Here, let me do it." She began to work the small object through his cuff. "Though what you would have done if I hadn't come along, I don't know." She shook her head and bent over his hand.

"I would have spent the evening with one hand thrust in my pocket," he answered smoothly. "Sort of a suave and continental stance."

"Oh, Tony." She looked up with a bright smile and shining eyes. "Sometimes you're positively cute."

A sound outside the door caught her attention, and she turned her head as Christophe walked by, paused for a moment to take in the intimate picture of the laughing woman fastening the man's cufflink, two fair heads close together. One dark brow raised fractionally, and with a small bow, Christophe continued on his way, leaving Serenity flushed and disconcerted.

"Who was that?" Tony asked with blatant curiosity, and she bent her head over his wrist to hide her burning cheeks.

"Le Comte de Kergallen," she answered with studied nonchalance.

"Not your grandmother's husband?" His voice was incredulous, and the question elicited a bright peal of laughter from Serenity, doing much to erase her tension.

"Oh, Tony, you are cute." She patted his wrist, the errant cufflink at last secured, and she looked up at him with sparkling eyes. "Christophe is the present count, and he's her grandson."

"Oh." Tony's brow creased in thought. "He's your cousin, then."

"Well…" She drew the word out slowly. "Not precisely." She explained the rather complicated family history and the resulting relationship between herself and the Breton count. "So, you see," she concluded, taking Tony's arm and walking from the room, "in a roundabout sort of way, we could be considered cousins."

"Kissing cousins," Tony observed with a definite frown.

"Don't be silly," she protested too quickly, unnerved by the memories of hard, demanding lips on hers.

If Tony noted the rushed denial and flushed cheeks, he made no comment.

They entered the drawing room arm in arm, and Serenity felt her flush deepen at Christophe's brief but encompassing appraisal. His face was smooth and unreadable, and she wished with sudden fervor that she could see the thoughts that lived behind his cool exterior.

Serenity watched his gaze shift to the man at her side, but his gaze remained impassive and correct.

"Ah, Serenity, Monsieur Rollins." The countess sat in the high-backed, richly brocaded chair framed by the massive stone fireplace, the image of a monarch receiving her subjects. Serenity wondered whether this placement had been deliberate or accidental. "Christophe, allow me to present Monsieur Anthony Rollins from America, Serenity's guest." The countess, Serenity noted with irony, had neatly categorized Tony as her personal property.

"Monsieur Rollins," she continued without breaking her rhythm, "allow me to present your host, Monsieur le Comte de Kergallen."

The title was emphasized delicately, and Christophe's position as master of the château was established. Serenity shot her grandmother a knowing glance.

The two men exchanged formalities, and Serenity was observant enough to note the age-old routine of sizing up, like two male dogs gauging the adversary before entering into combat.

Christophe served his grandmother an *apéritif,* then inquired as to Serenity's pleasure before continuing with his duties with Tony. He echoed Serenity's request for vermouth, and she stifled a smile, knowing Tony's taste ran strictly to dry vodka martinis or an occasional brandy.

The conversation flowed smoothly, the countess inserting several of the facts pertaining to Tony's background he had so conveniently provided her with that afternoon.

"It is so comforting to know that Serenity is in such capable hands in America," she stated with a gracious smile, and continued, ignoring the scowl Serenity threw at her. "You have been friends for some time, *non?*" The faint hesitation, barely perceptible, on the words "friends" caused Serenity's scowl to deepen.

"Yes," Tony agreed, patting Serenity's hand with affection. "We met about a year ago at a dinner party. Remember, darling?" He turned to smile at her, and she erased her scowl quickly.

"Of course. The Carsons' party."

"Now you have traveled so far just for a short visit." The countess smiled with fond indulgence. "Was that not considerate, Christophe?"

"Most considerate." With a nod, he lifted his glass.

*Why, you artful minx,* Serenity thought irreverently. *You know very well Tony came on business. What are you up to?*

"Such a pity you cannot remain longer, Monsieur Rollins. It is pleasant for Serenity to have company from America. Do you ride?"

"Ride?" he repeated, baffled for a moment. "No, I'm afraid not."

"*C'est dommage.* Christophe has been teaching Serenity. How is your pupil progressing, Christophe?"

"*Très bien,* Grandmère," he answered easily, his gaze moving from his grandmother to Serenity. "She has a natural ability, and now that the initial stiffness has passed"—a fleeting smile appeared, and her color rose in memory—"we are progressing nicely, eh, *mignonne?*"

"Yes," she agreed, thrown off balance by the casual endearment after days of cool politeness. "I'm glad you persuaded me to learn."

"It has been my pleasure." His enigmatic smile only served to increase her confusion.

"Perhaps you in turn will teach Monsieur Rollins, Serenity, when you have the opportunity." The countess drew her attention, and amber eyes narrowed at the innocence of the tone.

*The meddler!* she fumed inwardly. *She's playing the two against each other, dangling me in the middle like a meaty bone.* Irritation transformed into reluctant amusement as the clear eyes met hers, a devil of mischief dancing in their depths.

"Perhaps, Grandmère, though I doubt I shall be able to make the jump from student to instructor for some time. Two brief lessons hardly make me an expert."

"But you shall have others, *n'est-ce pas?*" She tossed off Serenity's counterploy and rose with fluid grace. "Monsieur Rollins, would you be so kind as to escort me to dinner?"

Tony smiled, greatly flattered, and took the countess's arm, though who was leading whom from the room was painfully obvious to the woman left behind.

*"Alors, chérie."* Christophe advanced on Serenity and held out his hand to assist her to her feet. "It seems you must make do with me."

"I guess I can just about bear it," she retorted, ignoring the furious thumping of her heart as his hand closed over hers.

"Your American must be very slow," he began conversationally, retaining her hand and towering over her in a distracting manner. "He has known you for nearly a year, and still he is not your lover."

Her face flamed, and she glared up at him, grasping at her dignity. "Really, Christophe, you surprise me. What an incredibly rude observation."

"But a true one," he returned, unperturbed.

"Not all men think exclusively of sex. Tony is a very warm and considerate person, not overbearing like some others I could name."

He only smiled with maddening confidence. "Does your Tony make your pulse race as it does now?" His thumb caressed her wrist. "Or your heart beat like this?" His hand covered the heart that galloped like a mad horse, and his lips brushed hers in a gentle, lingering kiss so unlike any of the others he had given her that she could only stand swaying with dazed sensations.

Lips feathered over her face, teasing the corners of her mouth, withholding the promise with the experience of seduction. Teeth nibbled at the lobe of her ear, and she sighed as the small spark of pain shot inestimable currents of pleasure along her skin, drugging her with delight and slow, smoldering desire. Lightly, his fingers traced the length of her spine, then moved with devastating laziness along the bare flesh of her back until she was pliant and yielding in his arms, her mouth seeking his for fulfillment. He gave her only a brief taste of his lips before they roamed to the hollow of her throat, and his hands moved slowly from curve to curve, fingers teasing but not taking the fullness of breast before they began a circling, gentle massage at her hips.

Murmuring his name, she went limp against him, unable to demand what she craved, starving for the mouth he denied her. Wanting only to be possessed, needing what only he could give, her arms pulled him closer in silent supplication.

"Tell me," Christophe murmured, and through mists of languor, she heard the light mockery of his tone. "Has Tony heard you sigh his name, or felt your bones melt against him as he held you so?"

Stunned, she jerked back convulsively from his embrace, anger and humiliation warring with desire. "You are overconfident, Monsieur," she choked. "It's none of your business how Tony makes me feel."

"You think not?" he asked in a politely inquiring tone. "We must discuss that later, *ma belle cousine.* Now I think we had best join Grandmère and our guest." He gave her an engaging and exasperating grin. "They may well wonder what has become of us."

They need not have concerned themselves, Serenity noted as she entered the dining room on Christophe's arm. The countess was entertaining Tony beautifully, currently discussing the collection of antique Fabergé boxes displayed on a large mirrored buffet.

The meal commenced with vichyssoise, cold and refreshing, the conversation continuing in English for Tony's benefit. Talk was general and impersonal, and Serenity felt herself relaxing, commanding her muscles to uncoil as the soup course was cleared and the *homard grillé* was served. The lobster was nothing less than perfection, and she mused idly that, if the cook was indeed a dragon, as Christophe had joked on that first day, she was indeed a very skilled one.

"I imagine your mother made the transition from the château to your house in Georgetown very easily,

Serenity," Tony stated suddenly, and she regarded him with a puzzled frown.

"I'm not sure I understand what you mean."

"There are so many basic similarities," he observed, and as she continued to look blank, he elaborated. "Of course, everything's on a much larger scale here, but there are the high ceilings, the fireplaces in every room, the style of furniture. Why, even the banisters on the stairs are similar. Surely you noticed?"

"Why, yes, I suppose I did," she answered slowly, "though I didn't realize it until now." Perhaps, she reasoned, her father had chosen the Georgetown house because he, too, had noted the similarities, and her mother had selected the furnishings from the memories of her childhood. The thought was somehow comforting. "Yes, even the banisters," she continued aloud with a smile. "I used to slide down them constantly, down from the third-floor studio, smack into the newel post, then slide to the ground floor and smack into the next one." The smile turned into a laugh. "Maman used to say that another part of my anatomy must be as hard as my head to take such punishment."

"She used to say the same to me," Christophe stated suddenly, and Serenity's eyes flew to him in surprise. *"Mais oui, petite."* He answered her look of surprise with one of his rare, full smiles. "What is the sense of walking if one can slide?"

A picture of a small, dark boy flying down the smooth rail, and her mother, young and lovely, watching and laughing, filled her mind. Her startled look faded slowly into a smile which mirrored Christophe's.

She helped herself to the raisin soufflé, light as a

cloud, accompanied by a dry and sparkling champagne. She felt herself drifting through dinner in a warm, contented glow, happy to let the easy conversation flow around her.

When they moved to the drawing room after dinner, she decided to refuse the offer of a liqueur or brandy. The glow persisted, and she suspected that at least part of it (she was determined not to think about the other part and the quick, tantalizing embrace before dinner) was due to the wine served with each course. No one appeared to notice her bemused state, her flushed cheeks, and her almost mechanical answers. She found her senses almost unbearably sharpened as she listened to the music of the voices, the deep hum of the men's mingling with the lighter tones of her grandmother. She inhaled with sensuous pleasure the tangy smoke of Christophe's cheroot drifting toward her, and she breathed deeply of the women's mingled subtle perfumes overpowered by the sweet scent of the roses spilling from every porcelain vase. A pleasing balance, she decided, the artist in her responding to and enjoying the harmony, the fluid continuity of the scene. The soft lights, the night breeze gently lifting the curtains, the quiet clink of glasses being set on the table—all merged into an impressionistic canvas to be registered and stored in her mind's eye.

The dowager countess, magnificent on her brocade throne, presided, sipping crème de menthe from an exquisite gold-rimmed glass. Tony and Christophe were seated across from each other, like day and night, angel and devil. The last comparison brought Serenity up

short. *Angel and Devil?* she repeated silently, surveying the two men.

Tony—sweet, reliable, predictable Tony, who applied
the gentlest pressure. Tony of the infinite patience and
carefully thought-out plans. What did she feel for him?
Affection, loyalty, gratitude for being there when she
needed him. A mild, comfortable love.

Her eyes moved to Christophe. Arrogant, dominating, exasperating, exciting. Demanding what he wanted,
and taking it, bestowing his sudden, unexpected smile
and stealing her heart like a thief in the night. He was
moody, whereas Tony was constant; imperious, whereas
Tony was persuasive. But if Tony's kisses had been
pleasant and stirring, Christophe's had been wildly intoxicating, turning her blood to fire and lifting her into
an unknown world of sensation and desire. And the love
she felt for him was neither mild nor comfortable, but
tempestuous and inescapable.

"Such a pity you do not play the piano, Serenity." The
countess's voice brought her back with a guilty jerk.

"Oh, Serenity plays, Madame," Tony informed her
with a wide grin. "Dreadfully, but she plays."

"Traitor!" Serenity gave him a cheerful grin.

"You do not play well?" The countess was clearly
incredulous.

"I'm sorry to bring disgrace to the family once again,
Grandmère," Serenity apologized. "But not only do I
not play well, I play quite miserably. I even offend Tony,
who is absolutely tone deaf."

"You'd offend a corpse with your playing, darling."
He brushed a lock of hair from her face in a gesture of
casual intimacy.

"Quite true." She smiled at him before glancing at her grandmother. "Poor Grandmère, don't look so stricken." Her smile faded somewhat as she met Christophe's frigid stare.

"But Gaelle played so beautifully," her grandmother countered with a gesture of her hand.

Serenity brought her attention back, attempting to shake off the chill of Christophe's eyes. "She could never understand the way I slaughtered music, either, but even with her abundant patience, she finally gave in and left me to my paints and easel."

*"Extraordinaire!"* The countess shook her head, and Serenity shrugged and sipped her coffee. "Since you cannot play for us, *ma petite,"* she began in a change of mood, "perhaps Monsieur Rollins would enjoy a tour of the garden." She smiled wickedly. "Serenity enjoys the garden in the moonlight, *n'est-ce pas?"*

"That sounds tempting," Tony agreed before Serenity could respond. Sending her grandmother a telling look, Serenity allowed herself to be led outside.

# Chapter 9

For the second time Serenity strolled in the moonlit garden with a tall, handsome man, and for the second time she wished dismally that it was Christophe by her side. They walked in companionable silence, enjoying the fresh night air and the pleasure of familiar linked hands.

"You're in love with him, aren't you?"

Tony's question broke the stillness like a rock being hurled through glass, and Serenity stopped and stared up at him with wide eyes.

"Serenity." He sighed and brushed a finger down her cheek. "I can read you like a book. You're doing your best to hide it, but you're crazy about him."

"Tony, I..." she stammered, feeling guilty and miserable. "I never meant to. I don't even like him, really."

"Lord." He gave a soft laugh and a grimace. "I wish

you didn't like me that way. But then," he added, cupping her chin, "you never have."

"Oh, Tony."

"You were never anything but honest, darling," he assured her. "You've nothing to feel guilty about. I thought that with constant, persistent diligence I would wear you down." He slipped an arm around her shoulders as they continued deeper into the garden. "You know, Serenity, your looks are deceptive. You look like a delicate flower, so fragile a man's almost afraid to touch you for fear you'll break, but you're really amazingly strong." He gave her a brief squeeze. "You never stumble, darling. I've been waiting for a year to catch you, but you never stumble."

"My moods and temper would have driven you over the edge, Tony." Sighing, she leaned against his shoulder. "I could never be what you needed, and if I tried to mold myself into something else, it wouldn't have worked. We'd have ended up hating each other."

"I know. I've known for a long time, but I didn't want to admit it." He let out a long breath. "When you left for Brittany, I knew it was over. That's why I came to see you; I had to see you one more time." His words sounded so final that she looked up in surprise.

"But we'll see each other again, Tony; we're still friends. I'll be coming back soon."

He stopped again and met her eyes, the silence growing long between them. "Will you, Serenity?" Turning, he led her back toward the lights of the château.

The sun was warm on her bare shoulders as Serenity said her goodbyes to Tony the next morning. He had already made his farewells to the countess and Christophe, and Serenity had walked with him from the coolness of the main hall to the warmth of the flagstone courtyard. The little red Renault waited for him, his luggage already secured in the boot, and he glanced at it briefly before turning to her, taking both of her hands in his.

"Be happy, Serenity." His grip tightened, then relaxed on her hands. "Think of me sometimes."

"Of course I'll think of you, Tony. I'll write and let you know when I'll be back."

He smiled down at her, his eyes roaming over her face, as if imprinting every detail in his memory. "I'll think of you just as you are today, in a yellow dress with the sun in your hair and a castle at your back—the everlasting beauty of Serenity Smith of the golden eyes."

He lowered his mouth to hers, and she was swamped by a sudden surge of emotion, a strong premonition that she would never see him again. She threw her arms around his neck and clung to him and to the past. His lips brushed her hair before he drew her away.

"Goodbye darling." He smiled and patted her cheek.

"Goodbye, Tony. Take care." She returned his smile, determinedly battling back the tears which burned her eyes.

She watched as he walked to the car and got in, and with a wave headed down the long, winding drive. The car became a small red dot in the distance and then gradually faded from sight, and she continued to stand, allowing the silent tears to have their freedom. An arm slipped around her waist, and she turned to see her grandmother standing beside her, sympathy and understanding in the angular face.

"You are sad to see him go, *ma petite?*" The arm was comforting, and Serenity leaned her head against the slim shoulder.

"*Oui,* Grandmère, very sad."

"But you are not in love with him." It was a statement rather than a question, and Serenity sighed.

"He was very special to me." Pushing a tear from her cheek, she gave a childish sniffle. "I shall miss him very much. Now, I shall go to my room and have a good cry."

"*Oui,* that is wise." The countess patted her shoulder. "Few things clear the brain and cleanse the heart like a good cry." Turning, Serenity enveloped her in a hug. *"Allez, vite, mon enfant."* The countess held her close for a moment before disengaging herself. "Go shed your tears."

Serenity ran up the stone steps and entered through the heavy oak doors into the coolness of the château. Rushing toward the main staircase, she collided with a hard object. Hands gripped her shoulders.

"You must watch where you are going, *ma chérie,*" Christophe's voice mocked. "You will be running into walls and damaging your beautiful nose." She attempted to pull away, but one hand held her in place without effort as another came under her chin to tilt back her head. At the sight of brimming eyes, the mockery faded, replaced by surprise, then concern, and lastly an unfamiliar helplessness. "Serenity?" Her name was a question, the tone gentle as she had not heard it before, and the tenderness in the dark eyes broke what little composure she could still lay claim to.

"Oh, please," she choked on a desperate sob, "let me go." She struggled from his grasp, striving not to crumble completely, yet wanting to be held close by this suddenly gentle man.

"Is there something I can do?" He detained her by placing a hand on her arm.

*Yes, you idiot!* her brain screamed. *Love me!* "No," she said aloud, running up the stairs. "No, no, no!"

She streaked up the stairs, like a golden doe pursued by hunters, and finding her bedroom door, she opened it, then slammed it behind her, and threw herself on her bed.

The tears had worked their magic. Finally, Serenity was able to rinse them away and face the world and whatever the future had in store. She glanced at the manila envelope which she had tossed negligently on her bureau.

"Well, I suppose it's time to see what old Barkley sent me." Serenity got up reluctantly and went over to the bureau to pick up the envelope. She threw herself down on the bed again to break the seal, dumping its contents on the spread.

There was merely a page with the firm's impressive letterhead, which brought thoughts of Tony flooding back to her mind, and another sealed envelope. She picked up the neatly typewritten page listlessly, wondering what new form the family retainer had discovered for her to fill out. As she read the letter's contents, and the totally unexpected message it contained, she sat bolt upright.

Dear Miss Smith,
Enclosed you will find an envelope addressed to you containing a letter from your father. This let-

ter was left in my care to be given to you only if you made contact with your mother's family in Brittany. It has come to my attention through Anthony Rollins that you are now residing at the Château Kergallen in the company of your maternal grandmother, so I am entrusting same to Anthony to be delivered to you at the earliest possible date.

Had you informed me of your plans, I would have carried out your father's wishes at an earlier date. I, of course, have no knowledge of its contents, but I am sure your father's message will bring you comfort.

M. Barkley

Serenity read no farther, but put the lawyer's letter aside and picked up the message her father had left in his care. She stared at the envelope which had fallen face down on the bed, and, turning it over, her eyes misted at seeing the familiar handwriting. She broke the seal.

The letter was written in her father's bold, clear hand:

*My own Serenity,*
*When you read this your mother and I will no longer be with you, and I pray you do not grieve too deeply, for the love we feel for you remains true and strong as life itself.*

*As I write this, you are ten years old, already the image of your mother, so incredibly lovely that I am already fretting about the boys I will have to fight off one day. I watched you this morning as you sat sedately (a most unusual occupation for you, as I am more used to seeing you skating down the sidewalks at a horrifying speed or sliding without thought to bruised skin down the banisters). You sat in the garden, with my sketch book and a pencil, drawing with fierce concentration the azaleas that bloomed there. I saw in that moment, to both my pride and despair, that you were growing up, and would not always be my little girl, safe in the security your mother and I had provided for you. I knew then it was necessary to write down events you might one day have the need to understand.*

*I will give old Barkley* (a small smile appeared on Serenity's face as she noted that the attorney had been known by that name even so many years ago) *instructions to hold this letter for you until such time as your grandmother, or some member of your mother's family, makes contact with you. If this does not occur, there will be no need to reveal the secret your mother and I have already kept for more than a decade.*

*I was painting on the sidewalks of Paris in the full glory of spring, in love with the city and needing no mistress but my art. I was very young, and, I am afraid, very intense. I met a man, Jean-Paul le Goff, who was impressed by my, as he put it, raw young talent. He commissioned me to paint a portrait of his fiancée as a wedding present to her, and arranged for me to travel to Brittany and reside in the Château Kergallen. My life began the moment I entered that enormous hall and had my first glimpse of your mother.*

*It was not my intention to act upon the love I felt from the first moment I saw her, a delicate angel with hair like sunlight. I tried with all my being to put my art first. I was to paint her; she belonged to my patron; she belonged to the château. She was an angel, an aristocrat with a family lineage longer than time. All these things I told myself a hundred times. Jonathan Smith, itinerant artist, had no right to possess her in dreams, let alone reality. At times, when I made my preliminary sketches, I believed I would die for love of her. I told myself to go, to make some excuse and leave, but I could not find the courage. I thank God now that I could not.*

*One night, as I walked in the garden, I came upon her. I thought to turn away before I disturbed her, but she heard me, and when she turned, I saw in her eyes what I had not dared dream. She loved me. I could have shouted with the joy of it, but there were so many obstacles. She was betrothed, honor-bound to marry another man. We had no right to our love. Does one need a right to love, Serenity? Some would condemn us. I pray you do not. After much talk and tears, we defied what some would call right and honor, and we married. Gaelle begged me to keep the marriage a secret until she could find the right way to tell Jean-Paul and her mother. I wanted the world to know, but I agreed. She had given up so much for me, I could deny her nothing.*

*During this time of waiting, a more disturbing problem came to light. The countess, your*

*grandmother, had in her possession a Raphael
Madonna, displayed in prominence in the main
drawing room. It was a painting, the countess
informed me, which had been in her family for
generations. Next to Gaelle, she treasured this
painting above all things. It seemed to symbol-
ize to her the continuity of her family, a shining
beacon remaining constant after the hell of war
and loss. I had studied this painting closely and
suspected it was a forgery. I said nothing, at first
thinking perhaps the countess herself had had a
copy made for her own needs. The Germans had
taken so much from her—husband, home—that
perhaps they had taken the original Raphael, as
well. When she made the announcement that she
had decided to donate the painting to the Louvre in order to share its greatness, I nearly froze
with fear. I had grown fond of this woman, her
pride and determination, her grace and dignity.
I had no desire to see her hurt, and I realized
that she believed the painting to be authentic. I
knew Gaelle would be tormented by the scandal
if the painting was dismissed as a fraud, and the
countess would be destroyed. I could not let this
happen. I offered to clean the painting in order to
examine it more critically, and I felt like a traitor.*

*I took the painting to my studio in the tower,
and under close study, I had no doubt that it was
a very well-executed copy. Even then, I do not
know what I would have done, if it had not been
for the letter I found hidden behind the frame. The
letter was a confession from the countess's first*

*husband, a cry of despair for the treachery he had committed. He confessed he had lost nearly all of his possessions, and those of his wife. He was deep in debt, and having decided the Germans would defeat the Allies, he arranged to sell the Raphael to them. He had a copy made and replaced the original without the countess's knowledge, feeling the money would see him through the hardship of war, and the deal with the Germans would keep his estates secure. Too late, he despaired of his action, and hiding his confession in the frame of the copy, he went to face the men he had dealt with in the hopes of returning the money. The note ended with his telling of his intention, and pleading for forgiveness if he proved unsuccessful.*

*As I finished reading the letter, Gaelle came into the studio; I had not the foresight to bolt the door. It was impossible to hide my reaction, or the letter, which I still held in my hand, and so I was forced to share the burden with the one person I most wanted to spare. I found in those moments, in that secluded tower room, that the woman I loved was endowed with more strength than most men. She would keep the knowledge from her mother at all costs. She felt it imperative that the countess be shielded from humiliation and the knowledge that the painting she so prized was but forgery. We devised a plan to conceal the painting, to make it appear as if it had been stolen. Perhaps we were wrong. To this day I do not know if we did the right thing; but for your mother, there was no other way. And so, the deed was done.*

*Gaelle's plans to tell her mother of our marriage were soon forced into reality. She found, to our unending joy, that she carried our child, you, the fruit of our love that would grow to be the most important treasure of our lives. When she told her mother of our marriage and her pregnancy, the countess flew into a rage. It was her right to do, Serenity, and the animosity she felt for me was well deserved in her eyes. I had taken her daughter from her without her knowledge, and in doing so, I had placed a mark on her family's honor. In her anger, she disowned Gaelle, demanded that we leave the château and never enter again. I believe she would have rescinded her decision in time; she loved Gaelle above all things. But that same day she found the Raphael missing. Putting two and two together, she accused me of stealing both her daughter and her family treasure. How could I deny it? One crime was no worse than the other, and the message in your mother's eyes begged me to keep silent. So I took your mother away from the château, her country, her family, her heritage, and brought her to America.*

*We did not speak of her mother, for it brought only pain, and we built our life fresh with you to strengthen our bond. And now you have the story, and with it, forgive me, the responsibility. Perhaps by the time you read this, it will be possible to tell the entire truth. If not, let it remain hidden,*

*as the forgery was hidden, away from the world
with something infinitely more precious to conceal it. Do what your heart tells you.*

*Your loving father.*

Tears had fallen on the letter since its beginning,
and now as Serenity finished reading, she wiped them
away and took a long breath. Standing, she moved over
to the window and stared down at the garden where her
parents had first revealed their love.

"What do I do?" she murmured aloud, still gripping
the letter in her hand. *If I had read this a month ago,
I would have gone straight to the countess with it, but
now I don't know,* she told herself silently.

To clear her father's name, she would have to reveal
a secret kept hidden for twenty-five years. Would the
telling accomplish anything, or would it undo whatever good the sacrifices made by both her parents had
done? Her father had instructed her to listen to her
heart, but it was so filled with the love and anguish of
his letter that she could hear nothing, and her mind was
clouded with indecision. There was a swift, fleeting
impulse to go to Christophe, but she quickly pushed
it aside. To confide in him would only make her more
vulnerable, and the separation she must soon deal with
more agonizing.

She had to think, she decided, taking several deep
breaths. She had to clear away the fog and think clearly
and carefully, and when she found an answer, she had
to be sure it was the right one.

Pacing the room, she halted suddenly and began
changing her clothes in a frantic rush. She remembered
the freedom and openness that had come to her when

she rode through the woods, and it was this sensation, she determined, slipping on jeans and shirt, that she required to ease her heart and clear her brain.

## Chapter 10

The groom greeted her request to saddle Babette doubt-fully. He argued, albeit respectfully, that he had no or-ders from the count to go riding, and for once Serenity used her aristocratic heritage and haughtily informed him that as the countess's granddaughter, she was not to be questioned. The groom submitted, with a faint mut-tering of Breton, and she was soon mounted on the now-familiar mare and setting off on the path Christophe had taken on her first lesson.

The woods were quiet and comforting, and she emp-tied her mind in the hopes that the answer would then find room to make an appearance. She walked the mare easily for a time, finding it simple now to retain com-mand of the animal while still feeling a part of it. She found herself no closer to resolving her problem, how-ever, and urged Babette into a canter.

They moved swiftly, the wind blowing her hair back from her face and engulfing her once more with the sense of freedom which she sought. Her father's letter was tucked into her back pocket, and she decided to ride to the hill overlooking the village and read it once more, hoping by then to find the wisdom to make the right decision.

A shout rang out behind her, and she turned in the saddle to see Christophe coming after her astride the black stallion. As she turned, her foot connected sharply with the mare's side, and Babette took this as a command and streaked forward in a swift gallop. Serenity was nearly unseated in surprise, and she struggled to right herself as the horse raced down the path with unaccustomed speed. At first all of her attention was given to the problem of remaining astride, not even contemplating the mechanics of halting the mare's headlong rush. Before her brain had the opportunity to communicate with her hands and give them the idea to rein in, Christophe came alongside her. Then, reaching over, he pulled back on her reins, uttering a stream of oaths in a variety of languages.

Babette came to a docile halt, and Serenity's eyes closed in relief. The next thing she knew, she was gripped around the waist and dragged from the saddle without ceremony, with Christophe's dark eyes burning into hers.

"What do you hope to accomplish by running away from me?" he demanded, shaking her like a rag doll.

"I was doing no such thing," she protested through teeth that chattered at the movement. "I must have startled the horse when I turned around." Her own anger began to replace relief. "It wouldn't have happened if you hadn't come chasing after me." She began to struggle away, but his grip increased with painful emphasis. "You're hurting me!" she stormed at him. "Why must you always hurt me?"

"You would find a broken neck more painful, *ma petite folle*," he stated, dragging her farther down the path and away from the horses. "That is what could have happened to you. What do you mean by riding off unescorted?"

"Unescorted?" she repeated with a laugh, jerking away from him. "How quaint. Aren't women allowed to ride unescorted in Brittany?"

"Not women who have no brains," he returned with dark fury, "and who have been on a horse only twice before in their lives."

"I was going very well before you came." She tossed her head at his logic. "Now just go away and leave me alone." She watched as his eyes narrowed, and he took a step toward her. "Go away!" she shouted, backing up. "I want my privacy. I have things to think about."

"I will give you something else to think about."

He moved swiftly, gripping her behind the neck and stealing her breath with his lips. She pushed against him without success, fighting both him and the whirling dizziness which flew to her brain. Gripping her shoulders, he drew her away, his fingers digging into her flesh.

"Enough! *C'est entendu!*" He shook her again, and she saw by his face that the aristocrat had fled and there was only the man. "I want you. I want what no man has had before—and, by God, I *will* have you."

He swept her up into his arms, and she struggled with

a wild, primitive fear, beating against his chest like a trapped bird beating against the bars of its cage, but his stride remained steady and sure, as though he carried a complaisant child rather than a terrified woman.

Then she was on the ground, with his body crushing down on hers, his mouth savaging hers like a man possessed, her protests making no more of a ripple than a pebble tossed into the ocean. With a swift, violent motion, her blouse was opened, and he claimed her naked skin with bruising fingers, his lovemaking filled with a desperate urgency which conquered all thought of resistance, all will to struggle.

Struggle became demand, and her mouth became mobile and seeking under his; the hands which had previously pushed him away were now pulling him closer. Drowned in the deluge of passion, she reveled in the intimacy of his masculine hardness, her body moving with the ageless rhythm of instinct beneath him. Urgent and without restraint, his hands traced trails of heat along her naked flesh, his mouth following the blaze, returning again and again to drink from hers. Each time, his thirst grew, his demands taking her into a new and timeless world, the border between heaven and hell, where only one man and one woman can exist.

Deeper and deeper he led her, until pleasure and pain merged into one spiraling sensation, one all-consuming need. Helpless under the barrage of shimmering passion, the trembling began slowly, growing more intense as the journey took her further from the known and closer to the unexperienced. With a moan mixed with fear and desire, her fingers clutched at his shoulders, as if to keep from plummeting into an eternal void.

His mouth left hers suddenly, and with his breath uneven, his cheek rested against her brow for a moment before he lifted his head and looked down at her.

"I am hurting you again, *ma petite*." He sighed and rolled off her to lie on his back. "I tossed you on the ground and nearly ravished you like a barbarian. I seem to find it difficult to control my baser instincts with you."

She sat up quickly, fumbling with the buttons of her blouse with unsteady fingers. "It's all right." She attempted but failed to produce a careless-sounding voice. "No harm done. I've often been told how strong I am. You must learn to temper your technique a bit, though," she babbled on to hide the extent of her pain. "Geneviève is more fragile than I."

"Geneviève?" he repeated, lifting himself on his elbow to look at her directly. "What has Geneviève to do with this?"

"With this?" she answered. "Oh, nothing. I have no intention of saying anything to her of this. I'm quite fond of her."

"Perhaps we should speak in French, Serenity. I am having difficulty understanding you."

"She's in love with you, you big idiot!" she blurted out, ignoring his request for French. "She told me; she came asking for my advice." She controlled the short burst of hysterical laughter which escaped her. "She asked for my advice," she elaborated, "on how to make you see her as a woman instead of a child. I didn't tell her what your opinion was of me; she wouldn't have understood."

"She told you she was in love with me?" he demanded, his eyes narrowing.

"Not by name," she said shortly, wishing the conversation had never begun. "She said she had been in love with a man all of her life, and he regarded her as a child. I simply told her to set him straight, tell him that she was a woman, and... What are you laughing at?"

"You thought she spoke of me?" He was once more flat on his back and laughing more freely than she had ever seen. "Little Geneviève in love with me!"

"How dare you laugh at her! How can you be so callous as to make fun of someone who loves you?" He caught her fists before they made contact with his chest.

"Geneviève did not seek you out for advice about me, *chérie*." He continued to hold her off without effort. "She was speaking of Iann. But you have not met Iann, have you, *mon amour?*" He ignored her furious struggles and continued to speak with a wide grin. "We grew up together—Iann, Yves, and I—with Geneviève trailing along like a little puppy. Yves and I remained her 'brothers' after she grew into a woman, but it was Iann she truly loved. He has been in Paris on business for the last month, only returning home yesterday." A small jerk of his wrists brought her down on his chest. "Geneviève called this morning to tell me of their engagement. She also told me to thank you for her, and now I know why." His grin increased as amber eyes grew wide.

"She's engaged? It wasn't you?"

"Yes, she is; and no, it was not," he answered helpfully. "Tell me, *ma belle cousine,* were you jealous when you thought Geneviève to be in love with me?"

"Don't be ridiculous," she lied, attempting to remove her mouth from its proximity to his. "I would be no more jealous of Geneviève than you would be of Yves."

"Ah." In one swift movement he had reversed their positions and lay looking down at her. "Is that so? And should I tell you that I was nearly consumed with jealousy of my friend Yves, and that I very nearly murdered your American Tony? You would give them smiles that should be mine. From the moment I saw you step off the train, I was lost, bewitched, and I fought it as a man fights that which threatens to enslave him. Perhaps this slavery is freedom." His hand moved through the silk of her hair. "Ah, Serenity, *je t'aime.*"

She swallowed in the search for her voice. "Would you say that again?"

He smiled, and his mouth teased hers for a moment. "In English? I love you. I loved you from the moment I saw you, I love you infinitely more now, and I will love you for the rest of my life." His lips descended on hers, moving them with a tenderness he had never shown, lifting only when he felt the moistness of her tears. "Why do you weep?" he questioned, his brow creasing in exasperation. "What have I done?"

She shook her head. "It's only that I love you so much, and I thought…" She hesitated and let out a long breath. "Christophe, do you believe my father was innocent, or do you think me to be the daughter of a thief?"

His brow creased again with a frown, and he studied her silently. "I will tell you what I know, Serenity, and I will tell you what I believe. I know that I love you, not just the angel who stepped off the train at Lannion, but the woman I have come to know. It would make no difference if your father was a thief, a cheat, or a murderer. I have heard you speak of your father, and I have seen how you look when you tell of him. I cannot believe that a man who earned this love and devotion could have committed such a crime. This is what I believe, but it does not matter; nothing he did or did not do could change my love for you."

"Oh, Christophe," she whispered, pulling his cheek down to hers, "I've waited all my life for someone like you. There is something I must show you." She pushed him away gently, taking the letter from her pocket and handing it to him. "My father told me to listen to my heart, and now it belongs to you."

Serenity sat across from him, watching his face as he read, and she felt a deep peace, a contentment she had not known since her parents had been taken from her. Love for him filled her, along with a strong sense of security that he would help her to make the right decision. The woods were silent, tranquil, disturbed only by the whisper of wind through the leaves, and the birds that answered it. For a moment, it was a place out of time, inhabited only by man and woman.

When he had finished reading the letter, Christophe lifted his eyes from the paper and met hers. "Your father loved your mother very much."

"Yes."

He folded the letter, replacing it in its envelope, his eyes never leaving hers. "I wish I had known him. I was only a child when he came to the château, and he did not stay long."

Her eyes clung to his. "What should we do?"

He moved nearer, taking her face in his hands. "We must take the letter and show it to Grandmère."

"But they're dead, and she's alive. I love her; I don't want to hurt her."

He bent down and kissed shimmering lashes. "I love you, Serenity, for so many reasons, and you have just given me one more." He tilted her head so their eyes met again. "Listen to me now, *mon amour,* and trust me. Grandmère needs to see this letter, for her own peace of mind. She believes her daughter betrayed her, stole from her. She has lived with this for twenty-five years. This letter will set her free. She will read in your father's words the love Gaelle had for her, and, equally important, she will see the love your father had for her daughter. He was an honorable man, but he lived with the fact that his wife's mother thought him to be a thief. The time has come to set them all free."

"All right," she agreed. "If you say this is what we must do, this is what we will do."

He smiled, and taking both her hands in his, he lifted them to his lips before helping her to her feet. "Tell me, *cousine*"—the familiar mocking smile was in place— "will you always do as I say?"

"No," she answered with a vigorous shake of her head. "Absolutely not."

"Ah, I thought not." He led her to the horses. "Life will not be dull." He took the reins of the buckskin in his hand, and she mounted without assistance. He frowned as he handed her the reins. "You are disturbingly independent, stubborn, and impulsive, but I love you."

"And you," she commented, as he moved to mount

the stallion, "are arrogant, overbearing, and irritatingly confident, but I love you, as well."

They reached the stables. After relinquishing the horses to a groom, they set off toward the château with linked hands. As they approached the garden entrance, Christophe stopped and turned to her.

"You must give this to Grandmère yourself, Serenity." He took the envelope from his pocket and handed it to her.

"Yes, I know." She looked down at it as he placed it in her hand. "But you will stay with me?"

*"Oui, ma petite."* He drew her into his arms. "I will stay with you." His mouth met hers, and she threw her arms around his neck until the kiss deepened, and they were only aware of each other.

*"Alors, mes enfants."* The countess's words broke the spell, and they both turned to see her watching them from the edge of the garden. "You have decided to stop fighting the inevitable."

"You are very clever, Grandmère," Christophe commented with a lift of his brow. "But I believe we would have managed even without your invaluable assistance."

Elegant shoulders moved expressively. "But you might have wasted too much time, and time is a precious commodity."

"Come inside, Grandmère. Serenity has something to show you."

They entered the drawing room, and the countess seated herself in her regular thronelike chair. "What is it you have to show me, *ma petite?*"

"Grandmère," Serenity said as she began moving in front of the countess, "Tony brought me some papers from my attorney. I didn't even bother to open them until he left, but I found when I did that they were much more important than I had anticipated." She held out the letter. "Before you read this, I want you to know I love you." The countess opened her mouth to speak, but Serenity hurried on. "I love Christophe, and before he read what I'm giving you, he told me he loved me, as well. I can't tell you how wonderful it was to know that before he saw this letter. We decided to share this with you because we love you." She handed the letter to her grandmother and then seated herself on the sofa. Christophe joined her, and he took her hand in his as they waited.

Serenity's eyes were drawn to her mother's portrait, the eyes that met hers full of joy and happiness, the expression of a woman in love. *I have found it, too, Maman,* she spoke silently, *the overwhelming joy of love, and I hold it here in my hand.*

She dropped her eyes to the joined hands, the strong bronzed fingers intertwined with the alabaster ones, the ruby ring which had been her mother's glowing against the contrasting colors. She stared at the ring on her own hand, then raised her eyes to the replica on her mother's, and she understood. The countess's movement as she rose from her chair interrupted Serenity's thoughts.

"For twenty-five years I have wronged this man, and the daughter whom I loved." The words were soft as she turned to gaze out the window. "My pride blinded me and hardened my heart."

"You were not to know, Grandmère," Serenity replied, watching the straight back. "They wanted only to protect you."

"To protect me from the knowledge that my husband had been a thief, and from the humiliation of public scandal, your father allowed himself to be branded, and my daughter gave up her heritage." Moving back to the chair, she sank down wearily. "I sense from your father's words a great feeling of love. Tell me, Serenity, was my daughter happy?"

"You see the eyes as my father painted them." She gestured to the portrait. "She looked always as she looked then."

"How can I forgive myself for what I did?"

"Oh, no, Grandmère." Serenity rose and knelt in front of her, taking the fragile hands in her own. "I didn't give you the letter to add to your grief, but to take it from you. You read the letter; you see that they blamed you for nothing; they purposely allowed you to believe that they betrayed you. Maybe they were wrong, but it's done, and there can be no going back." She gripped the narrow hands tighter. "I tell you now that I blame you for nothing, and I beg you, for my sake, to let the guilt die."

"Ah, Serenity, *ma chère enfant.*" The countess's voice was as tender as her eyes. *"C'est bien,"* she said briskly, drawing her shoulders up straight once more. "We will remember only the happy times. You will tell me more of Gaelle's life with your father in this Georgetown, and you will bring them both close to me again, *n'est-ce pas?*"

*"Oui,* Grandmère."

"Perhaps one day you will take me to the house where you grew up."

"To America?" Serenity asked, deeply shocked.

"Wouldn't you be afraid to travel to so uncivilized a country?"

"You are being impudent again," the countess stated regally as she rose from her chair. "I begin to believe I will come to know your father very well through you, *mignonne*." She shook her head. "When I think of what I allowed that painting to cost me! I am well pleased to be rid of it."

"You still have the copy, Grandmère," Serenity corrected. "I know where it is."

"How do you know this?" Christophe asked, speaking for the first time since they had entered the room.

She turned to him and smiled. "It was right there in the letter, but I didn't realize it at first. It was when we were sitting together just now, and you held my hand, that it came to me. Do you see this?" She held out her hand where the ruby gleamed. "It was my mother's, the same she wears in the portrait."

"I had noticed the ring in the painting," the countess said slowly, "but Gaelle had no such ring. I thought your father merely painted it to match the earrings she wore."

"She had the ring, Grandmère; it was her engagement ring. She wore it always with her wedding band on her left hand."

"But what has this to do with the copy of the Raphael?" Christophe questioned with a frown.

"In the painting she wears the ring on her right hand. My father would never have made such a mistake in detail unless he did it intentionally."

"It is possible," the countess murmured.

"I know it's there; it says so in the letter. He says he concealed it, covered by something infinitely more precious. Nothing was more precious to him than Maman."

*"Oui,"* the countess agreed, studying the painting of her daughter. "There could be no safer hiding place."

"I have some solution," Serenity began. "I could uncover a corner; then you could be sure."

*"Non."* She shook her head. *"Non,* there is no need. I would not have you mar one inch of your father's work if the true Raphael were under it." She turned to Serenity and lifted a hand to her cheek. "This painting, Christophe, and you, *mon enfant,* are my treasures now. Let it rest. It is where it belongs." She turned back to her grandchildren with a smile. "I will leave you now. Lovers should have their privacy."

She left the room with the air of a queen, and Serenity watched her in admiration. "She's magnificent, isn't she?"

*"Oui,"* Christophe agreed easily, taking Serenity into his arms. "And very wise. I have not kissed you for more than an hour."

After he had remedied the discrepancy to their mutual satisfaction, he looked down at her with his habitual air of confidence. "After we are married, *mon amour,* I will have your portrait painted, and we will add still another treasure to the château."

"Married?" Serenity repeated with a frown. "I never agreed to marry you." She pushed away as though reluctant. "You can't just order me to do so; a woman likes to be asked." He pulled her against him and kissed her thoroughly, his lips hard and insistent.

"You were saying, *cousine?"* he asked when he freed her.

She regarded him seriously, but allowed her arms to twine around his neck. "I shall never be an aristocrat."

"Heaven forbid," he agreed with sincerity.

"We shall fight often, and I will constantly infuriate you."

"I shall look forward to it."

"Very well," she said, managing to keep a smile from her lips. "I will marry you—on one condition."

"And that is?" His brow raised in question.

"That you walk in the garden with me tonight." She drew her arms around him tighter. "I'm so tired of walking in the moonlight with other men and wishing they were you."

\* \* \* \* \*